Salt and Honey

Also by Candi Miller

Kalahari Passage

SALT AND HONEY

Candi Miller

**Tindal
Street
Press**

First published in UK July 2006
by Legend Press
This edition published in August 2011
by Tindal Street Press Ltd
217 The Custard Factory, Gibb Street,
Birmingham, B9 4AA
www.tindalstreet.co.uk

A CIP catalogue reference for this book is available
from the British Library

ISBN: 978 1 906994 27 3

Typeset by Tetragon
Printed and bound in Great Britain by
CPI Cox & Wyman, Reading, RG1 8EX

To Yianno, who always believed

PROLOGUE

South West Africa, 1958

The guard dogs began to bark so insistently that Marta got out of bed and hurried to the window.

Unremitting blackness, not even the Southern Cross visible on the horizon.

Must be cloudy, she thought. With a bit of luck, tomorrow will be cooler.

She'd forgotten how hot it could be here in December. Bad for her feet, already swollen by pregnancy.

She heard frenzy in the Doberman's barking now, and even the ridgeback's usually token accompaniment sounded urgent. Not one of the ubiquitous jackal then, patrolling the farmyard fence in the hope of finding a way into the hen house. And it wouldn't be one of the servants. They wouldn't dare enter the yard until the dogs had been chained up for the day by their master, Etienne Marais.

But Etienne and all the other men were away for the night. Out in the veld somewhere, hunting. Marta looked at the shotgun propped up next to the window. Etienne, her brother-in-law, had insisted she take charge of it in the men's absence.

'Lettie's likely to put holes in one of her own toes if I leave it with her,' he'd said, winking in the direction of his wife.

'I want nothing to do with guns,' Marta had told him.

She left the room now without it, feeling her way down the dark passage towards the growing cacophony. As she struggled with the screen door she heard the Doberman yelp. Then a familiar voice, cursing it:

'Shut up, you blerry brak.'

'Are you boys back already?' Surer now, she hastened down the veranda steps, aware of shapes, animal and human. Impossible to distinguish anyone in the moonless night.

'Deon,' she called out to her husband, as a man, limping more badly than usual, came into view. 'Is everything alright?' Deon held a torch and in its shaky beam she saw a horse with two small figures astride it. Behind plodded an ox, dragging something heavy and inert on a litter. The dogs capered around, the ridgeback whining.

'Voetsek, jou fokken brakke,' she heard her nephew, André, swear.

Marta whistled for the dogs and when they came she grabbed each one by its collar, making them sit.

'Why are you back so soon?' she asked Deon.

'Beenah accident,' he mumbled, drunkenly. Marta's hands flew to the open neck of her nightdress, clutching it closed. The dogs bounded away.

'Mannie?' she whispered.

'Boy's awright.' Deon waved the torch vaguely in the direction of the horse.

Marta snatched it from him and stumbled over to her son. Her hand roved across the child's body, trying to discover what the weak beam could not.

'Are you all right, my boy?' He seemed it – cool; no fever; no wounds; no obviously broken bones. Thank God. She trained the beam on his fright-white face.

'For pity's sake, what's the matter?'

'Ma, Ma,' he said, gulping back sobs, 'it's not me, Ma. Check Uncle Etienne. Save him, Ma, please, Ma, cos it's my fault,' he said, choking. Baffled, she turned from her son.

Suddenly there was lamplight from the house, candlelight coming from the servants' compound, and above, on the veranda, the shrill tones of her sister-in-law: 'Liewe magies, what's going on?'

Marta trained the beam on the ox and gasped. On the makeshift litter, Etienne lay dead still, a maroon stain spread across his chest.

Marta froze. She should feel for a pulse, but she couldn't move.

'Ma, please! Do something quick. I think . . .'

She spun back to her son, spotlighting him. In the wider arc of light she now saw he was propping up a small body – slim yellow limbs, wide oriental eyes – a Khoisan child. But not from around here; that she could see from the child's traditional dress: a pubic apron and a cloak made of animal skin. It must be from a Kalahari Desert band. What on earth was it doing so far from home? And alone?

'Someone, help me get these children down,' she shouted, dropping the torch and running over to the horse.

As she reached up for the Khoisan child, it recoiled in terror and raised bound hands to fend her off. Marta stopped, horror-struck. 'Why is this child tied up?'

As soon as André had secured the dogs, servants began to pour into the yard in various stages of dress. Housemaids, never ever seen bareheaded this side of the compound fence, looked unfamiliar and naked despite having blankets or shawls draped modestly around them. Some carried their bleary-eyed children while their men milled about bare-chested, with knopkieries or lengths of metal pipe held at the ready. As elders tried to establish who should be in charge now the whites and Twi, the boss-boy, were preoccupied, two youths with initiation cuts still healing on their chests, set off to patrol the perimeter fence, burning logs held aloft. The dogs strained at their chains, barking ferociously.

The anxious human susurrus built until Marta could feel it down the back of her neck, like the rasping breath of a leopard.

'Give me a lamp, get a torch,' she shouted into the throng. 'And for God's sake, someone go start the generator.' She heard footsteps fly to do her bidding then Lettie's shrieks at the sight of Etienne, and André trying to soothe his mother. Marta kept her attention on Deon. 'Where did you find this child?'

'Out there; Mother Hills way.' His bloodshot eyes flicked towards a pair of hills whose stone summits had been eroded into nipples by the desert wind. Nestled in the cleavage between the hills was a secret pool of water. When the sun's rays reached it, it would shine like an aquamarine set against the red-gold rock. The pool, forbidden to all but the white landowners, was evidence of the abundant artesian wealth beneath the dull, dry earth.

South West African farmers had learned how to plunder this hidden hoard. None better than Etienne Marais. He of the banknote green cornfields that stretched around the farmhouse as far as the eye could see. Big, blond, broad Etienne Marais, an Afrikaner success story: master of all in the area and parliamentary representative of those whose skin colour entitled them to vote.

Now he lay dying, as Marta turned her back on him and struggled with the knots tying the Khoisan child to the pommel.

She was aware of André pushing past, carrying his father with the help of three black servants. Lettie Marais skittered alongside in kitten-heeled slippers, whimpering. She was wringing the lifeless hand that fell over the side of the stretcher.

'Marta, Marta, for pity's sake, come help. Make some muti or something. My Etienne's bad. Liewe magies, leave the damn child. It's only a kaffir.'

Kalahari Desert, 1950

Meat. Piles of it. Strips skewered on thorny branches drying in the doorways of grass-domed huts, slabs sizzling on every cooking fire. People laughed, called across the camp, teased the hunters, saying what a pathetic specimen the mighty giraffe was. Excitement flared like fat in flame as the hunters hacked at the giraffe carcass, slipping and sliding in a slush of sand and blood.

Zuma sat straight-legged on sand pinkened by the evening sun. In a gourd, she mixed giraffe fat with ground bark. It made a thick paste, satisfyingly red. Grinning, she began working it into her skin, determined she should look her best for the dance that would follow the feast. After all, she would be on show. She was the owner of the first arrow to hit the old bull.

'Mmm, the first cut of Tall Elegant Person's meat is mine. Tami's arrow-arm is strong – a good son-in-law. But my arrow, yau, a fine food-bringer, a meat-maker. People will remember I am a rain-season child. I must shine tonight. My skin must glow like the coat of a red buck.'

Zuma sensed a wind tapping at her shoulder – and she knew immediately what it was. She determined to ignore it. The spirits always chose inconvenient times to speak. Couldn't they wait until she took part in a trance dance? She shook her head to clear her ears of their whisperings. Her hair ornaments jiggled. She touched her cropped hair. Was the grey showing again? Maybe she should ask N‡aisa to shave her head.

The spirit wind nudged her. She ignored it, massaging away the goosebumps that had formed on her arms. The wind spiralled, collecting a cargo of sand. Too late Zuma closed her eyes against this dust devil.

Coughing, eyes an angry red, she capitulated, cocking her head to one side and listening to the message.

So, there were ǀTon at their tree-water. She would tell Khalʼan, her husband and a more experienced shaman, but he was old now for such a long journey. And what match were his arrows for ǀTon thundersticks? There'd been enough of fighting between her people and others. She shrugged. Perhaps it was her duty to add this episode to the Juǀʼhoan story. Make sure the children knew.

She rose, smoothed the hide apron that covered her groin and strolled over to nearby fires. She chatted to a woman here, flirted with a man in passing, all the while assessing receptiveness. Tonight the young ones wanted meat. They could smell it – everywhere. Who could begrudge them, after months of roots and berries? Zuma thought. But the meat wasn't ready yet. A story might distract them.

She fixed two feathers to the back of her head and, with arms bent backwards like folded wings, she began her kori bustard impression, pacing ponderously about the camp.

A big-bellied tot pointed at her, tugged at his mother's kaross, eyebrows quizzical.

'Kori woman has an egg she wants to lay,' his mother said, laughing.

His older sister scooped him up. 'Come, we'll follow her. She'll have a story to crack open.'

Other children joined them, trotting after Zuma as she high-stepped to a shady alcove under a baobab tree.

'Wum, wum, wum, wummm!' she cried.

Hearing her, older children abandoned their games and ran to join the group. Zuma n!a'an was a fine storyteller.

Zuma let them settle then, drawing her three-year-old granddaughter, Koba, onto her lap, she said casually, 'There's a new story, but you probably don't want to hear it.'

Her granddaughter cocked her head to one side, inclining a cowrie shell of an ear to the wind. 'I *can* hear,' she whispered, big-eyed. Her voice was drowned out by the chorus of the other children clamouring for Zuma to tell her tale.

'Well, it's new, but it begins long-back, after the time of the Early Race but before our time, when groups of we Real People lived all over this land – towards sun's-rising-place where the mountains have teeth' – Zuma bared her own, ground down by years of chewing on fibrous roots and sandy food – 'towards sun's-resting-place where the earth sparkles with bright stones.'

'Where's that?' a little girl with shining eyes breathed. Zuma pointed west and patiently explained the route between the camp and the Skeleton Coast, mentioning as many dunes, watering holes and other landmarks as she could remember. No child listened more intently than the long-eyed one on Zuma's lap. Koba was mesmerized by this hint of a world beyond the camp baobab.

Zuma's tone became mysterious. 'Then, into this land came strangers. They drove herds of tame animals before them and suffer-suffered when they found no water or grazing.

'Our people showed them where the water was and took their herds deep into the valleys to find grass. When the Jul'hoansi returned with the herds full-fattened, they were given tobacco and were glad. "Come and be our herdsmen," these Herero and Tswana tribesmen said to our people, "and we will give you plenty of milk." But the Jul'hoansi did not wish to. They preferred to follow the meat animals they loved.'

While the group nodded, Zuma felt for the beaded pouch at her waist and withdrew a pipe. She pushed tobacco into the bowl and dispatched a boy to fetch a light from the nearest fire. The children waited politely. All except Koba.

'More, more,' this tot pleaded, chubby fingers reaching to remove the pipe that stopped the story.

'Yau.' Zuma laughed, holding it out of reach. 'This granddaughter of mine is dry. She thirsts for stories like a root for water.'

The older children distracted Koba – pulling faces, tickling her, passing her from lap to lap. Once Zuma had a good draw going on the pipe, she continued. 'After the herdsmen came, the Jul'hoansi moved away. Game gone, you see. The farmers' herds were eating all the grass.'

She closed her eyes as she began the beloved litany: 'Eland, gemsbok, kudu, wildebeest, hartebeest, tsessebe, roan . . .' The children chanted along, many with their eyes closed, almost tasting the great meat animals. Zuma puffed contentedly. 'Now all these

– eland-gemsbok-kudu-wildebeest-hartebeest-tsessebe-roan – had to move off to find new food.' Zuma shook her head so the feathers wafted sadly. 'Juǀ'hoansi and farmers became enemies.'

'How did they become enemies?'

The old woman removed the pipe from her mouth and sighed. 'They fought each other for things – for grass, for tree-water, for the tame meat animals. The strangers had many things our people wanted. The Juǀ'hoansi took them with their arrows, but were chased off when the ǀTon arrived' – Zuma paused, rolled her eyes – 'with their thundersticks.'

Fear snaked through the older children in the group. Younger ones sensed the mood change. Koba demanded an explanation.

A boy jumped up, extended his arm at shoulder height, pulled an invisible trigger. The fire-fetcher joined him. Soon they were shooting at each other, competing to reproduce the perfect rifle report.

Koba began to cry. Zuma gathered her granddaughter to her, pressed the bobbled head to her red chest. 'Hush-hush. No thundersticks will find you here.'

'Dere, dere,' Koba insisted, pointing towards distant hills.

Zuma's face clouded as she recalled the whispering of the wind. But Koba was too young to have the Ear. Time to abandon the story. The new part might only confirm what frightened them both.

'Yau,' she exclaimed, clapping her hand over her nose, 'my what's-up-front – something's in it. Koba, Koba, can you see?' She thrust her wiggling nose close to the child's astonished face. 'It's pulling me, calling me.' She leaned away from the bemused group. 'A smell has got me by the nose. I must follow. Come, Koba.'

The older children caught on. Getting up, they sniffed the air. The smell of grilled meat was irresistible. 'It's ready,' they shouted as they dashed to their family fires.

Zuma came more slowly, cradling Koba and blowing softly into her ears to disperse any sounds there.

I

South West Africa, 1958

Koba stood at the Mother Hills, mesmerized by the water. She'd never seen anything like it. A pool of permanent drink, glowing yellow-green like a cat's eye seen in the firelight. At home, deep in the Kalahari Desert, water collected only after a rare downpour. It lay briefly in shallow, brown sheets, then vanished. 'Sipped by the sun,' said her mother. 'Swallowed by the sand,' said her grandmother.

Koba believed Zuma. Sometimes the old woman could find her a drink of cool water when she stuck a straw into the burning sand. No need now, not with all this!

Koba trailed pink-padded fingers in the water then dabbed at the skin above her anklet of ostrich eggshell beads. Balm for her barbed-wire graze.

'I left a piece of my skin hanging in the claws of the ǀTon fence!' Koba said to Zuma, who was crouched nearby.

Her grandmother shook her head. 'Sorry-sorry for it.' Zuma flapped at the flies paddling in the mucus of her infected eye. 'This tree-water belonged to us, long before the |Ton came. Now, uh-uhn-uhn . . .' Zuma hawked and spat. Green sputum spotted with blood stayed on her chin. Koba darted forward and wiped it with a corner of her hide apron. She hovered as her grandmother hacked out coughs.

Anxiously she studied the bowed head, noting how white the hair was. Now she came to think of it, her grandmother hadn't asked her to shave the ashes from it for a while.

Now Zuma dipped a whisk of bustard feathers into the pool. Koba watched her shake waterdrops onto her skin. They looked like stars on the hide of an elephant, she thought. Zuma rubbed the droplets into her skin, giving careful attention to the tired leather of her concave breasts. Still vain. Koba grinned, as she stepped into the pool to begin her own ablutions.

She scooped up the water with a minimum of splash. This place, where the sound of heat stored in rocks was the loudest noise, unnerved her. Koba bent to rinse her face, raising her buttocks to the afternoon rays. Then she waded ashore and flopped down on the rock to dry off. Her skin warmed, but she kept shivering. She didn't like this place, despite the abundance of water and plant-food.

'And why have Father and Mother gone for more food? Already we have enough meat to make our bellies swell like a snake that's swallowed a buck, yet they collect more.' She scowled at the pile of nuts her father had instructed her to clean. 'Are we termites trying to stock a nest?'

Zuma said nothing, just rubbed water into the folds of her shrunken belly. Koba waited. Zuma had an answer; she could tell from her grandmother's feigned deafness. The old woman's hearing was as sharp as a meerkat's. But no words came.

Koba stood up angrily. 'Yau, adults! Always-always ignore me.'

She kicked out at the pile of nuts. Several shot into the pool with plops that amplified as the sound echoed round the stone enclosure. A cloud of blue waxbills rose with a whirr of wings to settle in the safety of a thorn bush.

Koba gazed fearfully about, but nothing else moved except the creeping shadow of afternoon. Behind, she heard Zuma suck her few remaining teeth.

'You are like a calf butting the wrong end of its mother. Put your heart in the right place and your mouth will find milk.'

Koba sulked. Grandmother was her favourite relative, but trying to understand her when she was using nlom talk, words that came to her from the spirit world, was like trying to see the sun behind clouds. Something shining was up there; a person could feel it, almost see it, but it hurt to look too long. After a while she squatted down, slightly behind her grandmother. 'Grandmother n!a'an,' she asked respectfully, 'are there evil spirits in this place?' Zuma manoeuvred a stiff turn towards her. Her expression was grave.

'Uhn-hn, I don't feel them, child.'

'I feel something – like lions walking,' Koba whispered.

Zuma looked about agitatedly. 'Yau, do not mention clawed things. Not here. Not now.' Her bead and brass hair ornaments swung in front of her face as she shook her head.

Koba knew she'd done wrong. A person shouldn't speak directly of danger. It might awaken. But it wasn't her fault she'd been born as sensitive as a springhare's whisker. She tried to be like other children, tried to play catch-clap and feather flight out in the bush without hearing whisperings on the wind, but she did hear the voices of people who weren't there. Not distinctly, just as mumblings she didn't understand.

When she'd first told her father he'd deliberately tried to distract her. When she persisted with her questions, he'd gently chided her for concerning herself too soon with 'things the old people haven't told you about yet'. She'd taken her queries to her mother, who had referred her to Zuma.

'Could it be that, like you, she has the Ear,' N‡aisa said, trying not to sound proud.

'Why you want to worry the child with sky-things now? Spirits talk-talk-talk; does that mean she should listen? A person must be trained for these things; they must learn to receive nǀom. Nǀom is a fierce thing. It is too strong for children.'

Koba had been content to accept that anything she heard in the wind was not a message for her, and now she tried to ignore the near-cacophony of whispers her inner ear detected around the Forbidden Pool. The effort was making her irritable.

'What about your nut work, daughter of Tami?' Zuma reminded her. 'Your father asked you to clean them.'

'Too many to crack open and it takes too long with the hammering stone wrapped up,' Koba snapped. 'A mangetti won't open unless we're sharp with it.'

'Mangetti nut will be no match for you in that temper.' Her grandmother smiled, but Koba was remembering her father's enigmatic instructions before he left camp to go hunting.

'Muzzle the stone,' her father had said. 'No one must hear it talk or they will know we are in the Mother Hills.'

Koba knew people were afraid of this n!ore. She'd heard it spoken of in hushed tones around campfires. Was it because of its closeness to |Ton? she wondered.

She had never seen whites, let alone their homes. And even here they were so far from a |Ton house, no smoke was visible.

Perhaps |Ton don't use fire to cook, Koba mused. People said they had machines to do their work – and their walking. The machines were wondrous, people said, but the |Ton were ugly – chameleon skin – first white, then turning red in the sun. Coming off, like a snake's. Did that hurt? she wondered. And did |Ton truly have hair like winter grass – pale and straight? She wanted to see them – just a small look – but her father said they should leave as soon as possible.

To Koba's surprise, Zuma now spoke. '|Ton say if we walk on this ground or take even one springhare from it, we can be killed. '!Khui!' Zuma reproduced the report of a rifle. The sound sent a lizard scurrying for cover and left Zuma coughing. Koba hesitated in offering help – it served Grandmother right for making such a disturbance. When Zuma began scrabbling feebly for her pipe, Koba relented. Just sucking on it could soothe the old woman. Koba fished it from the beaded pouch. The stem was long gone, and the wooden bowl had two dark indentations where Zuma's fingers had gripped it for as long as Koba could remember. She handed it to her grandmother.

She waited while Zuma sucked her cough into submission, then she pleaded: 'Why-why have we come? It's safer in the desert – a person can hear things. Should we not begin to pack the food, Grandmother n!a'an? Then, when Mother and Father return, we can leave. Be away from here before night?'

'Child, child.' Zuma brushed off her beseeching hand. 'Do not worry me like a bee around a honey badger. I sit here until I die.'

'Die, *die* – yes, you will.' Koba gripped her grandmother's twig-like limb as hard as she dared. 'Haven't you seen the gemsbok Father shot, and the duiker hanging in the gai tree? The |Ton will come with his gun and kill us all!'

'Koba, Koba,' Zuma tsk-ed, 'be still. You are like a tumbling weed – fast-fast going nowhere. Sit. Sit. There is a story I will crack open to tell you.'

For Koba the words worked like a lullaby. She felt safe, secure as a seed encased in nut. It was almost as though she was little again and being cradled in her grandmother's lap. If Grandmother was relaxed enough to tell tales, there was nothing to fear, Koba thought. Grandmother could see beyond. Spirits talked to Zuma even when she wasn't in trance. She heard them clearly, so she would know about any imminent danger.

The old woman reached for a peeled mangetti and sucked on it, her milky eyes focused on the horizon. Koba moved the bag out of reach. They hadn't peeled enough yet.

Zuma squirrelled the nut away in one cheek and smiled, lopsided. 'Your grandfather, Khal'an, was very fond of this place. It was here that we first saw each other. There' – she gestured to where a beach arched over the eye of the pool like a blond brow – 'where medicine dances would be held when all the Jul'hoansi came. We women sat *there*, singing. The men answered from beyond the circle. Slowly, slowly they moved in, stamping, singing, the rattles on their ankles going so.' The old woman rotated her wrist. Bangle jangle approximated the sound of jiggling shells and beads.

'In the middle of the line I saw a young man, taller than the others.' Zuma reached for her feather bushel, began to trace dreamily along her leg. 'He had muscles like an eland, long and strong-strong. His chest. Yau! Bright in the firelight, golden like metal. When I saw his head – bent so as not to be boastful of his view above others – I knew him to be Khal'an, whose mother was Koba, she for whom you are named.'

The old woman removed the slimy kernel from her cheek and nibbled at it. Between swallows she spoke.

'Now Koba had the water rights to this hole, from when it was called ǀKaeǀkae, before it was Mother.'

Her granddaughter began to fidget. Perhaps Zuma was no longer kori-woman, best storyteller in the tribe?

'Koba had them from her mother, old Be, who was married . . .'

'Grandmother,' Koba blurted. 'What happened when you saw Grandfather?'

'Eh? Oh, Khaľan . . . Khaľan felt the interest of my eyes and I looked away.'

Koba nodded. It was proper behaviour. Zuma chortled. 'But when everyone was asleep, I met Khaľan up there.' Zuma gestured with difficulty to the ledge high above their heads. Koba craned her neck to see, but was blinded by the sun refracted off the rocks.

'I shall show you . . . when you have finished your work.'

'But, Grandmother . . .'

Zuma ran gnarled fingers around her gums to clear nut debris. 'Auck, child, it is hot now to climb so high . . . and the way is heavy with unfinished work to carry on one's conscience. We will look tomorrow.'

'But . . .'

'There is time.'

Zuma hummed while Koba sighed elaborately, but to no avail. She resumed work peeling the nuts, trying to conjure up the face of her dead grandfather. All she could remember were his fingers, feathered it seemed to her. Later she realized the feathers were because he was always plucking birds. Khaľan had been the best trapper in the village, adept at setting snares for gamebirds: guinea fowl, sandgrouse, even large kori bustards.

One day he'd disturbed an adder and had been bitten on the ankle. Zuma had bound the wound with strips of hide, but still the leg had ballooned. After a few days it looked taut and shapeless, massive as the branch of a baobab tree.

Soon the skin on Khal'an's limb had begun to break down, splitting into oozing sores which ate deeper and deeper into his flesh. No amount of poulticing had kept the rot at bay and finally maggots had set to work, eating the wound clean, but exposing the bone.

It was a relief when the leg eventually fell off below the knee. They'd buried it, as if it were a full corpse, moved away as custom dictated, and the wound had healed.

But Khal'an had lost his will to live. He lay in their hut day after day, his face turned from the door.

Zuma had discussed with her son-in-law, Tami, her wish to carry Khal'an to the rock painting. But without help from others in their group they could not manage it. And they could not insist that their kinfolk come too. A pilgrimage to what had become known to the band as the Mother Hills was just too dangerous.

Many medicine dances had been held for the healing of Khal'an, with Zuma entering a trance herself so that she could plead with the spirits to leave Khal'an with her a while longer. But they told her he wished to die, so Zuma had sat beside him as he wasted away, refusing on his behalf the choice meat young hunters brought to tempt him.

As though she sensed Koba's thoughts had made the same journey as hers, the old woman sighed. 'Uh-uh-uhn. I have lived too long without him. It's my time to die. Khal'an's spirit will come here to meet mine.'

Koba frowned to see Zuma contemplating her own emaciated arm. 'I long to feel him stroking me, but bah' – she sneered at her limb – 'this ugly thing. Once it was a python – smooth, shining, with beautiful markings. Many men wanted to stroke it.'

Her granddaughter shuddered. Everyone knew that Zuma had eaten food with many men. Her appetite was still big-talk around the campfires.

Zuma guffawed at Koba's prim expression. 'Don't worry; tomorrow you leave me on the ledge.'

Koba flung herself at Tami on his return. 'Father, Father, will we leave Grandmother here when we go?'

Tami's shoulders were red from the bloody gemsbok embryo he carried slung around his neck.

'Yes,' he said, gesturing for her to gather some branches so he could lay down the carcass. This meat he would cook tonight. It was so tender his mother-in-law might manage to chew it.

Koba was still at his elbow. 'What about the hyenas and baboons? I've seen their spoor.'

'That's why we'll leave Grandmother up on that ledge.' Holding the buck by its toy-sized back hooves, he slit along the belly. Fluid gushed out, falling onto the sand. Immediately flies fell onto the gore and began to lap at it. 'Rock at her back and a fire at her feet, she'll be safe until she chooses to let her spirit leave her body.'

'Safe perhaps from the hyena – but the baboon? That Tearing-tooth will douse her fire to get at her.'

'Koba, Koba!' Tami slipped the knife carefully into the sheath at his waist. Its blade was badly chipped but he didn't dare sharpen it – it was eggshell-thin already from all the filing. He needed metal to make a new one, but the only place to get that was at the trading store. He was reluctant to go there. ǀTon frequented it.

He set the buck down on a rock and pulled his daughter towards him. Looking into her eyes, he asked, 'What's the matter with you? You've seen old people sit down to die; or lie in their huts waiting. If a hyena hurries Grandmother . . .' He shrugged and stood up. 'If Zuma has spoken to you of her coming death, then she must also have told you how dangerous this place is for us. But not for her. We must go. She has chosen to stay.'

It was miserable around the campfire that night. Icy wind penetrated thin karosses, crêping flesh and fraying tempers.

'Animal hide is no good for such nights,' Koba's mother, Nǂaisa said. 'The cold stabs through into one's back.'

'Eh-ha.' Zuma nodded. Her back was full of scars, burn marks from years of lying almost in the fire in the search for warm sleep.

Tami looked up from the thumb piano he was strumming. 'Turn your backs to the fire, women. They will soon be warm.'

'And then our fronts will be frozen.' N‡aisa looked tired, the smooth of her brow ruffled with resentment. 'If we had proper clothes, wrap-right-round ones like the |Ton's, we could be warm all over.'

'You do not need |Ton clothes!' Tami snapped, pushing the crude keyboard away from him and dangerously close to the fire. 'Every time we come within a day's walk of the |Ton, you become long-lipped.' He stared at them all, firelight blazing in his brown eyes. The women dropped their gaze, he dropped his voice. 'Your karosses are as thick and soft as I could make them. Your aprons are beautiful with the many beads I have sewn onto them.'

Koba was surprised at her father's words. Almost boastful. Lucky they weren't in the village. People might think Tami was strutting.

'An apron takes a long time to dry after rain-soaking,' N‡aisa was saying. '|Ton clothes dry much quicker.'

Tami tore at his hair. 'Leave it alone. You're like a fly on a wet wound.'

The females stared. It was seldom the man people called 'Quiet Tami' became so irascible. 'Yes, it's cold . . .' N‡aisa and Koba rolled their eyes at each other. 'Bone-biting,' he admitted, his neck corded with the effort of control, 'but tomorrow the sun will shine. We'll walk away from here . . . with nothing to slow us down.'

He jabbed a finger at the women ranged around the fire opposite him. 'For too long our people have thought that |Ton ways are better than ours. They are not!' Tami banged his fist onto his knee. 'You must learn this, Koba; teach it to your children.'

Koba nodded solemnly. It was the first time her father had made a marriageable-age remark to her. Did this mean she had a suitor? She tried to catch her mother's eye, but N‡aisa was furiously mashing up the inside of the small green melon she gripped between her knees.

Tami walked around the fire and hissed at his wife: 'Yes, the |Ton have many machines – lorries, guns – but they are slaves to their animals! They cannot move away fast.' He glared, and then walked off into the darkness.

Koba stared at the fire, flames now sputtering because her mother had placed the moist melon into it. What was going on? Everyone was so careless.

'Bah,' N‡aisa grumbled, 'what do |Ton need to walk away from? *They* have freedom. We are prevented from hunting animals we've always eaten; we have wires across our paths . . .' The moisture in the melon was burning away. N‡aisa ranted on, regardless. Koba drifted off. Her mother was always grumbling. Being with her grandmother was better. But Grandmother was dozing again, or pretending to.

She walked in the direction her father had taken and found him picking leaves from an acacia tree. Irritably he shoved them into his pipe.

'My heart longs for tobacco.'

'I know.' She laid her hand on his knee as she squatted down next to him in the mauve moon shadow of the tree. The night was noisy with the 'nyaaaa' of the

31

jackal, comforting despite its tremulous sound. Koba waited for her father to speak. Instead he stood, smiled, and swung her up and over one shoulder, as he'd done when she was little.

Koba felt foolish riding high into camp. She was too big; too much of her torso protruded above her father's head. She felt unsteady. And she hated the sight of her grandmother from up there. She looked too small in her kaross, like a worm that couldn't fill its skin, Koba thought.

Koba scraped a little hollow for herself in the sand and lay down, curled up as close to the glowing fire as she dared. Above her the night sky dulled, the glittering banner of the Milky Way cloaked by clouds driven in by a violent wind. When the moon peeked briefly from behind the billowing black, baboon sentries were visible on the ridges above them. One began to bark.

'You have offended the People Who Sit on Their Heels,' Koba's father teased, reminding her of their noontime conversation.

Koba rolled over irritably. She didn't feel like jokes. How could her father not understand what was in her heart?

Seeing her tense back, he threw an extra log onto the fire and, despite his better judgement, blew it into flame. Koba relaxed.

Later, when her parents were asleep, unusually far apart on their sleeping mat, Koba crept across to Zuma.

Zuma closed her eyes as if to dismiss her granddaughter, then she opened them and gave one of her worn-down grins. 'Come lie here with me,' she whispered.

Koba scooted over and, with a sigh of relief, snuggled into the curve of her grandmother's bony frame. Almost instantly she felt the chilling tappings in her chest begin to warm, then gradually synchronize with her grandmother's heartbeat. The sensation soothed her, and somehow it was more than just comforting; it was emboldening.

'You know this tapping too, don't you, Grandmother?'

'I have known it. Now I am too weak and have lost the hearing in my Ear.'

'But can you tell me what the tapping means?' Koba asked, her voice less sure now.

'I can tell you only that it is a warning . . . from the spirits. What you must beware of, I can't say.' Zuma gave a long, tired sigh. 'I am sorry. I am too old now to help you hear this message.'

Koba's fear returned. Something was out there. Something dangerous. Her breathing quickened and her heart raced, its clamour drowning out the polite knocking of her tappings. Then she felt her grandmother blow onto her head. She inhaled the warm, Zuma-smelling breath. It was as pleasing as the smell of her favourite mangetti nuts roasting in a fire. Light as moth wings, her grandmother's hands fluttered down to cup her face. The dry old hands drew all the anxiety from her thoughts, and she began to relax.

'Time for sleep now, not for worry-worrying. Your spirit guide will come to help you when you need it, and it will be a powerful animal. This much I have always known.' Zuma began to croon an old lullaby. Her legs creaked up to cradle her granddaughter, and instantly Koba felt safely cocooned again.

Cosy here, with Zuma n!a'an protecting me from sand-spraying wind, she thought drowsily. Her lids began to close.

But the old woman was asleep before her. Mid-phrase the song stopped and Koba heard the rasp of Zuma's snores. She felt alone again. She lay watching for a break in the clouds so she could see the baboon sentries on the summit. While they watch, I can sleep, she told herself. Tomorrow, perhaps, my heart will be done with this. But when she thought of leaving Zuma, she began to cry. Her sorrow grew and shook sobs from her that she was sure would wake her grandmother. She didn't want that. The old woman should have her last family night in peace. She should be comforting Zuma, not the other way around.

Koba stifled her sobs, and in time was able to stop crying. She rolled away from sleeping Zuma, then stood up and stepped over her grandmother. Carefully she lay down again behind the old woman. She felt the sand spatter against her back, felt her skin contract against the cold, but her heart, pressed against her grandmother, swelled with warmth.

Cold at my front, Koba thought when she woke up. Aah, that was why – her mother was raking away the warm ashes. Auck, Koba sucked her teeth, the sun's not up yet. And where was her grandmother?

She sat up and was relieved to see her grandmother nearby, shoving things into her kaross. Zuma n!a'an looked stronger this morning.

Now she saw her grandmother shoulder a small bundle with no difficulty and turn towards the summit path.

'Wait!' Koba scrambled up. 'I want to come with you.' She picked up the sack of nuts, grabbed a fistful of meat strips drying in a tree and headed for the steep path. Quickly she caught up. The old woman was breathless, but merry.

'Wipe the worry from your what's-up-front. Look around you. See what the birds see.'

Koba leaned against a boulder and gazed out over the dawn landscape. Grass tousled by wind, dunes pink as the eyelids of newly hatched birds. The land looked soft from sleep. In a tree, truncated from this perspective, the hunched shapes of roosting vultures. With the first updraft of warm air they'd take flight, riding the thermals until they were spiralling well beyond sight. There to keep an eye on the day's dying.

'Mother' – N‡aisa appeared and took Zuma's bundle from her – 'walk carefully or you will kill yourself falling off this path.'

Zuma began to laugh, at first a wheezy snigger, then with hacking, howling mirth. N‡aisa looked mortified. Koba gave her arm a squeeze while she tried to hide her giggles. Her mother grinned sheepishly. They linked arms and continued up the path.

Once out of the gully they found themselves in sunshine. N‡aisa allowed herself a tentative smile while Zuma exulted. 'Aiee-eeee-aaaa!' she shouted, flinging her arms above her head towards the gold and guava sky.

The vultures shifted on their perch as if appalled at the old woman's vitality.

'Hush, Mother n!a'an!' Tami pleaded as he came into view carrying armloads of meat and utensils. 'Your voice will carry.'

'Let it,' Zuma wheezed. 'Let everyone know I'm home!' She scuttled forward. 'And here are the Early People.' She pointed to a rock wall, off to one side. It was covered in drawings, reddish-brown and black, human figures and animals.

They all stepped forward, transfixed. Reverently they peered at the rock painting. 'Did the great god make this, Mother n!a'an?'

'Some say so, but others say it was the Jul'hoansi, long-long-long ago.'

'Our people have never painted,' Tami said emphatically. He put his bundles on the ground and stepped closer. 'Hau, I see hunters. Didn't know them at first – so flat. But look, look how they stalk. N‡aisa, see, this one's ready with a spear should his friend's arrow fail.'

'And see this woman clapping.' N‡aisa traced around a figure with raised arms. 'They'll feast tonight!' She and Tami drifted off, chattering and pointing as they drew each other's attention to new wonders in the teeming mural.

Zuma tapped the rock close to a crowded scene. 'A trance dance, child. Full of power.'

Koba frowned. She saw figures in a line, but could they be people? They had the heads of buck and elephant-size penises. The female ones had tails. They leaked from their faces and were bent low like the old. 'I see no power.'

'You must feel it. Put your hand on that eland.'

Koba cupped her hand over the ochre line drawing of a powerful buck. The rock felt cold and hard. Only her back was warm with the sun shining on it.

'No, no, you must press skin with the eland. Use your head to learn his wisdom,' Zuma urged.

Gingerly, Koba leaned her forehead against the sandstone. It felt warm, as though the sun were now shining on her front. But that couldn't be. She was up against night-chilled rock. Yet there was something yielding against her forehead; she could have sworn it was pressed against an animal's abdomen. She could smell a musty male antelope. She pulled back from the mural and stared at the eland. He wasn't meat and blood. She turned her incredulous face to Zuma.

Zuma clapped her hands with joy. Though dim now, her inner eye discerned the mark of the eland on her granddaughter's forehead. The child would have a powerful spirit guide. She beamed, then drew the child towards her and blew over her face. Best if the experience was forgotten by Koba for the time being.

Koba opened her eyes a few seconds later when Zuma clapped again. 'Come. Put my sleeping mat here, son-in-law; this is where I shall lie.'

For the next hour Koba and her parents prepared Zuma's final camp. They stacked firewood and water containers, checked flints and food supplies, scraped out a sleeping hollow, swept the rock floor. They piled extra karosses onto her sleeping mat and arranged her essentials close to hand: tobacco pouch, fire fan, digging stick to use as poker or weapon.

Then there was nothing more to do, nowhere to look but at the faint footpath that led away from the Mother Hills back towards the desert. They all saw the wraith of smoke curled on the horizon.

'The |Ton's home-fire?' Koba asked.

'No, that is towards the west.'

Koba read anxiety in the set of her father's shoulders. 'It could be our own people, Father.'

'No, too big.'

'Maybe it's just a veld fire. Now is the time for them.'

Tami shook his head. 'The sun is not yet hot enough.' Then, seeing the strained expressions on his family's faces, he smiled. 'But perhaps it's yesterday's fire – walked this way in the night. Don't worry – far off.'

Koba was worried. She'd seen how soot stuck to the undersides of feet and left a trail across blackened bush. Even the |Ton would have no trouble seeing such a sign. They had to leave, quick-quick.

She flung her arms around her grandmother and held on, trembling.

'What's this I feel?' Zuma held the child at arm's length. She lifted the small chin in her shaky hand. 'A person who can shelter another in the night has nothing to fear.' Koba sniffed, but felt gratified. 'And you will have a guide. Now you will find your answers.'

'Not without you.'

'I'll be there, beyond the circle of firelight.'

Koba whispered, 'Something bad is going to happen. I can feel it.'

Zuma made to whisper back but Tami rushed forward. 'Stop feeding these notions of hers, Mother-in-law.'

'I say nothing she doesn't already feel.'

'No!' He put a hand on each of Koba's shoulders. 'These are feelings beyond her years. Come.' He turned Koba away. She felt a wrench that tore at her insides like a tree uprooting. She stood in agony, arms clutching her middle. Tami had to pick her up.

Nǂaisa pushed past and kneeled down to Zuma. She clasped her mother's hands and blew on them. Zuma pressed her daughter's head into her lap and murmured something Koba could not hear. Then, 'Go, go quickly.' Nǂaisa jumped up and ran, head down. Hearing her sobs stopped Koba's. She'd never seen her mother cry.

Tami saluted hurriedly and set off with Koba. She twisted in his grasp, stretched her arms out to Zuma. Tami forced her to turn. 'We must hurry.' They ran. Near the bottom of the path, Koba halted and looked back. High up, indistinct, she saw something. But it wasn't bright, like sun behind cloud. It was black and beetle-sized – Zuma with her arms raised to wave, her kaross flapping behind like shredded wings.

2

Mannie sat astride the stallion like a crown prince. He knew that even André, six years older than him, wasn't allowed up on Bliksem. Mannie hoped it was only a matter of time before his uncle, whose arm was clamped around his nephew's middle, would ignore Pa's warning about him being too young and allow him to take the reins.

The ride to the furthest reaches of the farm had been exhilarating. Etienne had given the huge horse its head and they'd galloped full tilt across the land, powdering labourers they passed with their imperial cloud of red-brown dust.

Now the horse stood heaving at the game fence, its coat damasked with sweat stains. Even at seventeen hands high, Bliksem's head did not reach the top barbed-wire strand of the massive construct that kept Etienne's kudu and other antelope out of his cornfields and cattle pastures.

The land beyond the fence was Etienne's too. Recently acquired for game, it was hundreds of hectares of uncultivated bushveld, hock-high grass dotted with thornscrub and occasional trees, which stretched all the way to the distant Mother Hills.

He had another game farm too, hundreds of miles away in South Africa. His brother, Deon, managed it for him.

Mismanaged it, Etienne had grumbled last time he visited and found even common impala buck too scarce to hunt. He'd been planning to write to Deon and give him an ultimatum – sober up and do the job properly, or move off the farm. But now that his boet-and-brood had turned up at Weltevrede, he'd have it out with the idler, face to face – just as soon as the opportunity arose.

Right now, though, there were too many other things that needed seeing to – in his constituency and around the farm. And to top it all, Twi said he had a poaching problem.

He glared down at his foreman. Twi was a wizened little man, whose slanting eyes suggested a Bushman heritage. Now they were downcast as he nudged a dead gemsbok with his splayed toes. She was sprawled against the fence, her soft, white stomach slashed, her uterus burgled of its calf. Blue-black flies fizzed around the mess of mucus and blood.

'Butchering abortionist bastards,' Etienne spat.

'What's a bortionistbastard?' Mannie asked, not missing the warning look his father gave his uncle.

He was thrilled when Etienne ignored it and kept on shouting and swearing, using words Mannie desperately wanted to remember so he could repeat them to the boys at school.

Etienne lowered his nephew to the ground then jumped off the horse. He bent over the buck. 'Didn't even want the horns or the hide, the bastards. Killed her for an embryo – a little scrap with hardly any meat on it yet. It's muti-murder, man. Some witch doctor's responsible for this.' The big Boer straightened up, inflated with indignation.

Twi was studying a small wound in the buck's chest. 'Not the witch doctor, baas,' he said, 'Jul'hoansi. One shot. Here, heart-near.' He nodded. 'A good arrow, a good hunter.'

Mannie thought his uncle was going to explode with rage. Etienne's face looked purple, his eyes bulged like ping-pong balls, and he was dancing round in the dust like a horse that didn't want to be saddled.

'Take it easy, boet,' he heard his father say. 'Overwrought and overweight is bad for your heart, hey.'

Etienne's boot lashed out, connecting with the mesh of the enormous fence. It twanged, the reverberation rousing the veld from its afternoon drowse. A butcherbird displaying a blood-red chest flew from the topmost wire with a tearing protest, and a snake slithered away towards some scrub. The stallion shied, but Etienne held on to it, all the while waving his free hand about, shouting at Twi: 'You telling me it's those wild cousins of yours? I'll kill the trespassing thieving Hotnots when I catch them.'

Twi remained silent, staring down at the sand. Mannie had the impression the little man wasn't as worried about his master's temper as he and Pa were.

Mannie backed away from the group. It was ugly to get that cross, the ten-year-old thought. Pa never did. Ma did a bit, but she did have reddish hair. The boy began drawing circles in the dun-coloured sand with a long stick, thinking that his mother got cross about strange things: him not eating cabbage – why was that so important? Pa said it was because she'd grown up German. Kraut. Sauerkraut was what he secretly called Ma when she was annoyed with him. Mannie spied a column of big black ants marching towards their hole. He placed his stick across their path. Soon they'd surge over it to get to the nest. Just like a Panzer division, he thought.

He supposed his ma felt a bit shy about being German. Not so much here, in South West – there were lots of people with Kraut accents around – but back at Impalala. Every time they showed a war film at the bioscope in Nelspruit, he had to fight in the playground next day when a boy said his ma was a Nazi. No good saying she grew up in Africa nowhere near any Tommies or Jews. Easier to fight.

Several yards away, Etienne was still shouting: 'Bliksemse Bushmen, they must *work* for food, just like everyone, or go back to the fokken desert.' A pulse pummelled on his neck. 'We can't have people helping themselves to another man's stuff like they're *entitled* or something,' he fumed. 'Hell, man, what are they? A bunch of Bolsheviks?'

Deon snorted. 'Here it comes – red peril propaganda. I tell you, boet, ever since you became the MP for Onderwater, you've become a cliché.'

Etienne whitened under his tan. Through clenched teeth he said, 'Use all the big words you like, boetie, but I'll tell you one thing, I didn't make all this' – he waved his arm across the endless horizon – 'by sitting on the stoep dopping all day.'

Deon looked away. Ja, Etienne had given him a job when the hotel laid him off, but did he have to be reminded of it every time they met?

Jissus, his leg hurt; he needed a drink. He shouldn't have come on the ride, shouldn't have come back to Weltevrede. He was only there because Marta wanted to visit her father's grave.

It had been more than ten years since old man Hoffman died – during the war, in an internment camp for enemy aliens. Enemy alien; Manfred Hoffman? That was a laugh. The old goat had lived in Africa for longer than he'd ever lived in Germany. The mission station, deep in Damaraland, was the only home Marta had known.

Deon had met her when she turned up at Etienne's farm, Weltevrede, collecting for the mission. Her dusty donkeys needed resting, and she herself must be dying for a bath, said Lettie, ushering the sunburned, windswept young woman inside.

'My dear, you *must* stay the night. I can make up a bed in two ticks, run you a nice, cool bath and . . .' Deon had known what was coming. Sure enough, it was a Lettie-foot-in-mouth classic. 'I can find you a pretty blouse to wear.'

He kicked his sister-in-law under the tea table. She turned guileless blue eyes to him then, registering: 'Not that your blouse isn't very nice. It looks very, er, hard-wearing . . .' she flustered.

Marta looked taken aback at the turn the meeting had taken, but she did her best. 'Um, yes, it is hard-wearing. Hemp, I think. One of my father's . . .' she trailed off.

'And I'm sure it looks very nice on him,' Lettie hastened to reassure her guest.

Marta looked more astonished than offended. Deon groaned. Then Marta started to laugh – a sound he found as refreshing as rain falling on parched earth.

Soon the blushing Lettie was tittering too and promising that she'd get a handsome donation for the mission station from her husband if Miss Hoffman would forgive her and accept her hospitality.

Marta Hoffman appeared that night, still in her father's shirt, but it had been washed and ironed and neatly buttoned up. A shame, Deon thought. He'd have liked another glimpse of the delicate freckles at the base of Marta Hoffman's throat.

'See how nice we did Miss Hoffman's hair,' Lettie said, showing how she'd tamed the red-gold mane into braids and looped it up, fräulein-style. Marta and Deon smiled at each other over Lettie's head.

That night Etienne's supporters gathered for a braai. They were celebrating some rugby success or other. Deon remembered how Marta had scandalized the women by leaving them to talk jam-making while she joined the men out on the veranda.

They'd been drinking brandy and Coke and talking the usual nonsense: 'Hey, you-ous. Heard what the kaffirmeid said to the bishop?'

'Faster master, here comes the miesies,' the men chorused. They stopped guffawing when Marta appeared.

'Would that be about the *Afrikaans dominee*, a Dutch Reformed minister, the government's church of choice, correct-me-if-I'm-wrong? And wasn't he the first person to be prosecuted under our wonderful new Immorality Act?' she asked innocently.

Deon chuckled from the shadows. 'Ja, I read about that one. Ironic.' Marta threw him a grateful green gaze, then watched with amusement as a few men stood up saying nature called, and others busied themselves refilling their pipes or topping up their drinks from a trolley manned by a uniformed servant.

Etienne stood his hallowed ground. 'Ja-well, the law's mos the law, Miss Hoffman,' he said.

'Ja, and a wonderfully flexible thing it is under the National Party, Mr Marais.'

'What do you mean?'

'Again, correct-me-if-I'm-wrong, but didn't the reverend gentleman receive a suspended sentence for this heinous crime?'

Deon kept in touch with the intriguing Miss Hoffman after that, using quiet duty-manager nights at the hotel to write her letters. When she wrote saying her father had died, he took leave and came up to Damaraland to convey his condolences in person.

But that was all before the accident that left him crippled and alcoholic. The booze helped the pain, he explained, but they both knew that was just an excuse.

He'd always been a drinker. Being around Etienne just made him worse.

But what could he do? He had to come. Marta wouldn't hear of delaying the trip, and she couldn't travel on her own, not on a seven-night train journey in her condition, and with carriage changes too. So he'd gone to the bar while she pawned her mother's jewellery to pay for their train tickets to Onderwater.

Tired out from the long gallop across the veld, the stallion ambled up the incline to the house. Young black children, vibrating with excitement, orchestrated the opening of the heavy, cross-barred gate. Some pulled, some pushed, most just rode the arc of its high, wide swing, squeaking with delight. Etienne threw down a sixpence as they passed. Dive, scramble, dust. When Mannie looked back the children were back on the gate, chirruping and rocking like birds on a telegraph wire.

The farmhouse was a tin-roofed stone building with a wide veranda that jutted out in front like a stubborn chin. An adolescent stood there, feet wide apart, arms folded across his broad chest. André scowled as his father lifted Mannie from the horse. 'I hope Pa-you-all had a nice ride?'

Etienne didn't look up. 'No. We've lost a gemsbok ewe – in calf.'

'How'd it happen?'

'Long story. Your cousin'll tell you.' Etienne threw the reins at André. 'Take Bliksem to his stall. Make sure it's Twi who rubs him down.' And Etienne was up the stairs two at a time, Deon trailing behind him.

Feeling André's cruel grip on its mouth, the horse plunged, chopped the air with a lethal-looking hoof, tried to shake free. André smiled and held on. 'Help me unsaddle him, pipsqueak,' he ordered as Mannie tried to slip away.

Mannie hesitated.

'Whazzamatter, hey? You scared of the big horsie?'

'I'm not scared.'

'Come on then, or do you expect me to be your kaffir-boy and do all the dirty work?'

The stallion reared up. André dragged him down with strength beyond his sixteen years. 'Don't think I haven't noticed how you suck up to my pa. Now he'll let *you* ride on his mad horse, but *I* can't.' He punched the stallion savagely in the chest. Bliksem shied, wild-eyed. Again André held him, and now he pinched the horse's upper lip between his thumb and forefinger, then twisted it sharply. Bliksem's eyes rolled, but he stood still.

'Come on, arse-kisser, now's your chance. I've got him.'

Gingerly Mannie approached the horse. It stood still, trembling violently. Gently he lifted the saddle flap. The girth buckle was higher than his head. He daren't ask for help. He stood on tiptoe, legs shaking.

Stretching, struggling, he didn't notice André lean against the horse's chest, forcing it to step backwards. It planted its huge hoof square on Mannie's toes.

'Ow, ow. André, he's on my foot. Eina, man.'

'Ag, isn't he a clumsy oaf.' André grinned.

The horse felt the child's struggles and made to move. André yanked up his other hoof. More pressure on Mannie's toes.

'Eina, eina!'

Bent low so he could see between the stallion's legs, André smirked at the boy's white face. Mannie tried wriggling his foot free. He felt the burn of broken flesh. He closed his eyes against the tears, but they slid treacherously out.

Just across the yard, the veranda door swung open again. 'What the blerry hell are you doing, André?' Etienne roared. André instantly dropped Bliksem's hoof and jerked the horse forward off Mannie's foot.

'Nothing, Pa.'

Etienne addressed Mannie: 'You all right, son?'

'Ja, um-jaaa . . .' Mannie swallowed. 'I'm er – f-fine, Uncle Etienne.' Mannie felt André's eyes boring into his back as he stepped away. He dared not limp.

'Okay then. André, didn't I tell you to put that horse away?' Etienne said.

Mannie kept his head down. He heard clip-clopping across the yard, loud footsteps, the screen door bang. Safe now to hobble and have that cry. He sat on the bench against the veranda wall, partly hidden by the golden shower creeper that fell over it. He whimpered, softly.

One day, one day soon, I'll be big enough to bugger up that André, effing bully, he thought. Then I'll hit him so hard he won't walk for a week!

Mannie sniffed and wiped his nose on his scrawny forearm. His toes were beginning to swell, but at least they didn't hurt as much. They'd gone numb. He decided to sit there for a bit, eyes closed.

*

'Ag, liebchen, was the ride so tiring?' Marta bent to kiss her sleeping son, her plait, still long, but less gold now, fell across her shoulder and the tip tickled his face. His eyes flew open. 'Only me,' she said as she straightened, hands in the small of her back to counterbalance her heavy belly. 'Have you been crying?'

'No . . . ja. Well, just a bit. I hurt my foot.'

'What happened? Let me see.'

'It's nothing.'

'Let me see anyway?' She patted her thigh where she wanted him to place his foot.

'Ag, Ma, don't make a fuss.'

She rolled her eyes. 'All right, little man.' She sat down next to him. 'So, did you have a nice ride? Did your uncle show you anything interesting?'

Instinct told him he shouldn't tell his mother about the afternoon's gruesome discovery. Not all of it, anyway.

'We saw a gemsbok. And Uncle Etienne let me ride up front on Bliksem.'

'That's nice.'

He found a loose thread at his buttonhole and began to pluck at it with filthy fingers. 'Ma? Ma, can Bushmen be cattle-rustlers?'

She flicked her plait back over her shoulder. 'It's rude to call them Bushmen, son. Remember it's Khoisan now. Steal cattle, hey? Why do you ask?'

'Just because.'

'Has that uncle of yours been filling your head with prejudice?'

'No.' The white thread was now grub-grey. He began to twist it. 'Yes. I mean, what's prejudice?'

'Prejudice is disliking a group of people for no reason other than they're different from you.'

'Ja, well, but do they kill, I mean *steal* people's animals, the Bush . . . Khoi . . .?'

'Well' – she put her freckled arm around his shoulders – 'the Khoisan don't call it stealing. They think God made all animals for all people. They don't understand about private property. In their community everything is shared.'

He yanked at the thread and it began to unravel. Ma was all right, but when she started on the stupid native thing, or what were they here, Bushmen . . . Khoikhoi – hoi polloi – whatever they were called!

The button flew off. He dived onto the ground after it. 'But why,' he said over his shoulder, 'would they kill a beautiful wild animal?'

'What beautiful wild animal?'

Mannie could have kicked himself. 'I dunno. Any one. Just, what if they did? Supposing they did?' He peeped up at his mother from under his fringe. His hair had the red-gold sheen of hers in her youth, but he was freckled only across his sunburned nose and cheeks. 'I mean, why would they, Ma, if they like animals so much?'

She tilted her head, studying him, her frown forming freckles into an arrow shape on her forehead. 'If they did it,' she said slowly, 'it would be for food, I suppose, son. Meat to survive on. They haven't got cattle and sheep like Uncle Etienne. They can't grow crops in the desert areas.' She waggled her long finger emphatically. 'But the Khoisan never kill unnecessarily.'

Etienne sat at his dining table that night with the Bible open in front of him. A few years before, in preparation for his bid for office, he'd plugged the holes in his Afrikaner pedigree by acquiring some of the accoutrements of a passionate Boer republican – an ox-wagon, reputed to have been used in the Great Trek (the restoration of which earned him valuable column inches in the local paper), and the Old Testament he was now thumbing through. Of course, the family tree on the title page was not his, but Maritz was close enough.

Attending the Bible-reading before supper was now obligatory for family and servants at Weltevrede. That night they heard Etienne read from Exodus 21, verses 12 to 24: '. . . he that smiteth a man, so that he die, shall be surely put to death,' without irony and in High Dutch. This was the only time they heard anything but Afrikaans from their master, whose linguistic dexterity meant he was fluent in English, Ovambo, Himba and several Nguni languages too, but whose new-found Afrikaner nationalism forbade their use on his farm.

After the staff filed out to their meal in the compound, Etienne made an announcement. 'We men are going on a hunting trip tomorrow. We'll take the old trekker wagon out, head towards the Mother Hills. Can you pack some padkos for us, Mother?'

Lettie Marais flustered prettily. She was the only child of the largest landowner in the area, a prize, not just because of her looks, but because locals thought she had style. She'd been to beauty school, in the city. She knew how to dress, do a manicure and set hair. And her milk tart won first prize at the country show every Easter.

She'd been wooed and won by Etienne shortly after his arrival in the Onderwater area and in due course he took over the running of her father's farm too.

Now she patted her perm. 'Liewe magies, Daddy, there's only the Christmas things in the pantry and we can't eat those. Tomorrow I could bake. But what about meat? If you waited a bit . . .'

'We don't need meat. We'll get a kudu. Weather's right for making biltong.'

Mannie noticed the inquisitive lift of his mother's eyebrows. 'One of your precious buck? Well-I-never!'

Uncle Etienne ignored her, nodded towards him instead. 'You coming tomorrow, little man?'

'Can I, Ma? Can I, Pa?' he pleaded, but he knew the decision was his uncle's. He'd be going.

Mannie puzzled over Ma's attitude to his uncle. She was always arguing with him, getting annoyed over things he said about kaffirs – mustn't-say-kaffirs – natives, things about natives. And about the government. Instead of staying in bed like she was supposed to with her pains, she seemed to seek Uncle Etienne out. 'To needle him,' Pa said with a laugh.

Uncle Etienne's funny too, Mannie thought. Most of the time he ignores Ma, but sometimes, when he thinks no one's looking, he stares at her. I see. Pa sees. It makes Pa's top lip twist tight as barbed wire.

3

'Okay, we've got everything. Let's go,' Etienne said. It was still dark as the party pulled out of the farmyard. A drover walked beside the oxen, holding a lamp. Mannie stood in the back of the wagon, among the spares and supplies: ammunition boxes; hunting knives; a fifty-gallon water drum; paraffin and more lamps; shovels and rope; tarpaulin; stools; bed rolls, cooking pots, tins and baskets of food tied up in muslin cloths to keep the dust off.

Mannie was in a sulk. He'd hoped they'd be going in the big wagon, the proper Voortrekker cart with a tent, pulled by ten oxen controlled by a whip as long as a rugby pitch, but his uncle said there wasn't time for that – they had to get out on the trail fast.

Why such a big rush, Mannie thought, and why did *he* have to ride in the wagon like a baby?

André trotted past on a high-stepping boerperd. 'Hey, pipsqueak, missing your ma already?'

Mannie shoved his fists into the pockets of his shorts trying to drag them down over his knees. It was colder than he'd realized, but he couldn't wrap his legs in the extra blanket Ma had given him. André would laugh. Mannie slumped down on the hard wooden seat next to Twi, shivering.

'Sun soon,' the driver said.

'Can I take the reins?' Mannie asked.

'No, basie. We must fast-fast.'

'I can make the bullocks go fast. I can, let me show you.' But Twi just cracked the short hide whip and laughed, his yellow face folding into even more wrinkles.

Dried-up old velskoen, Mannie thought crossly. But he forgave his companion when Twi handed him a spotlight and suggested he look for animal eyes.

There weren't many to be seen. The squeak and grind of the metal-rimmed wagon wheels frightened most wildlife off. But he did pick up a small group of kudu, a bachelor herd, said Twi, judging by the height of their shining yellow-green orbs from the ground. And, closer to dawn, they startled a big-eared steenbok, who zigzagged away, rump swaying. 'Marilyn Monroe arse,' said Etienne as he passed on Bliksem.

Eventually Mannie nodded off. He woke to hear Twi call, 'Hokaai, hokaai,' to the oxen, putting a strange click into the sound.

Etienne trotted over. 'We'll have coffee and watch the sun rise,' he said.

Mannie began to salivate – one of Auntie Lettie's rusks dipped into condensed-milk coffee. Mmm. But first he needed to pee. He sprang down from the wagon and hurried to a bush.

'So, little man.' André loomed out of the dark. 'Your first hunting trip, hey?' Mannie, midstream, ignored him. He felt André staring at his penis. Then he heard the older boy free his own.

'Excited?' André asked him.

Mannie sensed André's nakedness, but he couldn't hear his cousin peeing. He tried to concentrate on restoring his trickle to a spurt. A big gush would be manly.

'I said' – André stepped so close Mannie could feel him through his arm – '*Excited?*' Mannie didn't move. André's penis was long and thick and very nearby. André laughed. '*This* is what excited looks like.' He waggled his erection at the boy. 'See? See?' André reached for something behind him. 'Yours, is just . . . fish bait.' André stepped back and Mannie heard a swishing sound. Too late he recoiled. The thorny branch caught him, a long, white thorn ripping across his foreskin. He opened his mouth to scream, noticed André's gleaming eyes, closed it again. Tears spilled down his cheeks and over his lips, tasting of dust. He fled, tucking himself in as he ran. André's laughter hyenaed through the dark after him.

Day came instantly as they sipped their coffee. One minute the veld was veiled in subtle grey and mauve; the next, it lay exposed, brazen as the fireball sun burst above the horizon. The servants stowed the canvas stools, flasks and mugs – enamel for them, china for the whites – back in the wagon and the hunting party trundled onwards.

They were heading for the Mother Hills, Mannie knew; a spooky place, his cousin had said. The hills were on the horizon somewhere, but something, smoke or a mist maybe, was making them difficult to see. It wouldn't be ghosts – that was just André chaffing him – but could it be sea air all the way from the Skeleton Coast? he asked Twi.

'No, basie, veld fire. No rain; since two summers.'

'Have you ever seen the sea, outa?'

'No, basie.'

Mannie looked disappointed. He'd never seen the sea either, but then he lived much further inland than the Weltevrede-folk did. Ma said they'd stop at the coast on their way back to Windhoek. A Christmas present for him. It was a long detour down a branch line, but Walvis Bay had a nice beach, she said, and she was sure his grandmother, Ingrid, would have wanted him to see the sea. He'd never met Grossmutter Ingrid and knew nothing about her except she had some ugly jewellery and came from a seaside place in Germany. Ma didn't remember much about her either. She'd only been three when her mother died.

Pa worried about the expense of a seaside hotel in the Christmas season, but Ma said it was a treat they deserved, something the three of them could do together before the new baby came. Mannie was excited about the baby, but he was more excited about seeing the sea.

They'd left the dirt road now, and as the wagon bumped along they saw a pale chanting goshawk swoop low, red talons outstretched after a fleeing mouse. The distraction made him miss his prey and he swooped back up to alight on a camel thorn and glare down at the intruders with a fierce eye. Mannie was excited to see a herd of springbok running from them. There weren't any at Impalala and he'd always wanted to see one pronk. Now several obliged, one after the other, leaping high into the air, legs straight, backs arched, heads down.

Twi pointed out the fan of brilliant white hair that flared on every buck's back as it leaped. 'Smells,' he said, touching his wide, flat nose. Mannie sniffed; there was an odour in the air which could have been a secretion – it smelled rich and sweet and waxy. Soon the springbok were out of range.

Funny how none of the men seemed interested in shooting them, Mannie thought. Springbok was supposed to make the best biltong. But the riders kept their guns slung across their chests and their horses' heads towards the Mother Hills. Mannie picked at a scab on his knee, yawning.

It got hotter, the going even slower as the high orange grass hid dongas and antbear holes. When they weren't lurching into these, they were digging the wagon wheels out of soft, sucking sand.

Mannie flapped irritably at a fly trying to settle on his bleeding scab. He wished he'd stayed at the farmhouse. His penis smarted, but he couldn't examine his injury. André kept wheeling back on his horse to wink and joke and jeer.

Eventually, Etienne reined in next to the wagon. 'Smoke's closer,' he said as he climbed aboard from his horse's back. He tethered the animal behind the wagon and then returned to the chest that served as a seat. He stood on it, planting his big boots between Twi and Mannie. They were the same height so he held comfortably onto each head for balance, scanning the veld like a captain on his bridge. 'Fire's moved east,' he announced.

Mannie noticed the khaki cloud where his uncle was pointing. The sun looked greasy through it, like a butter stain.

Etienne sat down between them. The old wagon chest sagged. 'Head for the black,' he ordered Twi, pointing to a section of burned veld. And to André: 'Send the tracker ahead. If anything's been this way since the fire, we'll soon know about it.'

Mannie cheered up. The hunt would soon begin.

Oxen and horses moved reluctantly over the charred veld. Tussocks still glowed from the fire, while the remains of camel thorn trees showered sparks. Mannie began to cough. They were stirring up soot. It was getting into his nose. He spat, trying to get rid of the acrid taste in his mouth.

Now they saw no game, other than a tortoise, upturned and feebly flailing its legs to right itself. Using the butt of his rifle as a polo mallet, André whacked it into the air. Mannie was relieved to see it land upright and lumber off. To the left, an emerald-spotted wood dove pecked through the charred debris of a tree. Then she lifted her grey throat and ululated her lament.

They saw the Tswana tracker jogging towards them, soot all the way up to his knees, like long socks. 'Masarwa, Masarwa!' he panted.

Etienne jumped up. 'Where?' he demanded. The tracker gestured to the east of the now-visible hills. Etienne sprang down, untethered Bliksem, and mounted. 'Whip these blerry oxen up,' he shouted to Twi before he galloped off.

To Mannie it seemed ages before the wagon reached the huddle of men. He jumped down, shoved his head through the palisade of legs, but could see no animal tracks. Only footprints. One was perfect – five small toe pads and a curve of heel, like a signature stamped in the soot. 'Masarwa – Yellow Ones,' the tracker was saying, holding up three fingers.

Mannie couldn't see. 'What is it, what is it?' he asked, but all the men were staring in the direction the tracker was pointing.

'Opsaal!' The circle broke up on Etienne's command. Men sprinted for their horses. Mannie felt himself scooped up like a toddler. His uncle dumped him back in the wagon. 'Come on,' he said, 'or we'll never catch them.'

Catch *them*? How many leopard were there? 'Do you think it's a mother with cubs, Twi?' Mannie asked. 'Do you think she's the one that killed the gemsbok? Uncle Etienne wouldn't kill her if she's still feeding the cubs, would he? Hey, Twi, hey?'

Twi stared straight ahead, the expression on his San features neutral.

*

The veld fire had forced Koba's family to detour. They were making slow progress through the blackened stubble because Tami insisted they step only on tussocks to avoid leaving footprints.

Koba's soles, not as hardened as her parents', burned as she leaped from clump to clump. It was like jumping on red-hot hedgehog. Occasionally she cheated – cooled her feet in sooty sand, leaving an obvious print. Her chest was pounding – from the exertion or from what Grandmother had called her signal, she couldn't tell. And the soot made it difficult to breathe. Black, throat-tickling clouds puffed up every time she landed. To add to her misery, a wind spiralled about her, winnowing sparks from ash, fanning smoulders into spiteful little flames. Eventually she stopped, gasping.

Then she heard it, in the distance – a creak. Voices?

Real ones? she asked herself. But her parents had heard them too. Tami was on all fours, his cheek pressed to the ground. Now Koba could feel the rumble of hooves through her seared soles. Animals – galloping their way – and a chasing cart, with men.

The family ran. The water shell in Koba's sling thumped painfully against her leg. She stopped to rearrange it. Tami sped back to her, grabbed the shell and threw it onto the sand. It cracked. Koba froze, staring. Abandoning water?

Her father grabbed her hand. 'Run, or you'll never need water again.' He pulled, so fast she didn't have time to tussock-hop. 'Faster,' Tami urged.

They ran without stop until Tami held up his hand. Mixed with the thump of their hearts, the sound of hooves. Closer.

'We must hide,' Tami said.

Nǂaisa's words came in squeaks as her ribcage accordioned with the effort of breathing: 'You do not know . . . that the people with hooves . . . mean to harm us. Let's go forward . . . greet them in friendship. Perhaps . . . tobacco.'

'No!' Koba shrieked. Now her fear had a name and pair of blue eyes. 'ǀTon . . . – I hear, feel, lions' paws. We must get away!' She set off like a hunted buck. Now she was pulling her parents along in her wake.

'It's Bushmen, definitely Bushmen. Once you seen those little footprints you never forget them.' Etienne spurred his horse.

Deon, astride a thick-necked mare, bounced next to him. The chase was sobering him up. He'd need another drink soon. 'Still find them this far west, hey?'

'Not often, man, not unless they've come to raid.'

They didn't gallop for long. The tracker had lost the spoor. They reined in, watching him zigzag across the ground like a jackal seeking a scent. He cowered when André berated him for his carelessness. Far behind, the wagon lumbered along.

'Do they give you trouble, these Bushmen?' Deon asked, unscrewing the top of his hip flask.

Etienne frowned. 'Plenty. Stole a prize heifer from Wiengaard's place last month, and yesterday, well, you saw the pregnant gemsbok ewe.'

'Marta says it's not stealing.' Deon took a swig. 'Bushmen don't understand about private land or animals.'

Etienne's look hardened. 'I suppose she thinks we should just let them help themselves, hey?'

Deon took another swig. 'Ag, you know her. She believes farmers should allow the Bushman into the livestock in a drought.' He offered the flask to his brother. He shrugged at Etienne's indignant snort and said: 'They only kill what they eat.'

'Bullshit!' The jerk on its mouth made the stallion rear up. Etienne drew its powerful neck down, turning the horse in tighter and tighter circles until it looked as though he sat astride a prancing dust devil in the middle of a soot storm.

That woman, he thought. He'd never met anyone who infuriated him as much as Marta. He remembered his first meeting with her, her chest heaving inside a man's shirt as she asked for money for her father's missionary work. Old man Hoffman had been one of those Kraut busybodies, Etienne recalled, stirring up the natives with talk of their rights. Still, Etienne found himself handing over money to the Kraut's statuesque daughter, even though he disagreed with her views and disapproved of the way she banged her fist on his table to get them across. But he'd come to respect that courage and passion. Hell, a person couldn't resist it. She burned red-hot, did Marta.

Transferring the reins to one hand, he used his forearm to wipe his brow. Ja-well, Marta was off-limits – his brother's wife and all that. A shock to see her big-bellied.

Who'd have thought old Deon still had it in him after all the boozing?

'Listen,' he said, letting the horse relax, 'Marta wasn't here fifty years ago –'

'Nor were you, boet,' Deon said slyly.

Etienne ignored him and continued in stentorian tones: 'She wasn't here when Piet Schoeman's father found his entire herd with severed hamstrings – alive but crippled. In agony, hey. The old people still talk about it. I ask you, is that the behaviour of people who respect animals and only kill what they need? No, siree.' He flicked the reins, causing the stallion to shy. As he battled to control it, he shouted over his shoulder: 'The Bushman's a savage. No better than a wild animal!'

Deon sat easy in his saddle, smiling. When Etienne's mount stood still but quivering, he said, 'So you want revenge on the Bushman, hey? This is punitive; a hunting expedition, just like the old days. And . . .' He tapped the side of his nose.

'Listen, man, there was nothing illegal or even secret about those expeditions. The government even ordered a few. Hell, around then you could even *buy a licence* to shoot a Bushman.'

Nowhere to hide in the singed savannah – no grass, no rocks, and the trees had lost their leaf cover. The family's tracks showed in saffron relief against the black sand.

Tami steered them to an abandoned termite mound. It stood tall and pointed on slightly elevated ground. At its base was an antbear hole. 'In there.' He shoved

Koba towards it. She resisted. 'Something may be inside – warthog, hyenas, a snake!'

Tami grabbed a branch and scraped inside the hole, tearing the silken lid off a small, deep burrow. A baboon spider scuttled out, hairs bristling. 'Only a spider. Gone now. Get in, get in!'

'There might be babies. The mother might come back.'

He gripped her shoulders, his knuckles shining white through yellow-brown skin. 'And you might get bitten. It will hurt, but not kill you. Koba' – she'd never seen her father look so desperate – sweat streamed down his forehead, his eyes were wild: 'there is nowhere else. You must hide.' He pushed on her shoulders, forcing her down. 'You are more than water. You are our future. Now hide!'

Koba backed gingerly into the hole. 'Where will you be?'

'Leading the strangers from here. I'll run – down there. Over the burned ground so they can see my tracks.'

'But they will catch you!'

'Yau, not on these cheetah-legs.' He almost grinned. 'Your mother will run the other way . . . which to chase first?' He saw his daughter's face crumple. 'No worry-worry. We will have time to hide. But promise you will not show yourself.' He looked hard into her eyes. They were huge with fear. He steadied his own to reassure her. 'We'll come back for you when the strangers have given up the search.'

Koba started to cry. 'What if you don't?'

He put his hands on her heaving shoulders, spoke rapidly. 'If we don't return for you by dark, follow the fat hunting star – towards the dawn – every night, until three sunrises have passed. Keep the salt pan on your left. You will come to our village. Do you understand?'

Koba nodded.

'Good. You will find the way, I know . . .' He hugged her quickly. 'Crouch-quick, so we can cover you.'

'Wait.' Nǂaisa ran up. 'Take this, my Koba, to cover your head.' She handed Koba her skin cloak then blew tenderly into her daughter's frightened face. Koba gulped at a sob that threatened to choke her, then retreated further into the hole as Tami dragged thorny branches across the opening and Nǂaisa swept the sand, eradicating their footprints.

Take me with you; run is better than hide, Koba wanted to scream. But she forced herself to lie still and quiet. Her grandmother had once said that Juǀ'hoan power lay in endurance, but to patiently wait *now* felt like foolishness. Had Zuma n!a'an foreseen this terrible danger? No. If she had, she surely would have warned them. Too late Koba realized the ǀTon threat was what her tappings had been about. The earth drummed with hooves. All she could do now was hide.

'Go with the wind,' she called to her parents' fleeing footsteps.

Back in the wagon, Mannie held on with two hands. The four oxen trotted at full tilt, the wagon jouncing behind. André rode alongside, grinning at Mannie's discomfort. Nevertheless, Mannie wanted to talk to him. 'Hey André,' he had to shout above the clanging and thumping, 'your pa's not going to kill the leopard and her cubs, is he?'

'What leopard?' André looked surprised.

'The one we're chasing, with cubs. The boy said there were three.' Mannie held his fingers up in imitation of the tracker's signal. André still looked puzzled. 'The Yellow Ones, man. The boy found their spoor and . . .'

Laughter exploded from André like a shot. 'The Yellow Ones are Bushmen, fool. We're tracking Bushmen.' He came closer and, dropping his voice, said: 'And when we find them you'll need your knife to get a souvenir for your ma – something small, like an ear!'

Mannie recoiled, turned quickly to Twi. The driver didn't seem to have heard. With a sick feeling Mannie realized André was telling the truth. They *were* tracking people, probably the people his uncle was so cross with for killing the gemsbok. He picked nervously at his scab, ignoring his cousin as André cantered off, still laughing.

Okay, thought Mannie, if we find those people with the small feet and they are the poachers, what's the worse Uncle can do? Give them a hiding, he supposed. André once said his pa smacked naughty native boys. He wondered if Twi had ever had a hiding from Etienne. André said Twi was very sly. Mannie glanced at him out of the corner of his eyes. What does sly look like exactly? he wondered.

Ahead, his saw his father sitting slack-backed on his ambling horse, his brandy flask in his hand. Ag no, Pa wasn't going to drink until he fell off, was he? 'Pa. Hey, Pa!' Deon turned and waved amiably, but he didn't come towards the wagon. 'Can Pa come here? I want to ask Pa a question,' he called. But the horse ambled on. 'Pa!' Mannie shouted at the top of his lungs: 'B-U-S-H-M-A-N?' he asked. Deon turned, waved the flask, and let the horse lead him on.

Mannie sat down, shoved his hands into his pockets, grabbed a fistful of fabric there and twisted. It'd be all right, he told himself. He didn't have to worry. Uncle Etienne would see to Pa. And the Bushmen. They'd chase them off the farm. That was all.

He unclenched his fists.

Come to think of it, seeing wild Bushmen would be bakgat. Maybe they'd have poison arrows with them and they'd give him one.

From within her lair, Koba felt the ground vibrate to the rhythm of racing hooves. She held her breath, closed her eyes. A rider passed so close she could smell him – sour sweat with pretend-fresh over. '|Ton keep their smell in a bottle,' Grandmother had once said. Koba wrinkled her nose, squeezed her eyes shut even tighter. The smell faded, the vibrations receded.

Slowly, Koba lifted a corner of the cloak and peered through the branches. From her vantage point she could see a black man scampering in front of some pale riders, eyes sweeping along the ground as though he'd lost something. Probably their spoor; Mother was a thorough sweeper. But now the black monkey was chattering, pointing. Had he spotted Mother and Father? She eased further out of her hole. There, in the distance, was her father, running deliberately slowly to draw the hunters away from her mother.

'Yau' – she held her hand to her heart – 'the |Ton have seen him. They've turned their tame animals. Even if Father flies he won't escape them now!'

Tami stopped running. He turned and faced the riders, an arrow in his hand but not in his bow. He raised his other hand in the traditional Jul'hoan greeting.

Etienne slowed the stallion to a walk some distance away from the Bushman. Turning to Deon, he said, 'Bet that old blunderbuss can't hit him from here.'

'That tiny little man? What you want to shoot him for?'

'Not shoot him dead. Just give the bugger a fright. He'll be one of the poachers. Come on, see if you can put a bullet near his thieving feet.'

Deon fingered the 6.5 Mannlicher Schoenauer protruding from his saddlebag. He was a good shot, but he'd been drinking. He might hit the Bushman.

'Bet you can't do it,' Etienne goaded.

'I'm not a betting man, ouboet. Nor are you!'

Etienne eyed him slyly. 'Some things are worth gambling on, hey?'

Deon nodded slowly. 'Some things are.'

Etienne threw back his head with laughter. 'Now you talking, man. Okay, I bet you a case of brandy you can't hit that Bushman from here.' Deon shook his head. 'Two cases?' Deon ignored him. 'Ten? And I'll make it cognac.'

Suddenly Deon felt disgusted. With himself, mostly. 'You know what? After this I'm going on one of those.' He jerked his thumb towards the wagon.

Etienne snorted. 'That I'd like to see. And so, bet-my-balls, would your lovely wife.' Deon tried to stare him down but Etienne had spurred the stallion forward and was making it spin around his brother's mare. It made Deon feel even dizzier. 'Tell you what, kleinboet, hit the kaffir from here, give up the booze and I'll give you Weltevrede as well as Impalala.'

Deon looked hard at him. 'You're going to give me Impalala? To do with what I like?'

'Ja. And my home farm, Weltevrede.'

'Ag, kak.' Deon laughed.

'I swear it,' Etienne said, 'on the head of my son. But the way you been knocking back the brandy I reckon both farms are safe.'

Deon shrugged. He hated farming, but if Impalala could be his own, if he didn't have to be Etienne's gamekeeper and could sell the farm, well hell, he'd move his family to the city – to Pretoria, probably – and start a hotel. Just a small place.

He shook his head, trying to clear it. Dreams. His brother was bluffing. Bastard. He'd like to see Etienne squirm.

Deon dismounted and pulled his rifle free of the bag. 'Let's play, ouboet.' Slowly, he inserted a cartridge, his eyes on Etienne. Etienne smiled down at him from the high horse. Deon put his rifle to his shoulder and took aim. He could see the Bushman in his sights. The man looked unreal, stick arms and legs, like a child's drawing of a person. He looked across the barrel towards Etienne, waiting for him to retract his offer. He heard the wagon pull up, oxen blowing.

'Pa!' Mannie screamed. 'Don't . . .'

Deon lowered the rifle. 'Just testing Uncle Etienne's nerve.'

A shot rang out. The Bushman dropped. Deon let his rifle fall, staring at it in disbelief. 'But I never even . . .'

'Uncle Etienne!' Mannie howled.

Etienne lowered his smoking gun. 'Did you see that? He was stringing his bow.'

Deon stumbled across. 'Are you fokken mad?' He grabbed Etienne's gun. 'What the hell did you shoot him for?'

Etienne snatched the rifle back. 'Listen, boet. All it takes is a graze from one of his poison arrowheads and it's tickets.' Etienne buffed the barrel of his rifle with his shirt-sleeve. 'The stuff gallops straight to your bloodstream. There's stories of men trying to hack off their arms or legs to get away from the pain. But there's no cure for it.'

'Pa? Uncle Etienne?' Mannie called from the wagon, his voice frightened.

Etienne trotted his horse over. 'Now don't you worry, little man. Keep your head down while I go . . .'

'Mannie.' Deon arrived ashen-faced at the wagon. 'I was never going to shoot him, I swear. I was just calling your uncle's bluff. I . . .'

'The Bushman didn't know that,' Etienne said impatiently, 'that's why he began to arm. Lucky I had him in my sights.'

Mannie was crying. 'Is he dead?'

'No, boy, I just winged him. Twi, keep the basie in the wagon with you. I'll go see.'

Loud-bang. Thundersticks? I must look, thought Koba.

She pushed the twigs off the lair's opening. She saw her father kneeling on the ground. He was hurt, but the ǀTon seemed in no hurry to get to him. She wanted to call out, but didn't dare. She noticed her father using his knee to string his bow. His arm must be injured. She trembled, wondering if the ǀTon had seen. Now a black man was running towards Father.

Tami let an arrow fly. It landed in the chest of the tracker. He fell, rolled in the sand, plucked at the shaft, gibbering like a monkey. Stupid man; harder to remove the arrow tip now. Koba watched a big man canter over to him, lean down from the horse, shout. The other ǀTon raised his gun and pointed it at Tami. Again she saw her father struggling to string his bow. She couldn't watch. Koba stuffed the corner of the kaross into her mouth and sank back into her hole.

She heard the rifle crack, but didn't listen for a cry from Tami. There would be none. A Juǀ'hoan did not let his enemy hear his suffering.

Mannie was shaking as Etienne galloped back to the wagon.

'I can't shoot straight from that bloody horse the way it's cavorting today. Here, hold this,' he said, thrusting the smoking Mauser at Mannie. 'Twi, there's two

73

more out here. Let's find them before this turns into a massacre.'

Twi gathered up the reins, very, very slowly.

'What have you done? What? Why?' Mannie shrilled.

'Hey?' Etienne looked puzzled.

'You shot a man, dead!' Mannie shrieked.

'It was self-defence, son. That man was a poacher – a scavenger who rips babies out their mothers' bodies. That's not what nice people do. It's not even what people do; it's animal behaviour.' He wiped a fleck of spittle from the corner of his mouth. 'Anyway, I didn't plan to kill him. He was going for your father.' He made to put his arm around Mannie's shoulders; the child wrenched free. 'I'm sorry you had to see, little man. It was an accident, though, believe me.'

Neither Mannie nor Twi would look at him. Etienne sighed. 'Okay, get this wagon moving, outa.' He turned back to the child hunched in misery beside him. 'I understand how you feel. I saw my father beat a black man to death when I was a sprog. He didn't mean to. He was drunk.'

'You beat natives,' Mannie shouted.

'I've never beaten a kaffir in my life. It wouldn't be a fair fight.'

'You do, you do,' Mannie sobbed. 'André said.'

'Ag, André. That boy needs a good clip around the ears. But first I must sort this mess out.' Etienne clambered down.

'I hate you,' Mannie said.

Etienne sighed. 'Look, son, I didn't start this thing, hey?' He held the boy's eyes with his own and gave his

74

words time to sink in. Mannie stared at him. Pa! It was Pa who'd aimed at the Bushman. Blerry-dronkie-boozing-bastard. What would Ma say? She'd never forgive him. She'd make him leave.

Etienne was still talking, softly now: 'You saw how the little blighter aimed at us. And how he got the tracker. Hey? Did you know that?' Mannie shook his head. 'Got him with his poison arrow. Poor Philemon. Part-Bushman himself. He'll vrek, and a bloody painful death it'll be too. Ja-no, a wild Bushman's a different kind of animal altogether, no matter what romantic stories your ma's been telling you.'

Koba heard the wagon rumble away. She stuck her head out. She could see her mother in the distance, but so could the |Ton. A man on horseback sped towards N‡aisa, whipping up dust. N‡aisa wheeled and ran the opposite way.

Koba realized he was herding her towards the wagon.

With the wagon blocking off one escape route and André another, Etienne knew he could grab the Bushman woman as she tried to run past him. Effortlessly he flung her over one shoulder and dumped her into the wagon.

Deon offered the tracker, Philemon, some water, then he and Twi helped the man over to the shade under the wagon. The arrow out, the wound looked small and innocuous. But the man would not accept Deon's assurances that he would be all right.

'Masarwa poison no good. Black mamba better! Two steps . . . dead! Masarwa? Two hours – makulu pain. Give gun, baas. Better to shoot.' Deon quickly walked away, leaving Twi to tend the man.

In the back of the wagon Etienne towered over the small, half-naked woman. André had her arms pinned behind her back. 'Here's a pretty little thing for you,' he shouted to Deon. 'Smells a bit – they rub animal fat on their skin, but you can always give her a bath.'

'Give me a bloody drink,' Deon said, climbing into the front.

'So this is you "on the wagon", hey?' Etienne laughed as he produced a bottle of brandy. Deon ripped the lid off and sucked at it, hollow-cheeked.

'What you going to do with her?' he said, pointing the bottle unsteadily at the woman.

'Take her home. They make damn fine servants. Not afraid of hard work . . . see' – he turned her round. 'Small, but strong. Feel the muscles in that back.'

Nǂaisa shrank from his finger. Her skin shone with sweat. Her sides heaved.

Mannie looked nervously at her and saw a pulse fluttering in her neck.

'And have you seen this?' Etienne lifted the Bushwoman's skin cloak.

Mannie saw a pair of coffee-coloured buttocks, out of all proportion to the woman's slim legs.

'Now you see where a Bushman stores his water,' Etienne said. André laughed.

Deon looked away. 'It's called steatopygia,' he said.

'Okay, Mr Big Words, here's something you've never seen before. Bend her over, André.' Despite N‡aisa's struggles the boy succeeded.

Mannie turned away, facing front.

'Open your legs,' Etienne shouted and tried to force them apart with his rifle. N‡aisa lashed out at him, connecting his chin. 'Shit! Kaffir bitch.' He rubbed his jaw.

Mannie saw him struggle to control his anger.

'I'm not gonna hurt you, woman – just a biology lesson. André!' he barked. 'Get the woman on her back.' With practised ease, André kicked her legs from under her.

Mannie heard the thud of her fall and closed his eyes.

'Now, hold that knee. I'll do this one. That's right. Pull them apart . . . we want a good view. But keep her down, dammit – she's thrashing like a bloody crocodile!'

André gasped, then giggled at the exposed vulva. His small eyes glittered with excitement and bright spots appeared on his cheeks.

Deon looked up and was surprised to see two skin flaps protruding from the woman's genitals. The flaps were hairless and darker than the skin around her pubic area.

With his splayed thumbs Etienne pinned back the extended labia. 'Pink inside, just like any other, hey?'

Deon stared at his brother with revulsion. 'For pity's sake, leave her alone,' he said as he jumped down from the wagon.

*

77

The sound of squeaking sand made Mannie open his eyes. Wriggling towards the wagon, on his belly, was the Bushman – the one Uncle Etienne had shot. His left arm dragged at his side and, behind him, a trail of dark-stained sand. The Bushman grimaced with every effort, but slowly and surely he was inching forward – to within shooting range.

Mannie glanced about. Had the grown-ups not seen? Nor André? He dared not tell them. Heaven knew what they'd do to the man. But what about Twi round the other side? Mannie leaned over the brake to look for him.

The movement caught Tami's eye and he reared up on his good arm like a cobra.

The gazes of San man and boy met in surprise. Mannie lowered his eyes.

Tami struggled to the lead ox and pulled himself up-right. Using his teeth, he strung his bow, ignoring the spurt of blood that every movement caused.

Mannie felt nausea storm up from his stomach. He dared not move. Silently his breakfast gushed out of his mouth, until only bile dribbled down his chin. But Tami was not looking at him, but down the shaft of his arrow. Mannie heard a whistle of pierced air, then:

'Arghh! What the hell? Jesus Christ, I've been hit!'

Mannie turned to see Etienne with the Bushman's arrow sticking out of his stomach. His eyes were goggled like a cartoon character's. Etienne collapsed into the food baskets.

Mannie threw himself out of the wagon, hit the sand, and ran.

Meanwhile, André grabbed a rifle from the box of spares. Shaking, he loaded it. At twenty yards he couldn't fail to hit the attacker. But Tami saw him and began to scramble away between the legs of the oxen.

'You little yellow bastard,' André screamed, firing wildly into the team. A shot thudded into an ox's flank. It bellowed and surged forward, throwing the team into chaos. Stamping, lowing, four oxen pulling in different directions, the brake screeched its protest. Tami crouched amid the bovine riot and André fired again. The lead beast fell, his dead weight splintering the yoke. His team-mate broke free, but at the cost of a severed hamstring. Its bellows were pitiful and, almost automatically, from where he stood some way off, Deon lifted a rifle and silenced the ox.

Etienne roared from the back of the wagon. 'Will you two swines stop shooting? How the blerryhell do you think you are going to get me back without the team to pull this fokken cart?'

'But, Pa, he's getting away,' André shouted as the San man broke cover. He fired, hitting the back of Tami's head, blowing the front of his face off.

Nǂaisa screamed, jumped out the wagon and ran towards her husband. André shot her in the back. She buckled and then pitched face-first into the red sand. There she lay, one arm flung up in a parody of the traditional greeting.

Mannie was leaning against a termite mound. His stomach heaved violently, but nothing came out. Suddenly, the base of the mound exploded, spewing twigs, earth and an assailant.

Mannie felt his face being clawed as he was pushed over. A weight on his chest and something pressing on his windpipe. He fought for his life, trying to heave the hissing, scratching, pressing leopard off him.

Then he saw an eye – wild, but human – a child, no bigger than him. Maybe even a girl. Jissus, she could fight!

Koba scratched and bit while they rolled in the dirt. She was going to kill this |Ton cub, with her bare hands if she had to. As they tussled she spat out every curse and obscenity she knew: the |Ton boy was a dry-season child and his seed would never populate the earth; his penis was a worm that even carrion flies wouldn't piss on; his father was a man who couldn't eat meat, who had nǂah seeds coming out of his arse; his mother's womb was a withered winter melon.

But by now the fight had gone out of the children. Mannie bit his lip and let the girl pummel his chest with her small fists. When she sprang up and ran away, he followed her.

He'd never seen anyone move like that. Her two slender legs were like four, so balanced was she as she tore down the rocky incline, leaping bushes in her path. When she got to the scene of the carnage, she tore across to a body lying dead still in the sand.

Koba threw herself onto Nǂaisa and laid her head on the blood-spattered chamois of her mother's chest.

Mannie stood dazed. Dead and injured oxen, André and Twi trying to catch the scattered horses, Etienne flinging the contents of the cart out onto the sand and three brown bodies – the tracker and two wild Bushmen. The girl was lying across the breast of one, her shoulders shaking, but he could hear no sound from her.

And where was his father?

'Snakebite serum. Find it. Somewhere here.'

André began ripping through the baskets and boxes lying on the sand. 'Where, Pa, where?'

'Somewhere. Keep looking, damn you!' Etienne sat against a wagon wheel, his face grey, his shirt faintly pink from the arrow puncture. The mid-afternoon sun was searing, but there was no time to rig up the tarpaulin to provide some shade. The serum was his only chance, and even then it wasn't a proven antidote to the Bushman poison. Twi had said the toxin came from the pupae of a special beetle. The hunters rubbed their arrow tips in it. He'd heard it took antelope a long time to die once the stuff got into their bloodstream. About men, he didn't know. Perhaps if he stayed still, didn't shake the stuff up too much and they got him to a doc in time? Ja, surely. He was big and strong and he'd cut the wound open immediately and poured water and brandy in it. Bliksemse thing was stinging now, though.

A shame about Philemon. A good boy. But maybe a wagon wheel going over your neck was easier than dying from the fokken Bushman poison? Ja-well, he didn't intend to find out.

'Did you check the tin with the bandages? I usually put some of the serum in there.'

'I checked, Pa. Twice, Pa.'

'We left in such a fokken hurry this morning I didn't have time to double-check. Hey, have you looked in the saddlebags?'

'All except Bliksem's, Pa. He's gone.'

'Probably back at the farm now. Where's your uncle, and Twi?'

'Uncle Deon's just sitting out there, near the bodies, watching Twi dig a hole, Pa.'

'Bastard's probably still drunk. Jissus, how did I get so unlucky? The one time, the *only* time I need to depend on my family, they let me down. I can't believe you fokken shot the oxen; and all for a thieving little kaffir!' André started to snivel. 'Don't you fokken cry. You get that uncle of yours and make a plan to get me to the doctor fast.'

André plucked at Deon's sleeve. 'Jissus, Uncle Deon, help me, man,' he begged.

Deon struggled up as if from a deep, dark well. His shirt clung to him, uniformly wet, as though he'd been immersed in water. Yet it was hot, stiflingly hot, and dry. Was it blood? He glanced down. No . . . sweat. He didn't remember sweating like that. He shivered and listlessly followed André back to the cart.

Again they turned the entire contents of the wagon upside down, emptied all the saddlebags onto the sand, but no sign of the serum. 'Twi, you bastard,' André shouted, 'stop digging fokken graves and come help us. Can't you see your baas is dying, man?'

Now they went faster, scrabbling through tool boxes, ammunition, under tarpaulin. They even upturned the milk tart Lettie had stayed up half the night to bake. They checked tins, baskets, pockets in trousers and jackets. Finally, all had been triple-searched. There was nowhere else to look.

André stood in front of his father, biting his lip. 'It's not here, Pa.' He swallowed. 'I don't think Pa packed it in.'

André and Deon couldn't bear to watch as Etienne started to laugh. His belly wobbled, the pink patches on his shirt began to seep red. 'Me, the big provider . . . forgot to provide the one thing that could save *my* life. Ha, ha. You've got to find it funny, hey?'

'Don't worry, boet, I'll make a plan,' Deon said.

'Ja-ja, you make your plans while you sit dopping on my stoep there at Impalala. Do you know' – he pointed a shaking finger at Deon – 'I was going to fire you, you drunken bastard, and now' – he laughed harder – 'now you get your very own farm to run into the ground. Good job it's only Impalala, hey? Ja, dankie tog you were too chicken to shoot that Bushman, otherwise, *all this* would be yours to booze away too.' He sank back, sweating profusely. André fanned him with his hat.

'Come, we must build a litter,' Deon said quietly to Twi.

An hour later he and Twi had Etienne on a makeshift litter that could be pulled by the remaining ox. By now, Etienne was in pain. He clenched his teeth, but didn't writhe. Deon passed him the brandy bottle and opened another for himself.

4

Koba wasn't sure how many sunrises she'd slept through. She hadn't expected to wake up.

She had confused memories of a journey with |Ton who smelled of drink and fear and death; and a boy's body, the |Ton cub, tied to hers, to keep her on the tame animal that walked so slowly in the dark, away from the Mother Hills, away from the hunting star her father had told her to follow.

She had kicked the tame animal as she'd seen the |Ton do, to try and make it run with her, but the limping |Ton shook his head sadly at her, and tied her ankles to the cub's and her hands to the seat. He made the cub hold her so she wouldn't slip off.

Koba had the sense that the sorrow of these two – were they father and son? – rose to meet her own pain when their eyes met. They said words she could not understand, but whose meaning she sensed: shock; sorrow; pain; guilt. When the boy |Ton saw that she couldn't bear his skin to touch hers, he tried to lean as far from her as the tame-animal seat would allow.

She must have fallen asleep on the long, dark, death journey. She woke to find herself leaning against the boy as a light shone on her. This was a world of evil spirits for sure. Strange faces in flickering light; shouting, crying, dangerous animal sounds; smells, lots of unnatural smells, and eyes staring at her with hate. Then a pair of kind hands, untying her. She was pulled from the tame animal and carried away in the dark. From the light of a burning torch she saw the ǀTon boy stare after her, his eyes as big as a frog's. And wet.

She was thrown into this place that smelled of animals and ugly faces loomed above her, jeering and spitting. But perhaps that was just a dream? Was the other, too? The one where her father had half a face and her mother lay on the sand, waving?

She pulled her mother's kaross more tightly around her. She was alive and this was no dream. She was alone in this dangerous place and she had to get away and back to the Mother Hills to find Zuma before it was too late. Together they could set off back to their n!ore.

She tried to straighten up, but her wrists and ankles were hobbled together and tied to a sturdy post. Koba struggled against her bonds. She froze as she heard footsteps approach. A stranger, dressed in black. Koba relaxed a little when she discerned a woman, very big, but clumsy as an eland cow in calf.

At the sight of the hobbled child, Marta broke into a run, one hand holding her belly and the other jamming her funeral hat onto her dishevelled hair. 'Who did this to you? Who?' She flung open the gate of the pen and immediately began to attack Koba's bonds with furious fingers. 'I'm sorry, ag, I'm so sorry.' She touched the girl's small arm.

Koba recognized the kind hand, but this was a chance. She sank her teeth into the spotted flesh and tried to run. Her ankle bonds held. Quickly she worked the knots.

Marta was staring at her scalloped wound. 'I'm sorry.' She rubbed her hand. 'You must be frightened and I . . .'

But Koba was free. She vaulted the gate and ran for the high green growth she could see some distance off.

Marta disliked having to disturb her sister-in-law in the middle of the funeral reception but she didn't feel she could organize a search party without Lettie's permission to approach the servants, who stood gathered outside the back door in their Sunday best.

Inside, the front rooms had been stripped of Christmas decorations and the mantelpieces were draped in black crêpe. Both rooms were packed with dignitaries – some local, some parliamentarians Etienne had worked with. Lettie was holding court in front of a huge flower arrangement, smiling bravely at sympathizers and dabbing her swollen eyes with a pretty handkerchief.

Marta thought Lettie was going to run her through with a cake fork when she explained what she needed. She felt someone take her elbow and steer her firmly away. It was Deon, pale and shaky, but sober. Marta shook his hand off. She wanted nothing to do with him after the way he'd behaved out at the Mother Hills, his excuses about bluffing notwithstanding. Yes, he had an inferiority complex about his brother – what man wouldn't have? – but she'd married him because she sensed a basic decency about him. His drinking seemed to have washed all that out of his character.

Chagrined, Deon went outside. A quiet word, some shillings passed round, and men kicked off uncomfortable shoes, handed their hats to their wives and set off to find the child.

It didn't take them long. Koba had left a trail of trampled cornstalks. Grinning, they dumped the struggling girl into a storeroom Marta had prepared.

Koba scurried to a corner of her new jail and huddled there, her back to her captors. The men laughed. 'Out,' Marta said, shutting the door firmly on their interested faces.

She approached the girl cautiously, a bowl of warm Dettol-water in her hands. Gently she placed it on the stone floor. The child winced at the clunk. 'I only want to clean you up, little one, come on, I won't hurt you.' She touched the tiny shoulder.

This time the child did not bite, but she was trembling so violently Marta decided it was kinder to leave her filthy. 'I'll fetch someone who can talk to you,' she said. Taking the blanket from the camp bed she placed it round the child's shoulders and left, locking the door behind her.

She found Twi sitting alone outside his hut in the servants' compound. He was wearing a suit that had belonged to Etienne in his slimmer days. Nevertheless, it looked six sizes too big on this scrawny man. Twi's wrinkled head poked out from the jacket like a tortoise's from its shell. He had the trouser legs rolled up into thick cuffs and he was, as ever, barefoot. Marta smiled. She'd seen the minister frown at this when he spied Twi among the black mourners at the back of the big white church.

'Sorry to disturb you,' Marta said, 'but that Khoisan – Masarwa – child you brought back, I need some help with her.' Twi remained seated and stared down at his feet. 'I want you to tell the child we mean her no harm,' Marta explained.

Twi's snort astounded her. This was rudeness like she'd never experienced from a servant before. But he wasn't her servant, Marta thought, and he had been through a lot out at the Mother Hills. That much was obvious from his haggard look.

'Please,' she said, stepping forward. The man looked up at, and then through, her. Twi was staring at the chicken coop some distance from the compound. He was thinking about Etienne.

Twi had come to Etienne's newly acquired farm one August night to steal chickens. Hearing the squawking commotion Etienne had pounded out with a shotgun. He saw he didn't need it for the inebriated little man who cowered before him in the coop. Instead he grabbed him by the scruff of his tattered shirt and thrashed him, using the butt of the gun like a paddle across his back and bottom. Afterwards, while the man crouched in a corner, sobering up fast and blubbering what sounded like abject apologies, Etienne felt he owed it to the toerag to at least listen. It wasn't dignified, spanking a grown man, but what else could he do to teach the fool a lesson? The big Boer leaned against the wire gate and gave the man a hearing.

'That I, a man who could trap any bird in the bush, should find myself so small as to steal one from another man's cage . . . huw-ah!' Twi lamented.

'So why did you do it then, man?'

'Big-big hunger, baas.'

Etienne stamped one brown-booted foot. 'So come and knock on my door, for fok's sake. It would save me having to come out here in the middle of the damn night. Jissus, kaffir' – he banged his fist on the chicken wire causing renewed panic among the hens – 'I've never turned a hungry man away. We'll make a plan. I feed you, you do some small job for me, then neither one of us can feel bigger or smaller than he should.'

It was too dark for Etienne to see the shrewd interest in Twi's eyes. The Jul'hoan studied the big blond man, his brain clearing with every throb of humiliation. Twi was wary of whites, and this one was a real animal, but not *that* dangerous. The bellowing |Ton had chosen not to use his gun. Not to shoot with, anyway.

The beating had shocked more than hurt Twi, though his buttock stung like he'd sat on a swarm of bees. Huw, if he'd had a poison arrow to hand he would have stabbed the big eating stomach, no matter what the consequences.

But it was a long time since he'd had anything to do with bows and arrows. Thankfully – hunting was a hard,

hard way to fill one's belly and there was no beer in the bush to slake a thirst like he had. Maybe the lion on the other side of the cage could be declawed and persuaded to share his plenty with little Twi?

When the Jul'hoan saw Etienne lean forward the better to study him, he decided to gamble on honesty. With a touch of theatrics, Twi rubbed his sore buttocks then dropped his chin to his chest. 'My hunger is not for food, baas,' he mumbled, 'it's for the beer. Since I left my n!ore for the town, the beer-hunger has clawed at me. See my hands' – he held out a genuinely shaking brown pair, small-boned as a child's – 'these hands could string a bow, or skin a giraffe. Now they shake-shake-shake and can't even hold a spade.' He shook his head and tried to see from under lowered lids what effect he was having. 'I am sick.'

Etienne snorted, so powerfully that Twi was convinced the dust rose obediently in two columns, summoned by the massive nostrils. His jailer stood up, but had to remain stooped to stop his head touching the roof.

'Ja-ja-ja, I've heard it all before,' Etienne said. 'Too sick to work, but not to steal, hey? Now listen, I'm giving you one chance and one chance only. Here's your chicken.' He reached for one of the hens still fluttering frantically. Wringing its neck without taking his eyes off the black man, he handed the limp fowl over. 'If you're still here in the morning, with all the birds alive except this one, you can work for me.'

Twi eased his aching shoulders as his eyes swept up the length of the man bent over him. No doubt the lion had counted his fowl and would keep watch from his house, gun at the ready. But, true to his word, he was giving food. Twi began to pluck the chicken.

Etienne laughed. 'Ja-jong, kaffir, don't you worry. Stay and work by me and I'll keep you so busy you won't have time for the beer-hunger to ever catch you again. And we'll see if we can put a bit of meat on those bones of yours, hey? Jissus, man, you're as thin as a bloody mielie stalk.' With that Etienne smacked him playfully on his burning back and left.

Twi became Etienne's most indulged worker. Twi pilfered tools, clothing, tobacco, seed, fencing, fertilizer. As the labour force grew at Weltevrede, newcomers learned they could buy or barter whatever they needed in Twi's hut. But not alcohol. The blind eye Etienne turned regained sight when Twi used alcohol on the farm.

'I have enough grief from my brother. I'm not putting up with a drunk boss-boy on my home farm,' he told Twi.

So Twi's thirst drove him to a shebeen in town. Occasionally he was too drunk to return in time for work. Then Etienne asked friends in the police force to locate Twi. His foreman understood the trade-off – he was never to let slip that the baas called on a certain Mrs Du Pree and stayed behind her closed curtains all afternoon.

And now the big genital was gone. Killed by an arrow from Twi's own people. Twi shook his head. Who'd have thought he'd miss Baas Big Belly? But he would, he would. Etienne had been his father – father to all the other workers on the farm too. He looked after his people. Gave them food; medicine when they were sick; helped them bury their dead. Twi's face puckered like a sultana as tears slid down his yellow cheeks.

In the storeroom, Twi stepped softly towards Koba. She shrank from him, retreating again into the corner of the room. He touched her, spoke quietly. To Marta his talk sounded like the rapid clicking of a touch typist. Koba kept her back to them.

Twi shrugged. 'Her throat is closed. Must be she fears things.'

'What things?'

'|Ton – white peoples,' he spat out. 'Dangerous things.'

'But I'm not dangerous.'

Twi's look was implacable.

Marta bowed her head. 'I'll wait outside.' She turned back at the door. 'Please – make sure she understands she's not in jail. I'll lock her in, but just for the time being, for her own safety.'

Twi looked at her with interest. Marta brushed hair that wasn't there from her eyes. 'Ohh, I don't know, just a feeling I have.' She shrugged. 'Anyway, I'll get her back home, I promise. You tell her.' She left the room.

Twi squatted down in front of Koba, slowly gave her Marta's message.

Koba found it impossible to stop the shivering down her back, the shaking in her legs. The muti Leopard-woman had left in the room smelled strong – like poison. Would it kill her slowly, or just take the run from her legs? She wanted to ask the uncle, but her voice would not come. More |Ton magic? What were they doing to her?

Tears slid down her cheeks, snailing through the grime. She felt herself sobbing, heard it in her head, but knew no sound was coming out her mouth.

The man was talking. Talk-talk, talking, but she found him difficult to understand. He has my face, but only half my tongue, she thought. And I have no tongue at all. The |Ton have taken it. She gesticulated at her throat, shaking her head, crying harder and faster.

Twi stared helplessly at her. Eventually: 'Yau, perhaps you are speechless.'

He squatted back on his heels, studying her. Perhaps this child was deaf too. That was why she didn't respond to his questions. Better if she'd been blind, he thought. Him too. He wished he hadn't seen that mess out at the Mother Hills. But it was not of his making and it was none of his business – especially if he wanted to keep his position under his new, murdering boss. He could advise this kin-child, that was all.

He tried to speak clearly, keeping every word distinct: 'The woman who was here, she with the spots, will not harm you. She bids me tell you this is not a prison. She locks you in to keep you safe. She says she'll send you home.'

Koba looked baffled. Twi shrugged and he stood up. 'My heart is sore for you, little closed-throat, but what can I do? I can't help you here. The new baas doesn't like us. But you go with the big spotted woman. My baas used to like her. She is soft. She will help you. Stop your

94

shake-shaking now. Drink some water. The woman will help you. You are not in prison.'

Koba had understood just one word the man said: 'prison'. It was the new word Grandmother had used at the Mother Hills – the one which put such fear into her. Now Zuma's explanation came back: 'Sometimes, ǀTon do not *kill* fence-crossers. Sometimes they bury them alive. ǀTon tie a person's hands and trap the person behind high walls. You cannot escape. Men guard you with thundersticks. You are caught, tighter than a sandgrouse in a snare. Worse-worse is' – Koba could picture her grandmother's bony finger wagging – 'they do not kill you. You cannot join your ancestors. No,' she had said, shuddering, 'they feed your body, but inside your spirit shrivels from the hunger. Uh-uh-uhnn. That is what I know. That is what I have heard. Prison, they call it.'

Koba pushed the water bowl away, spilling the cleaning solution. She fell back on the bed, rigid with fear. A tiny window set high in the wall, but barred. As she gazed, the walls shifted, seemed to draw closer together. The ceiling sank. The sky through the window was far, far away. Koba felt a tightness in her chest. Breathing became difficult. She began to gasp. The room was shrinking, soon there would be no air for her. Panting, she felt her head spin. She mustn't faint. She had to get to Zuma.

5

The day after the funeral, Mannie heard his mother step into his room.

'You awake, liebchen?'

He lay tense, eyes shut. Were the police here? Had she come to call him for questioning? If he pretended to be sick would they all go away and leave him alone? He didn't want to have to talk about the shootings, to say he saw the Bushman crawling towards the wagon. He didn't want to have to say what the grown-ups were doing to the Bushwoman in the back of the cart. Even now his cheeks burned at the thought and he felt sick.

The funeral had been terrible, but not as bad as before, when Uncle Etienne had lain in that open coffin and he'd had to stand there with Ma and Pa and Auntie Lettie-and-them pretending it had all been a terrible accident.

He'd never explained to Ma what he'd said the night they came back from the hunting trip, when she'd been fussing him instead of helping Uncle Etienne. Ma seemed to have forgotten how he'd sobbed it was his fault Etienne was dead. But it was his fault really, Mannie knew, and he'd have to keep the terrible secret to himself for ever.

So he couldn't go out, couldn't get up, had hardly managed to hand koeksisters round at the funeral. Every time André came into the same room as him, he'd had to leave, cake plate shaking so violently the koeksisters nearly landed on the floor.

Now he pulled the blanket over his head, even though it was sweltering in the room. He heard his mother walk over to the window. A scratchy, sliding sound as she drew open the curtains. He was aware of the intense brightness of the day, even through his covers. Ma was coming back. He squeezed his eyes shut. She flicked back the blanket and rested her hand on his cheek.

'Magies, but you are hot. Have you got a temperature? Mannie' – she shook him – 'Mannie, wake up.'

'Ag, leave me, Ma,' he grunted.

'I'm going to get a thermometer. If you've got a temperature I'll have to brew up some leaves.' Marta was mentally running through the dispensary available to her out in the veld. She knew a lot about the healing properties of plants, knowledge acquired on Impalala from the Tsonga women. They, like her, wouldn't dream of going to the trading store for pills and potions. But would she find something for fever here amid vegetation that had become alien to her? She felt her son again. His forehead felt a bit cooler. Perhaps if he got out from under the bedclothes? 'C'mon, c'mon. It's too hot for lying in bed. Sit up so I can pull your 'jama top off you. You're sweating in it. C'mon.'

Mannie sat up, scowling. His mother was wearing a black dress he hadn't seen before. She looked too pale in it. Even her freckles looked as light as sesame seeds.

'You've missed breakfast, but it's nearly time for lunch. Get washed and dressed and come.'

'Don't want any lunch.'

'Mannie.' She reached for his hand. 'You must eat.'

He shook her off. 'Not hungry.'

She leaned towards him. 'This has got to stop. You can't keep hiding in this room, Mannie. What are you so afraid of?'

She hadn't forgotten.

He tried to control the trembling in his hands by plucking at the crumpled sheet, balling it up in each fist. Marta watched him and let the silence grow. They heard the rattle of crockery as the maid carried a lunch tray down the passage to her mistress's room. Lettie had rallied for the funeral, but, show over, she was inconsolable and was being kept sedated. Marta said they should extend their stay to keep an eye on her. It meant having a very quiet Christmas, no celebrating, and they wouldn't be able to go the seaside. Mannie found he didn't care.

Once the footsteps had passed, the loudest sound was the ticking of Etienne's grandfather clock out in the passage. Ticking, tocking, steadily, like a heart, thought Mannie. Wasn't there a song about a clock that stopped when the master died?

He longed for things to be as they were: tractors coming in from the fields; workers splashing at the water pump; the cook banging a spoon on the huge, blackened pot to call them for their midday meal of pap and boiled meat. And Uncle Etienne banging one boot against the other to get the dust off before he stepped onto Auntie Lettie's polished floors.

Now it was so quiet he could hear the wind wafting the curtains. And still Ma said nothing.

'Have the police been yet?' he asked in a small voice.

'Yes.'

'And they didn't want to talk to me?' He unclenched his fists slightly. His mother looked grave as she sat down heavily beside him.

'No, my boy. Nor to me. They were only interested in the death of the MP for Onderwater. Snakebite is what's been put on the certificate as the cause of death.'

'But, Ma . . .' He knew his voice sounded young, like it did last week, before all this. 'Mama, what about the dead Bushmen? Do they know about those?'

'I told them, but I doubt they'll even drive out to get the bodies.' Marta's head was bowed. He could see red blotches on her neck. She always got them when she was upset. 'The thing is, the Bushmen – Khoisan – aren't white. Or even black. And they were trespassing and André is the son of the MP, so . . .' She swallowed hard and when she lifted her eyes they were filled with tears. 'I argued, said I'd write to the minister, said I was prepared to put you on the witness stand to say what happened, but . . .'

Mannie gasped then started to sob with fear. 'I can't, I can't. Mama, don't make me.'

'Ag, baby.' She gathered him into her arms and held his trembling body. 'There, there. Toemaar now. There won't be a court case. It's over now. But, son' – she held him away from her – 'I need to know you understand that what happened was wrong; very wrong. Mannie?' He nodded vigorously. 'Good.' Then Marta began to cry, tears coursing unchecked down her cheeks.

Mannie put his arms around his mother and rocked her as best he could. He patted her back. Somehow it made him feel better that someone else felt as sad and helpless as he did. After a while he felt her give a shuddering sigh and pull gently away. 'Ag, I'm sorry. Don't know what's the matter with me, crying every five minutes. And I haven't even been to Opa Manfred's grave yet. Don't know how I'm going to fit that in now.' She wiped her cheeks with the hem of her dress and her reddened eyes held Mannie's. 'Now, I'm sure you'll be very kind to the little girl when we take her home with us.'

He sat back in surprise. To feel sorry about the way bad grown-ups carried on was one thing, but to have to face that girl every day, knowing what his family had done to hers, was another. 'I don't want her to come back to Impalala,' he said.

'Manfred, I'm surprised at you. Our family are now responsible for this girl. We orphaned her, remember? It's a guilt we'll bear for the rest of our lives.'

'But it wasn't Pa who shot anyone. It was Uncle Etienne and André!'

'I know, I know. But all André will promise is that Twi can take her back to where you found her.' She twisted a strand of escaped hair round and round in frustration. 'That's not going to help her find the rest of her group, is it? She's obviously from the Kalahari – that's many, many days' walk away. She might not survive out there on her own while she wanders around trying to find people who have probably moved on by now.'

'Why can't Twi take her in a truck?'

Marta tucked the strand behind her freckled ear. 'Ja-well, that would be the best thing; if Twi or someone else set out on a proper expedition, carrying enough supplies with them. If you people had done that in the first place instead of setting out like some boy scouts on a play-play adventure, Etieinne might still be with us . . . Anyway, whatever kind of expedition, it takes time, money and men.' Marta frowned. Keeping her tone as neutral as possible she said: 'André doesn't want to commit to that now when there's so much he has to see to around the farm.'

'Can't *we* take her then?'

Marta stroked his cheek with the back of her hand. 'Ag, liebchen, I wish we could, but Pa . . .' She trailed off and looked out of the window at the horizon beyond the cornfields. Ludicrous to think of Deon coping alone out there. He had no bush-sense at all. He got lost on their own farm. And out in the Kalahari Desert there were no signs for those who couldn't read the searing sand. There was just heat and thirst and shimmering mirages that lured unwary vehicles to rusty graves in the vast salt pans. 'But when this baby is big enough,' Marta said, touching her bulge, 'and I've saved enough money, I promise I'll take the girl back to the Kalahari myself. You and me, we'll take her. Won't that be an adventure, hey?'

Mannie would not be drawn. It could be months, years even before Ma gathered enough in the jamjar – even if they found a hiding place for it that Pa wouldn't find. Mannie remembered hearing his mother say how sad it was to see Bushmen losing their bush ways. He reminded her of this.

'Khoisan, Mannie. You must start using the proper term. And don't you worry. I've got a plan for the girl that will keep her pure Bushman. Er, Khoisan.' She gave a light laugh. 'Now come on. Get dressed. And I'd like you to come and say hello to the girl. She's scared, just like you. Everything's so strange to her. But at least you'd be a face she recognizes.'

Mannie kept his head down. The silence began to build again. Marta stood up with some effort.

'Well, my boy, I won't force you. But you know going to see her would be the kind thing to do.'

Oh-ja, he thought after the door closed, imagine what the Bushgirl'll think when she sees me. What she'll remember.

6

With Lettie in her room and Mannie and Deon avoiding her, Marta spent more and more time in the storeroom. The child fascinated her. She was so delicate with her neat features and graceful limbs. Marta would have liked to draw her to try to capture her extraordinary bone structure – the acute angle between cheekbone and jaw, the high, smooth forehead – but the quiet dignity of this small person seemed to forbid it.

She hasn't reached puberty, Marta decided. She could be Mannie's age or a few years older, at most; maybe a young twelve?

Koba, meanwhile, was assessing the person she'd come to think of as Leopard-woman. If she understood the skinless Jul'hoan man, this |Ton was her way out of prison, her route to survival. And Koba meant to live. But to live without people; without someone to press against in the night, or call to as she gathered food in the veld; without someone to tell her stories of the Early Race, or braid ornaments into her hair; without someone to tell her she was more precious to them than water. That emptiness filled her with fear, a fear that made her insides ache, like winter-morning fingers, it gripped them and numbed her. It made her struggle for breath, like she had that first night in this room.

Grandmother had said it was best to make a friend of what one feared. She would learn to like her aloneness. She would tell herself stories, about all the things she remembered from her n!ore. She would say the names of her playmates, remember who was good at catch-clap, who made the best bird sounds, who could climb to the top of a baobab the fastest. She would list all the things abut her mother, her father, grandmother and all their kin, so that when she got back she would know them all, and they would know her as one of their own.

She wouldn't fear the tappings in her chest. She would listen and learn to understand them; use them as antenna, like grasshoppers did to keep themselves out of harm's way.

Koba sighed. It was strange how a person's life could change between one sunrise and the next. At the Mother Hills she had felt like a child and now, in this new place, only part of a moon later, she was older and needed to consider things for herself. Like this |Ton woman.

Koba steeled herself not to shiver when the woman touched her with her pale, spotted claws. She tried to eat the unpleasant food Leopard-woman put out for her – thick white paste, too hot to keep in her mouth if she ate it immediately, too stiff to swallow without gagging if she let it get cold.

Misunderstanding her dislike of the porridge, Marta brought some honey and drizzled it onto the child's breakfast. She rubbed her stomach and licked her lips, pushing the bowl towards the girl.

Koba tasted it tentatively and immediately gagged. How could she tell this ǀTon, on whom she must depend, that she hated honey? What she longed for was salt. It made most things palatable.

Christmas came and went and Marta became increasingly concerned about keeping the girl cooped up. But she couldn't risk the child making another bid for freedom that would most likely result in her death. She reckoned on having to stay another week at Weltevrede to help Lettie, and then she could take the child back to Impalala where she could put her plan into action.

In the meantime she began to bring bits of the bush into the storeroom, ostensibly to draw them. She left them behind afterwards, and once saw how eagerly the child grabbed a croton tree branch and crushed the silvery leaves under her nose, breathing in the lavender smell. She'd heard that Khoisan women dried and powdered the leaves to make a perfume.

Koba watched Marta carefully as she drew. She saw how the woman was in pain from her pregnancy, how an arrow formed between her brows when the pain attacked. She noted Marta's straight hair, even admired its colour – like red grass. She wondered what it would feel like to touch.

Leopard-woman's sketchings intrigued her. She craned her neck, trying to see into the lap across the room. Was Leopard-woman making a leaf? Could she make people, animals? Figures like those in the great painting?

One day Marta brought an empty tortoise shell, set it down and began to draw. Koba could resist no longer. She stood up, walked over to Marta's chair and gazed at the sketch. She saw a flat tortoise, without movement.

'Tortoise,' Marta said, pointing to the reptile. Instinctively Koba tried to copy the sound. Nothing came. Quickly she turned her face to the wall.

Marta kept talking. She placed her hand on her breast and said her name. She pointed to the plate of food – 'porridge'; to the sickly sweet – 'honey'.

Koba pouted. She didn't want these strange words, this horrible food. She wanted to be back with her people, eating mangetti nuts and monkey oranges and meat. She didn't want to be older. She wanted her father and her mother and the time before the Mother Hills. She pulled her mother's kaross over her head and sat tented inside it. She heard the Leopard-woman packing up her things. She noticed a sliver of light shining through a tear in the kaross. She stuck her finger through and waggled it about. Then she thought better of it; she mustn't tear it further, she had no way of fixing it. She heard Leopard-woman leave the room.

Ten minutes later, Marta returned with a needle and thread. She showed them to Koba. She saw something like comprehension cross the girl's face and she seized the needle and jabbed at the skin cloak. The child pricked her finger but didn't flinch. Gently, Marta indicated that she would sew it for her. Koba hesitated then handed over the kaross.

Marta was surprised at how soft the hide cloak was. It smelled of plants. She supposed it had carried a lot of veld food – berries, tubers, bark; Khoisan women used their karosses as slings for their children too. Had the girl been carried in it by her mother? Was this her equivalent of a treasured cot blanket?

Marta spread the cloak nervously over her knees and plunged in. The needle broke. She rethreaded another and broke that too. This was a job for an expert sewer, like Lettie, but she couldn't ask her for help; not now. Marta felt the solemn gaze of the child beside her. She tried harder.

Her first repair was clumsy; the stitches too far apart. She pulled them out, aware of the intense concentration of the girl.

Half an hour and another needle later, Marta had done it. The tear was mended with neat, even stitches. She handed the cloak back.

Koba took it without a word, but for the first time she met Marta's eyes.

7

The long journey from South West Africa to Nelspruit, in the north of neighbouring South Africa, was a nightmare for Marta. It wasn't the length of the trip: a thousand miles or more as the train went south, then east across the breadth of the African subcontinent, then north again. Nor had there been any trouble getting the awestruck girl onto the train. The problem was the conductor, a little man with brilliantined hair, who checked their tickets in Windhoek and refused to allow the girl into their reserved compartment.

'Third class,' he'd said, pointing to the carriages closest to the smoke stack. Marta had anticipated the problem. She put on her most educated accent.

'I think you'll find we *all* have tickets for this compartment, my good man.'

'Ja-but, this . . .' The man floundered, unable to categorize Koba. 'They must go third class.'

'This Khoisan child – Bushman, from the bush – has never been on a train, so I'd be most grateful if you'd oblige me by letting her remain in the compartment with us. Otherwise she may feel frightened.'

'Sorry, lady. We can't make no exceptions or we'll have kaffirs sitting everywhere. They're getting very white these days, wanting places up front on the buses and things.'

Marta realized the man would not be cowed. 'Look, if we're prepared to pay the price for a first-class ticket . . .'

'Listen, lady, I don't make the rules. I's only doing my job.' But, noticing how Marta pressed a hand to ease the pains in her lower back, he softened. 'Tell you what, you put her where she belongs and I'll give you a refund. I'm authorized.'

'I am not leaving this child on her own; not on a three-day journey.'

'Ag, don't worry. I'll tell one of the kaffirgirls to keep an eye on her. They can be very motherly, you know.'

Marta turned to Deon. 'Can you believe this man?' she asked in English.

Deon lifted his head from his paper and winked at his wife. 'Don't make a fuss, Martjie, this Boer will make a plan.'

'What plan?'

'When the train gets going, I'll find him, slip him ten bob and . . . bob's your uncle!'

'You mean you'll bribe this odious little servant of the apartheid system? You'll collude with him so he benefits from this immoral law in every respect? Not on my account you won't! And certainly not with my money, thank you very much.' She sat back in her seat, her neck aflame and glared at the clearly fascinated conductor. She couldn't leave it there. She leaned towards Deon again and hissed: 'By virtue of his colour, Mr Unskilled White over there probably has the job that some better qualified black man used to have before job reservations, and now you . . .'

Deon glanced quickly at the conductor. Judging from his blank look the English had been too fast for the man to follow. Nevertheless, Deon felt himself redden. 'Must it be *now* you get on your soapbox, Marta? You knew the law when you insisted on buying that ticket for her. If you carry on like this, I won't be able to help you and *he* won't feel like it, not even for *twenty* bob.'

Marta began to gather up her belongings. 'Good,' she said, 'because I want nothing more to do with men who don't seem to know what's right any more.' She stood up and addressed the conductor in Afrikaans. 'This child is my responsibility, so if she can't stay here with me' – she heaved herself off the seat – 'I'll go to third class with her.'

The conductor looked appalled. 'You can't!'

'Why not?' she demanded. 'Is there some rule about that, too?'

'Ag-no. It's just that . . . well, you'll be uncomfortable, lady. The seats is wooden, and it's crowded, hey. Place stinks of them!'

Marta stepped towards the man, so close he was obliged to look up at her. 'I don't suppose it ever occurred to you that *they* might think *you* stink.'

The conductor spluttered, patted the ticket dispenser on his belt, removed his pencil stub from behind his ear and tugged his jacket straight. He addressed himself to Deon: 'Mister, you better keep this wife of yours in check, man. Railways reserves the right to put troublemakers off the train.'

Deon laughed. 'Good luck, man.'

Ignoring him, the conductor glowered at Koba. 'Pasop-jong, don't let me catch you here when I come back, hey?' he said and banged out of the compartment.

Taking the girl's hand, Marta turned to Mannie. 'Coming?'

Mannie squirmed on the green leather seat. He should go with Ma, he knew, but blerry-bugger, no! He didn't think the Bushgirl should be here with them either – not in this compartment, not on the train, not in their lives. Just looking at her standing with her hand in Ma's made him want to hit her.

He knew that was unfair. She didn't want to be here any more than he wanted her to be – if Ma hadn't kept such a tight hold on her at the station she probably would have run away.

But no-way did he feel like sitting in a dirty carriage – he wanted to be here, with room to spread out, his own hand basin in the corner with its golden plughole. Tonight the steward would come and let down the bunks and make up beds for them, with starched white sheets. Pa said they'd go to the dining car, now they'd saved the money they would have spent on a hotel in Walvis Bay.

So Mannie said nothing. He simply shook his head at his mother's enquiry without meeting her eyes. Then he turned towards the window. The world outside was still dark, so his mother and the Bushgirl were clearly reflected in the glass. They stood together, bodies almost touching, then slipped from view, just like the dark shapes flashing past the train window as it gathered speed.

Marta felt ill as she and the girl lurched down the swaying corridor. The baby inside seemed to somersault. Marta clutched her stomach as a band of pain tightened around it.

I must stay calm. I've brought this situation on myself, she thought.

By the time she reached the dimly lit passage approaching third class, Marta could hear the din. She leaned against the interleading door, clutching her bag to her, her eyes wide and showing white in a face already sooty.

'I must sit down a minute,' she said to Koba as she sank to the filthy floor.

Why, oh why did she get herself into these situations? Of course it would have been better for her and for Koba to stay in Whites Only. The last thing she wanted to do was spend days and days in a dirty, overcrowded carriage, assuming it was as bad as that horrible little conductor had said. But now she'd made it impossible for Deon to come and rescue her. She dropped her head into her hands.

Standing in the inter-carriage space, Koba wanted to scream her panic. She was in the carapace of a metal monster and she was not safe. There were gaps in the body of the giant creature and through them she could see ground, dark and rushing, as the monster raced over it. It puffed bad smoke up through these holes and ate the metal beneath it with clacking teeth. She wanted to get out, go back to the room they'd just left, even if Hyena lTon and his cub were there. Leopard-woman had to take her. She must make the woman move.

Koba tugged at Marta's hand.

Marta looked up with a tear-stained face. 'Okay. I've made my bed, now let's go lie in it.' She struggled up, wiped her face, took a deep breath and depressed the greasy handle of the third-class carriage.

The noise was stupendous as the compartment door swung open – several languages all spoken at once, all at open-market volume. Babies cried, card-players whooped, transistor radios blared kwela music.

To the left, a housewife was haggling with a hawker over the price of the live chicken he dangled before her. She prodded it, seemed satisfied and, dipping into her bra, produced several coins. As he took them, the hawker made a lewd remark about their warmth.

'It's because they have lain with me,' the housewife said coyly.

'I'd like to be in their place,' he said, leering.

She sized him up. 'Cocky fellow, counting chickens. But you aren't high-born enough for this.' She tapped her ample bosom.

'You are mistaken, missus. I am a big, big man. All the ladies know,' he said, winking.

The women around her cackled. 'Big, but not a *king*,' one of them said as she undid her blouse. She showed him her coin-studded cleavage. Then she prised a penny off her skin and displayed the imprint – a perfect bust of Queen Elizabeth II on hers. 'See, to lie with the queen you must be a makulu.' Everyone guffawed.

The laughter stopped suddenly. Haggling halted, babies were shushed and blank stares from dozens of dark eyes met Marta's nervous smile.

She stilled her panic and tried to catch an eye, any eye. All looked away.

Near the door, a group of men, miners probably, Marta thought, coughed over a game of dice. No good approaching them for a seat. Towards the back she spied two young men with slick hair and switchblade-sharp sideburns jiving on an empty carriage seat. Two-toned shoes flashed beneath their baggy trousers. A Herero matron in full Victorian dress was bearing down on them, demanding sitting space. Beckoning to Koba, Marta followed, clambering over the bundles and cardboard suitcases that blocked the aisle, narrowly avoiding a backhand from an onyx-cheeked mother who flung her arm wide to untie the blanket that kept her wailing baby strapped to her back. With practised ease she swung him round to her front and slipped her dark nipple into his mouth.

Marta walked in the matron's wake, watching as the woman's wide, hooped skirt brushed hats off laps and even swept the transistor from the carriage bench. Finally the woman plumped down and, spreading her skirts, nodded apologies to her neighbours. Her turban looked like a vibrantly upholstered anvil.

Marta stopped next to her, greeted her formally, then whispered, 'If you could move up, just a little, we could squeeze in.' The woman, together with every other person there, looked at her in frank astonishment.

'The madam wants to sit here?' Marta nodded. Resentment replaced wonder on the woman's face. 'Why you don't sit with the whitepeoples?' she asked in a loud voice. Marta shrugged. The woman made a great show of peering round her at Koba. 'I see why.' Her disapproval rippled out across the rows of benches. 'Masarwa, Masarwa' echoed all around.

Marta turned to go. Wouldn't Deon laugh to see her now? she thought. She felt a tap on her shoulder. An elderly man, one of the passengers who'd had his hat knocked off by the Herero woman, stood up.

'Sit here,' he said, speaking English with a rural black accent.

'Oh, I couldn't take your seat.'

'I've been watching for you,' he said. 'I heard your words with the conductor. Me also.' He pulled a first-class ticket from his waistcoat pocket.

'I don't suppose you were offered a refund before you were chased in here?'

The man's laugh was terse. 'I know better. I do it only as a matter of principle . . .' Marta nodded vigorously. 'I am a lawyer, but to them' – he jerked his thumb conductor-wards – 'I am a baboon in a suit.' Marta made to protest. The man dismissed the gesture and indicated impatiently that she should sit down.

'Thank you. Thank you very, very much. I can't tell you how grateful I am to you for speaking to me.'

Touching his hat, the man bowed. 'Have a good journey.'

Pulling Koba down beside her, Marta sank against the hard backrest.

Koba's knuckles shone like the undersides of cowries as she gripped the edge of the bench. Now she'd seen the joints of this metal monster, she did not want to be inside it. Not even in a big room like this. People hated her here. And the ǀTon woman, too. But she was too tired to worry about what would become of her and if she'd ever see her tree-water again. She let her grip loosen, her spine relax. Her body swayed with the movement of the train. As her head emptied she tuned in to the rhythm of wheels, the puff of the pistons, finding music there – sa-ka-pa-ka, sa-ka-pa-ka, clack, clack, clack. Sa-ka-pa-ka-sa-ka-pa-ka, clack, clack, clack. It reminded her of the beat of a trance dance. When there was trouble in the camp, people would build up a large fire and gather round it. Zuma often started the clapping. Other women would join in and begin to chant. Some would stand up, shuffle round the circle, skin skirts flapping. Men would wind dance rattles round their ankles and begin to stamp, round and round, wearing a path in the sand, churning up dust that shone like copper gauze in the firelight. And she'd be there, lolling against her mother, or an aunt, or laying her head on Zuma's bony breast the better to feel the old woman's conviction that healing was on the way.

She began to feel that peaceful anticipation now, knew she could abdicate responsibility for her survival for a time. Leopard-woman's smell was beginning to sit comfortably in her nose – it was salty. She allowed her heavy lids to close. Soon she was asleep against Marta's shoulder.

8

Bushveld, South Africa

Impalala wasn't a big farm by South African standards and it lacked an accessible underground water supply like Etienne Marais'. What it did have was a boundary with the Kruger National Park, the largest game reserve in southern Africa. Smaller game, like warthog, steenbuck and duiker, passed freely between the farm and the game reserve, while inquisitive giraffe peered over the high fence as they grazed in the tree canopy along the boundary. Breakouts of the bigger wildlife – elephant, lion, buffalo and rhino – were rare, but not unheard of. A bush walk had to be taken with caution. Mostly, the farm was stocked with impala buck, dainty tan-coloured antelope with elegantly curved horns. The resident population of leopard and, occasionally in the past, Etienne and his guests, kept the numbers down.

Now, thanks to Etienne's unexpected bequest, Deon planned to turn Impalala into a guest farm for the growing number of Kruger Park tourists – people who wanted to shoot animals only with cameras. Over the next few weeks, Deon busied himself designing a complex of rondavels with accommodation, laundry and braai facilities, a dining room and a small supply store.

Marta sat in silence in the Impalala kitchen, watching Deon bubble with enthusiasm. The room was small and dingy, with corrugated iron walls and a cooking range so old it could have had pride of place in a museum. Deon had always promised her a better house with a modern kitchen, but he'd never done anything about building one. Marta didn't mind about the kitchen; she disliked cooking – the housemaid, Selina, did it all. But a house with proper brick walls would have been nice. These tin ones contracted in the cold, the metal shrieking in disbelief at the temperature differential between night and day so near the Tropic of Capricorn. Marta, never a sound sleeper, found it disturbing.

Now she raised an eyebrow as Deon mentioned building an outdoor cinema for what he was already calling 'the game lodge guests'. She was sceptical about his ability to follow through on a project. With reason, she thought, remembering the sieves and sorters stacked in one of the derelict outbuildings. Those were the legacy of Deon's interest in alluvial gold. He'd spent weeks up at Pilgrim's Rest, panning in the river, but he lost interest when all he found was fool's gold. Next he decided they could supplement their income with biltong. He built huge drying boxes and butchered a few impala, seasoning the meat deliciously, she thought. But every farmer in the area made biltong, so there was no market for it. He tried keeping bees; the hives still stood like an apian ghost town in a camel thorn copse near the koppie. Then he thought about hand-making veldskoens.

Marta sighed. There was a half-built reservoir round the back of the house where Deon had started a swimming pool for Mannie, but she decided not to mention it. She was too tired for argument and maybe, just maybe, this project would amount to something. Deon had been a very good hotel manager – when he was sober.

To Koba, the bushveld looked astonishingly lush. So many big-canopied, broad-leaved trees: some with long, soft branches that swept to the ground, others with striking, fever-yellow trunks, one festooned with bright red flowers, and several with fearsome-looking knobs on their grey trunks. And the grass – so high, birds so plentiful and a smell of wet in the air. Here, food would hang from the trees, not hide itself underground. A shame she would not be staying.

The hill she was being taken to now looked strange, protruding up on an otherwise flat landscape. Later she would learn the hill was called Pasopkop – Beware Hill – and that it reminded |Ton who lived across the sea of something called a castle. They said its summit looked like battlements. In due course she would also learn that the local Tsonga people shuddered to hear the word 'Pasopkop'. They swore the hill hid a monstrous mouth, fangs bared to the sky, and was capable of eating people.

On Koba's first sight of it, she simply thought, 'egg'. Where shell-smooth curves should have met to form an apex, she saw gnawed edges. A snout or beak had feasted on the life inside. Nothing could live up there. Certainly she couldn't. She would run away just as soon as she could.

Next to her, Marta was struggling up the steep slope. 'Home,' she panted, waving her arm to indicate a view clear across the bushveld. The land was covered in bleached blond grass high enough to hide elephants. Thorn trees poked through, opened against the sun like dark umbrellas.

'Now, I want you to understand I'm putting you up here for your own good. It's not that you're not welcome down at the house – you are, any time – but I don't want you to lose your Khoisan ways before I can take you back to your people,' she said.

'Ag, Ma, save your breath. She doesn't understand.' Mannie was worried by the exhaustion on his mother's face. 'You stop here, Ma. I'll take her.'

Marta nodded her gratitude. Her womb felt like dead-weight dragging on the muscles of her lower back. She handed Mannie a torch and a box of matches and indicated to the girl that she should follow him.

Koba pouted. She did not want anything to do with this ǀTon boy. She turned her back on him and continued to log her strange surroundings. The boy capered around her, gesticulating comically, rolling his eyes. He seemed to be able to make them protrude, like a frog's. She almost laughed. She watched him explain in sign language that up on the hill was a place for her to sleep. Would there be food there? she wondered. She was very hungry.

As they climbed she noted several plants that looked promising, but first she'd better find a safe place to lie. There were leopard prints here.

It took longer to reach the summit of the hill than it should have. Koba kept leaving the path to investigate plants, snapping leaves between thumb and forefinger to sniff or rub them. She picked up dried buck drop-pings, investigated wallows and even followed a lizard hot-footing it across a sun-baked rock. Mannie began to droop in the broiling heat.

Finally they reached the top and he indicated that Koba should slip into a rocky gully, one of several that made the summit look crenellated. Koba obliged reluctantly and was surprised to see a shallow bowl of lush vegetation spread out before her – bushes of all shapes and sizes, and the odd wildly contorted fig tree that had forced its way between rocks. And there was fruit on these trees. She strolled over and studied a wizened-looking fig. She had no intention of picking, let alone tasting it. It might be poisonous, but she sniffed it cautiously. The fruit smelled sweet – too sweet for her. She looked around. Which direction would the Mother Hills lie in? she wondered. She scampered along a rocky ledge she thought might serve as a lookout.

'Girl,' Mannie shouted impatiently, 'come to the cave.'

Koba turned towards the sound. No Frog-boy. She blinked. He'd been there, just behind her, but now, where was he? Intrigued, she approached the ragged line of bushes where he'd been standing. Yau, a chasm in the rock floor.

From below, Mannie saw her peer into the fissure, her body partially blocking out the sun. 'Come on. What my mother wants you to see is in here.'

Koba dropped into the cave like a cat. Mannie swept the beam around the space then held it steady on the far wall. He heard the girl gasp and clap her hands as she caught sight of the painting. Then she was beside him, clicking nineteen to the dozen and running her hands over the stick animals and people. He wasn't pleased when she snatched the torch from him, but when he realized she had tears streaming down her face, he let her keep it. He wondered if she knew why the men in the drawing had buck ears and hooves. And what did she make of that snot streaming from their noses and the sticks through the ends of their piepies?

He pulled a box of matches out of his pocket and struck one so he could see the girl better. She was kneeling in front of the painting his mother said was Khoisan rock art. He supposed it was, seeing how excited the Bushgirl was about it, her tongue click-clacking like knitting needles. He had the feeling she wasn't talking to him, but to the painting.

Mad. She kept touching her throat and blowing at the rock art like someone in church or something. He lit another match and three more after that, so he could keep an eye on her. Ma would want a full report.

Eventually the girl sat silent in front of the painting.

'Ja-well, I should go now – Ma'll be waiting.' He took the torch from her. 'Sorry, but Ma said to leave you with *these*.' He put the matchbox on the cave floor. 'A torch is too *western*, or something.'

When he'd left, Koba pressed her forehead against the mural. As she'd expected, it didn't feel hard or rough like rock. It was soft and slack, like the skin on her grandmother's cheek. Zuma was here, somewhere. She couldn't leave now.

9

This land is dangerous, Koba thought to herself the next morning as she stood on the edge of the summit warming herself in the sun. A person could sense danger in the grass that covered this land. It was the same colour as lion's fur.

Was she right not to run away? she wondered. She could leave tonight, take her chance with lions and follow the hunting star. How long would it take to get back? The metal journey had disorientated her. She'd tried to keep track of the number of sunrises, of the direction they were travelling, but the stifling air and the swaying seat and the music of the wheels had made her too sleepy for much of the time.

Now she squinted and tried to see beyond the scrub-studded horizon. No sign of anything resembling the Mother Hills out there. She could walk and walk and walk, but if she didn't die from hunger or thirst, would Zuma still be alive when she reached the ledge?

She knew the answer. Zuma was dead. How else could she have felt her last night in the rock? She must wait until her grandmother's spirit sent her a message.

In the meantime, she must eat. The flat white food Leopard-woman had given her was all gone.

Below the hill, she could see a circle of huts with thatched, conical roofs. Cooking fires burned outside some of them and black figures moved around inside a reed fence. There was no path tramped through the bush between the compound and the hill so she assumed the locals avoided the place. Would they avoid her too? Judging by the hostility of the black people on the journey, she assumed they would. She did spy a grey path leading from the huts to a |Ton house in the distance. From the hilltop it looked like a long scar in the lion's pelt. Better not walk that way either. She must find her own path while she waited for Grandmother n!a'an.

Little by little, Koba arranged her new home. For sleeping, she cleared a flattened section of cave floor, sweeping the bat droppings into a far corner with her grass bushel broom. Here she spread her mother's kaross as a sleeping mat. Next to her mat she placed two empty tortoise shells for use as food bowls. She was proud of them. Prising the shells off their owners had been no mean feat – the big leopard tortoise had to be drowned as the horny armour of his legs proved impervious to her stabbing stick. Once he was dead, it had been a battle removing his body without damaging his shell. The little tortoise she had simply asphyxiated in her fire. He'd tried to walk away until she smothered him in hot ash and coals. He was soon deliciously baked.

Only water was proving a problem. When it rained, she could collect it from various rocky hollows on the hill, but in dry spells she had to fetch her supply from the river. It was a long walk.

Koba's two most prized possessions had appeared mysteriously at the entrance to her cave one morning. One was a battered zinc bucket, which reduced the frequency of her walks to the river. The other was a pocket knife. Koba marvelled at its folding blade and the efficacy of the small hook for opening nuts. If only Father could have seen these tools, she thought.

While she polished the blade on her pubic apron, she considered the gift. It couldn't be hxaro or the giver would have identified himself so she could return the favour – a gift without obligation, then. Must be from a person with many riches. Must be from a |Ton. Which one?

Not Leopard-woman; she gave nothing but words when they met in the veld – strange words that she repeated at Koba so often they began to crop up in her dreams. Maybe Frog-boy? He avoided her – they'd had no contact since that first day – but she was aware he watched her from a distance, believing himself unseen. Ha, the |Ton. As noisy in the bush as raindrops on dried leaves. That left only the quiet |Ton as her benefactor – the one with the dragging leg. Hyena |Ton, she called him. If he'd been up here, he'd been careful not to step on the sand – she had looked for his footprints.

Koba's days were busy. She had to familiarize herself with new plants and animals and birds and insects, noting their behaviour and habitat. The wildlife around the river was the most interesting to her. She'd heard of crocodile, from Jul'hoansi who had travelled north to the great Okavango, but she had never seen them. Now she sat for hours waiting for them to leave the water where they drifted like logs, just eyes and snouts showing. Their short, bandy legs made them so clumsy on land, but the lightning snap of their jaws made her believe quite readily that they were more dangerous even than lion. Hippo amused her, with their ridiculously small ears and fat, tame animal bodies. She imagined they'd be very tasty, but how to get past their big snapping jaws? Easier by far to get the flapping silver food she secretly observed young Tsonga boys pulling from the brown water. But she would need tools like they had.

One dawn she boldly ventured to the edge of the compound where the Tsonga lived. Their refuse heap was a treasure trove: twine and a scrap of fishing net, enough for her to learn to weave from. Now she too could pull the shining food from the river and throw it onto a fire until it turned black and smelled mouth-wateringly good.

Koba never allowed herself to be seen by the Tsonga. She was afraid of these people with their black-black skin, their loud voices and their powerful magicians.

There was a story, told around Jul'hoansi campfires, about her father's uncle's cousin, who was cheated by a black witch doctor. Koba's kinsman had demanded the witch doctor pay him fairly for the cobra skin he'd brought him, but the man refused. Eventually the witch doctor's headman was approached, and reluctantly the witch doctor paid up. But he'd cursed the coins, and from the moment the kinsman touched the money, his hand began to burn. Hot-hot pain. His hand became paralysed and, though trance dances were done for him, his whole body was soon poisoned and he died. No, she did not want to be near the Tsonga. She was safer up on her hill.

Nights were the worst for Koba. Then she watched her fire cast long, threatening shadows on her walls and she felt her unprotected back prickle. She daren't allow herself to sleep soundly. She might not hear clawed things coming.

On nights when she did hear the low cough of a prowling leopard, she threw logs on her fire until the flames leaped all the way up to the roof entrance. It made the chamber very smoky, but it was better than being a clawed thing's prey.

On very bad nights she would hide under N‡aisa's kaross and smell her mother there. But she wouldn't let herself cry. Tear-time was over.

Now I must just live and live, she told herself.

One night, in a dream, Koba sensed a bony back against hers. She saw her dreaming self leap out of the cave and tear down the hillside, shouting: 'I must run-run-run until I find the metal track, then follow it back to the Mother Hills.'

'Easier to find a tear in a pool,' said a stiller Koba, floating above. Dreaming Koba ignored her and flew across moon-silvered sand until she saw the Forbidden

Pool. Above, on the ledge, she saw bones – a neat pile, the spine intact and curved like that of a very old woman.

Koba howled then, waking herself up with cries that scared off the prowling leopard and woke baby Tsongas tucked up in their huts. The terrified children knew now that tales of the tokoloshe were true. 'He lives on Pasopkop, Mama, with the Yellow One. Maaa, he comes.'

Up in her cave and fully awake now, Koba felt certain her grandmother was dead. But Zuma was not absent. Koba could feel her as certainly as if she lay cradling her bony back. Death had given her grandmother back to her. Her heart lifted. She sat up.

'Greetings, spirit of Grandmother n!a'an,' she said into the less-lonely darkness.

10

'Koba, Koba!' Mannie heard his mother call. He was helping her gather a selection of spring flowers for a drawing she had planned when they spotted Koba some distance off.

'What's "Koba"?' he asked.

'Her name,' Marta said. 'At least, I think it is. She taps her chest and makes this "Koba" sound every time I say I'm Marta.' His mother strode ahead swinging her basket.

Mannie ran to catch up with her. 'Has she said anything else?'

His mother stopped, turned a sad face to him. 'Yes. She wants to go home. She's indicated "home".'

He almost whooped his relief. 'So when's she going, Ma?'

'As soon as we've got money to spare, son.'

'I thought we had. From Uncle Etienne?'

'He left Pa the farm, but no money. Pa's having to borrow from the bank to build the guest facilities. Even if he sticks with this project, it could be years before we've paid the loan back and have anything to spare.' She sighed. 'No. We're no better off than we were, I'm afraid.'

Koba reached them. She seemed to be wearing a grey, feathered scarf, dotted with blue. Closer up, they realized she had a pair of dead guinea fowl slung over her shoulders.

'I see you've already got tonight's supper? Well done, Koba.' The girl just looked at her solemnly. 'Er, I'm collecting these, see . . .' She showed the contents of her basket. 'This red one we call Barberton daisy, the wild pear blossom you may have seen before . . .'

Koba nodded, understanding from Marta's manner that Leopard-woman was relaxed today, without the pain that put an arrow between her brows. A good time to strengthen their alliance, then. She looked around for an offering for the basket. She pulled a small branch off a thorn tree, pointed to the pink and yellow catkins dangling from it.

Marta beamed at her. 'Yes! Yes, sickle bush, *dichrostachys cinerea* – *dichrostachys* because of its two colours.' She saw but ignored her son's grimace – she'd have a word later. 'The Tsonga people call this plant "tassels for the chief's hat" . . .'

'Muti,' Koba said and made her forearm rear up, hand cupped like a spitting cobra.

'Oh, for snakebites. Yes, yes, I understand.' To Mannie she said, 'She'll know all *sorts* of plant remedies. And I bet she could teach you to snare guinea fowl too.'

Like I need some *girl* to teach me, Mannie thought. Marta noted his scowl. 'Ag, these feet of mine. I must sit down. Let's find a place next to the river.' They didn't have far to walk. Once Marta had scanned the canopy of the mahogany tree to ensure it was leopard-free, they settled in its shade. Mannie fiddled sulkily with a thick, woody pod he'd found. He split it in two, exposing pithy compartments for the eight scarlet, black-tipped seeds.

His mother prodded him gently with her toe. 'Show her,' she said.

Reluctantly he handed a seed to Koba. Marta prodded him again. 'Lucky bean,' he muttered.

Koba turned the seed over on her yellow palm. She'd seen these before, but in shorter pods. People collected them if they went a few days' walk from her n!ore. They looked pretty strung on a necklace. She ignored the surly boy and began collecting pods for herself.

Marta let them get on with ignoring each other. They'd be friends in time. Green shoots piercing through the earth, flame creeper cascading down the riverbank and pink in her son's cheeks. First time he's looked well since that hunting trip, she thought. And Koba too – skin glowing, clear eyes, no bald patches in her cap of woolly hair. Her diet must be good, thank God. It was hard resisting the urge to feed her from their table, especially when Deon kept questioning her decision.

They'd been sitting around the kitchen table, the atmosphere between them still tense. Selina, their maid, was clearing the table. She'd remarked that the Tsonga on the farm weren't happy about having the 'Yellow One' around. Marta said nothing.

'It's true,' Deon said. 'Having a wild child dressed in skins, hunting for food in this day and age is damn funny. What were you thinking of, bringing her here? I mean, she could end up being a tourist attraction.'

Marta flushed with fury. 'Do you seriously think I would allow that? Can't you see I'm simply trying to do the right thing for that little girl? Have you forgotten how much this family owes her?' She looked at Deon, green eyes glittering like emeralds in the haft of a drawn dagger. Selina scuttled from the room as fast as her bulk would allow and Deon stared down at the tabletop, his thin face pale. Marta tried to keep her anger in check; agitation might be bad for the baby. '*I* think the *right* thing for Koba is for us to ensure she doesn't become acculturated before we can take her home.'

Deon pushed his chair back. 'Take her home, hey? And what are we going to use for the train fare? The building's taking every penny we've got . . . and plenty we haven't!'

Her lips taut with the effort of speaking calmly, Marta said, 'But eventually . . .'

'Eventually she'll become a miserable, tame Bushman just like that one on Weltevrede.' Deon stood up. 'Face it, Marta. You may as well put her in a doek and let her start living with the Tsonga. At least she could do some work around here.'

Marta faced him across the table. 'No! She is not a servant. It won't cost us a penny to keep her; she'll be totally self-sufficient, you'll see. Her people have been living off land a lot less abundant in food and water than what we've got here. And they've survived. For thousands of years! She'll adapt. She's Khoisan.'

'She's a child!'

Marta's resolve had wavered then. But she had to be strong, for the girl's sake. 'You leave her welfare to me. I'll make a plan just as soon as the baby's come.'

That afternoon she sat down and wrote to A. D. Donker, a publisher of books on South African wild flowers. She sent them some of her drawings and asked about the possibility of a commission. If she got work, the money could go towards Koba's train fare, she thought. Deon would contribute what he could, she knew, when things calmed down. His bark was far worse than his bite. And even the bark was easier to bear, she admitted to herself, now that he was so involved with the building project.

Back on the riverbank, Marta thought idly about writing to Donker's again. It was two weeks since she'd sent off her samples. Perhaps they'd got lost in the post? Ja, she must see to it before the baby came.

She pulled two oranges from her pockets and peeled them. She handed one to each child in turn.

Koba sniffed hers. Yau, delicious-smelling! Without bothering to break it into segments, she bit into the orange ball. Yau-yau-yau! This was like monkey orange, but much, much better. Juicy and tart and meaty, all at the same time. She let the juice run down her chin, over her hands and along her forearms as she pushed the fruit into her mouth with both hands. Her cheeks bulged and her eyes watered with the effort of chewing and swallowing such a mouthful.

Mannie began to laugh.

'Manfred,' Marta growled; then sweetly to Koba, 'Have another orange.'

Koba peeled it, seething. Frog-boy had laughed at her. How dare he, he who had plenty-plenty, and family? Taking careful aim, she bent a segment between thumb and forefinger and pressed. As she'd anticipated, this Ton orange worked even better than a monkey orange. Frog-boy winced and began rubbing his eye. Good, Koba thought. That would make it sting more.

'Koba,' Marta gasped, 'you did that on purpose!' Koba laughed, exposing unchewed orange chunks in her mouth.

Mannie leaned over and shoved the annoying Bushgirl, both hands on her chest.

Koba hadn't spent her years wrestling other boys and girls in camp without learning something. She grabbed his hands and rolled backwards, pulling him off balance.

'Stop it, stop it, you two.' But the fight was on as the children locked together, Mannie grunting, Koba hissing as they tussled in the dirt, rolling down the riverbank and landing in a pool with a double splash.

'Crocodiles!' Marta shrieked, scrambling down after them. But she could see the water was too shallow to hide such a large reptile.

The children looked sheepish as she scolded them. Stealing a sidelong look at each other, they grinned.

Marta couldn't help noticing how they sat, arms almost touching, brown indistinguishable from white because of mutual mud.

Marta winced. A strong contraction; if that's what it was. She still had weeks to carry this baby, surely? She fiddled with the blank paper in front of her. She should draw. The flowers were wilting. But her hands were swollen – she'd be unwieldy with pencil or paintbrush. Her stomach felt hollow, as though she was famished, but she couldn't face the thought of food. She was too nauseous. She stood up, bent forward to relieve the discomfort in her back, sat down again but couldn't settle.

I'm like a pregnant bitch trying to find a place to pup, she thought. Maybe I've got my date wrong?

She became conscious of a wetness between her thighs. Waters breaking? She grabbed a tea towel, shoved it up her skirt and dabbed. A rosy-coloured stain. Here goes, she thought, with rising excitement. Not long now and I'll meet her; it is a her, I just know it.

An hour later, Marta was alarmed to see the sheet she'd put down stained with a greeny-black mucus. Meconium? Her contractions were still more than ten minutes apart. This baby was in distress.

She lurched to the bedroom door and said to Mannie, playing marbles in the passage:

'Please-please, fetch Pa. Quickly, son.'

A week later, Koba saw Mannie standing next to a small, newly dug grave. He was quivering like a sapling in a stiff breeze. Leopard-woman's baby, Koba thought. She crept away. It was bad where he was standing, downwind from the graves. The death spirit would blow onto him and make him sick. Perhaps Frog-boy was already sick? He looked thin, with frightened eyes.

But where was Leopard-woman? Koba hadn't seen her about. Only Hyena |Ton, and he no longer whistled as he worked with the men building huts. Koba began to worry that Marta might be sick somewhere and soon another, bigger grave would appear. How then would she ever get back home?

The girl climbed the jackalberry tree. It gave her a view of the small cemetery. She watched the boy. His skin was paler, so she knew he wasn't outside in the sun as much. Was he tending his sick mother? Koba felt a stab of guilt. She'd known the Leopard-woman would do badly with the baby. She'd even told Zuma of her fears. Zuma had pointed out that there was nothing she could do about it. The girl-baby was too weak for the world.

Seeing the boy looking so forlorn now, Koba decided being |Ton must be lonely. They lived in such small groups and kept too much to themselves. From what she saw, a |Ton child had only one mother and father. Jul'hoansi children had a whole tribe full. When the women and children had gone out foraging, she, as a toddler, had been as comfortable in the sling of an aunt or a cousin, as she was in her own mother's. If she was tired, or hurt or just sad, she could turn to any adult or older child in her n!ore for comfort. Even when she was far too big to be carried. And with Grandmother never far away, she almost didn't need N‡aisa.

An emerald-spotted wood dove called across the veld, a mournful arpeggio of notes that Koba remembered her grandmother saying was a lament for dead children. The girl shook herself out of her reverie. It was the |Ton's fault that she had no mother and was even lonelier than them here in this ugly place. Why was she wasting pity on them?

She climbed down from the tree so fast she took skin off her shin. As she set off across the veld she heard the wood dove call again. This time she was sure the bird sang that it wasn't Frog-boy's fault that her parents were dead.

Koba shrugged. She still didn't like him, but it would do no harm to keep him near her eye.

It wasn't difficult. Next morning, Mannie began following her as she foraged. She paused, idly kneeling to lick a rock as she allowed him to catch up. His shadow fell across her.

'What you doing?' he asked.

She thought she understood. She tried a Marta-word: 'Taste.' She indicated the white deposit on the grey stone.

'What is it?'

She scraped a bit off with her nail. 'Ihn,' she said, offering salt to him. He dabbed some onto the tip of his tongue, then spat. Koba laughed. Mannie scowled.

'You don't need to lick it off rocks, you know. There's an earthworks for salt nearby. The Tsonga have been working it since the olden days.' He stopped. The girl had understood little of what he said. 'Listen,' he tried again, 'you like?' He indicated the deposit. Koba nodded vigorously. 'If I bring you salt will you give me honey?'

Koba understood the ǀTon word 'honey'. Getting it was no problem on Impalala, unlike in the Kalahari. There, unraided hives were scarce. Here, a honey guide would often land on a branch in front of her, making its rattling 'quick-quick, honey-quick' call. It would flutter, agitating for her attention, then fly off, low, trying to lead her in the direction of a hive. Sometimes she'd follow and smoke the bees out, just to please the bird. It was a long task, best done in the early morning when the bees were immobile with cold, but even so a few stings were inevitable.

Even though she didn't like honey, she'd chew on a lump of beeswax, remembering how fond her father had been of it. Tami would be proud to see how well she managed to clear the hive, how she remembered to reward the bird. It liked the bee larvae in the wax, so she always tossed those towards the honey guide.

Tami had told the story of Dàbè Stomach, who ate all the beeswax, leaving the bird only liquid. On his way home Dàbè had stepped on a puff adder. That was the last time he was able to climb a tree to steal honey.

Koba cocked her head, considering Mannie's proposition. Plentiful salt was worth a few bites from the buzzings.

A few days later she handed over a large shellful of honey. She watched Mannie plunge two fingers into the shell, snatch at the dripping liquid with his mouth, then close his eyes as he sucked his fingers clean. Quickly he opened them again. 'Sorry.' He held out the shell. 'Did you want some?'

She shook her head.

Soon the two children were bartering not just salt and honey, but anything Mannie could spirit away from the farmhouse: a blanket for some crocodile eggs, the tiny reptiles live and squeaking inside them; a matchbox for a puff-adder skin; a tin mug for an evening around Koba's fire. They gave each other things of little value to themselves, never guessing how the other prized the gift.

'Ma's back from the hospital. She won't come out her room, though. Will you come see her? Pa says you might cheer her up.'

Koba understood the gist of Mannie's request, but more interesting to her was the cost to him of making it. He could not meet her eyes; his fingers twisted the corner of his sand-coloured shirt. She knew he'd resented any time his mother spent with her. Often he'd hovered between her and Marta, twittering like a honey guide, trying to distract her when she spoke to the |Ton woman. Now he was begging her to.

'If you come I'll give you watermelon – that pink food.' Koba pulled a face. She'd tried it – much too sweet for her.

'I know.' Mannie's face lit up. 'I'll give you an avocado pear. We've got a tree at the back of the house. I'll find a ripe one. Avo's delicious with salt. You'll love it. But you must come to the house.'

*

Koba hesitated on the threshold of the farmhouse door. Was it safe to go into this ǀTon place? It was as dark as a cave, but it stank. A pungent, waxy smell, but not from real bees. And there was the big black woman who always glared at her, on her hands and knees, rubbing the floor. Yau, it was *her* making the horrible smell, with that paste from her pot. Was that avocado? She wasn't going to eat that!

'Come on,' Frog-boy called from the gloom.

Koba stepped inside, not looking at the big black woman.

Selina stopped polishing and sat back on her wide haunches, staring at the Bushgirl.

Perhaps the Yellow One was as mad as was whispered in the kraal? Ancestors-only-knew what her husband, Gideon, would say when he got back from the mines. He always had a fund of Bushman stories, telling tales of the old days when Bushman's poison arrows killed Tsonga. Huw, the white people were mad to invite this dangerous person into their home. She shook her head and went back to her buffing.

Deon appeared from the bedroom door. 'It's all right. Don't be afraid,' he said, taking Koba's hand and leading her into Marta's room.

Koba was surprised by the sight of the ǀTon woman, thick-necked, puffy-faced, as though stung by a swarm of bees. She had a tiny pink garment clutched to her chest.

She is so-so white, even her spots have paled away, Koba thought. And the bright has gone from her hair. This is not Leopard-woman.

Marta stared at Koba as though she couldn't remember who she was. Koba took the opportunity to look around the room, saw zebra stripes where sunlight sneaked through the shutters, saw a roof sky-high above her head, saw a sleeping place with four clawed feet she knew would give her nightmares. The room smelled of sweet and sick and sadness. She winced as Deon crossed to the door, making the floorboards shout.

'Make yourself comfortable,' he said, pointing to a chair wearing the hide of a tame animal. Then he left the room.

Koba heard the bed groan as Marta tossed in it.

'He blames me, you know. He hasn't said so, but I can tell from the way he looks at me.' She struggled up onto one elbow and glared through a tangle of wilted hair. 'I don't need him to make me feel guilty. I'm sick with it.' She flopped back, lay staring at the ceiling.

Koba wondered what she should do. Most of Marta's words were a mystery to her – too strange, too fast, as though the ǀTon woman had bad spirits controlling her tongue. There should be a medicine dance for her. A nǀomkxao should trance and drive out the pain.

'Well, I suppose I was careless.' Marta's voice was low. 'Now I can see there were signs – I can see I ignored them.' She shifted her legs irritably under the covers. 'The nearest hospital's far away and there was so much going on; Etienne's accident' – she pulled herself upright and tried to smile – 'finding you and getting you settled here. What were a few headaches; some foot swelling? Doctor said it wasn't my fault. She'd have died anyway.

But that doesn't help . . .' Marta lay slowly back. After a silence in which the loudest sound was that of a bluebottle trapped between the insect netting and the window, she began to cry.

Koba settled herself down on the floor. Grief she knew about – it needed accompaniment. She began to keen, a mournful 'Ehay-oh' like a descant to Marta's sobbing, but she did not look at the woman. Her role was not to see. Now was the time to help a woman bear her burden.

Time passed. Koba rocked, crooned, kept up her hypnotic chorus, never varying the pace or the volume, until Marta quietened.

Eventually, Marta sat up, smoothed her hair off her face and looked at Koba, lucidly. 'The baby, Ingrid, would have been good for Deon and me. Now, I don't know what will happen . . .' A long, shuddering sigh. 'You know, I never expected to have another child. I was so pleased I even taught myself to knit!' Marta reached for the pink matinee jacket, laughing unnaturally. 'I'm all thumbs when it comes to housewifely skills, you know. Selina does the cooking. The mending . . .' She shrugged, smiled ruefully. 'Well, you saw how I struggled with your kaross. I grew up without a mother to show me these things, you see. But I knew the baby was a girl, so I bought a pattern and some pink wool' – she held the miniature jacket up – 'too ambitious for a beginner, this cable, but I thought I'd be able to work it out. Selina taught me the basics, knit one, purl one – but she was baffled by a pattern.

'I should have gone to the woman in the wool shop – asked for her help. But I was shy. She's a real Women's

Federation type, you know – very traditional. Well, I felt ashamed about admitting I couldn't knit. All the women around here can. They still sew shirts for their husbands and bake for the church fête.'

Koba shifted her weight from left haunch to right. Her eyes wandered across the flower-patterned wall behind Marta's head.

'I'm sorry.' Marta slapped her fingers over her bloodless mouth. She was talking too much, and to a person who couldn't be expected to understand her.

Of course she'd thought of talking to Deon, but she'd found it impossible, despite his solicitude – all that plumping up of her pillows, spooning broth between her lips, fresh flowers on the dressing table – and all the time his heart was breaking. She just wasn't strong enough to support his grief too. She felt her lip tremble, knew she was going to cry from self-pity.

Koba came over to the bed and picked up the matinée jacket. 'Mooi,' she said solemnly.

Marta blinked. A word; an Afrikaans word. She swallowed, blew her nose and dried her eyes. Automatically, she began to braid her dishevelled hair, thinking of all the things she could teach Koba now.

The girl watched, fascinated. Hesitantly, she put out her hand to touch the plait. Marta held it out to her. Koba fingered the silky tip. It was softer than she'd expected. Not like grass at all. And she could see strands of silver where there had been gold. She dropped the braid and stepped back, smiling sadly at Marta.

On her way out of the house, Mannie thrust an avocado pear into her hand and some salt in a twist of paper.

After that, Koba often came and sat with Marta. She wandered round the room as Marta spoke, looking at things, touching them as she became bolder – the springy mattress she longed to bounce on, the bed linen whose fineness she liked to feel. Marta's tortoiseshell hairbrush amused her, but most marvellous of all was the mirror on the dressing table. She stared in it for hours, pulling faces, checking views of herself to left and right in the wing mirrors.

Marta didn't mind talking to the back of Koba's head. There was freedom in being heard by someone who didn't understand and who wasn't sufficiently interested to try to. So she relaxed, made Koba privy to her most contradictory, illogical and even ungenerous thoughts. Slowly, mad grief ebbed away. She became less self-absorbed, began to ask questions Koba could understand: about veld food and weather and animals. A stilted dialogue began.

Later, when Marta was well enough to receive Koba in the kitchen, the girl's greatest delight was turning the tap on and off. Yau, to have the power to summon water with the twist of a wrist, she thought. She shoved her whole head under the gushing stream, slurping ecstatically at the cool, emerging with a tiara of liquid diamonds.

Marta touched her hair's springiness and laughed, surprised that there were still things that gave her pleasure.

I I

Summer was almost over by the time Marta felt well enough to sit outside. Deon placed the wicker chair in the deep shade of the veranda and helped her to it. She leaned comfortably against him. Strange how her weakness seemed to give him strength, she thought. It was as though Ingrid's death had sobered him up, permanently.

He settled her in the chair and left. As she watched him move from the shade into the bright sunshine she realized that the change had probably begun with Etienne's death; she'd just been too distracted to notice her husband stepping out of that shadow.

She gazed into the canopy of the old avocado tree nearby. It was older than the house, grew higher than the wind pump, and was home to a colony of weaver birds. Hundreds of them. Every branch was festooned with the pear-shaped nests.

Marta had planned to write to Lettie this afternoon. She'd received a long letter from her sister-in-law – was she still her sister-in-law? Marta wondered – offering her commiserations. Lettie ended with a postscript urging her to bear in mind that grief was very ageing.

Marta chuckled. But how to respond tactfully, especially when Lettie was so obviously worried about her son and Marta had the feeling a few words of reassurance would be very welcome. The trouble was, she didn't think André would grow out of what his mother called his 'wildness'. The boy was a brute and it could only get worse now he had power.

She sighed. She didn't feel up to being diplomatic yet. She preferred to just sit and think; about Koba, mostly.

Perhaps Deon was right? Perhaps she shouldn't keep Koba separate from everyone. But *her* wildness was special. Marta felt it gave the child an insight into nature that others had long lost.

She flapped irritably at a fly circling her head. Deon accused her of treating Koba like something from a Tarzan film – a noble savage. That was nonsense, of course. If anything, she was probably treating Koba more like one of them; like a daughter perhaps.

Was that why Mannie had seemed so resentful when she'd mentioned at supper last night that she'd started teaching Koba to read?

'I thought you didn't want to spoil her,' Mannie had snapped.

Feeling too fragile for confrontation she let his impudence go. 'Well, I've been thinking that perhaps Koba was sent to us for a reason; perhaps I'm meant to educate her, get her used to western ways. *Then* send her back to her people equipped to help them.' She smiled cajolingly at the two men. 'You see, I'm beginning to agree with Pa that the Khoisan can't stay untouched by civilization for ever, even out in the desert. So,' she said, winding a strand of hair around her finger, 'wouldn't it be better if one of their *own* becomes familiar with western ways, then goes back to help them . . .'

Marta had caught Deon and Mannie rolling their eyes at each other.

She found she was envious of the new closeness between them. She'd seen how Mannie sought Deon out first when he got back from school. She watched them walk the building site together, talking and laughing. Mannie never said what they discussed. For her, Mannie kept the stories of his school day: what book they were reading; what the little madam, Katrina Botha, from the farm next door, had got up to on the school bus.

Marta found her most relaxing times were with Koba, reading stories to the girl from one of Mannie's fairytale books or hearing Jul'hoan myths told in Koba's soft vernacular. The extraordinary range of click sounds she used was almost as fascinating to Marta as the girl's skilful imitation of the animals who featured in her stories.

Deon came into view. He had instructions for the labourers. They gathered around, cheerful and willing. Even they seemed to respect this new Deon, Marta noted. He was friendly, but authoritative. Despite his crippled leg, she'd watched him match them brick for brick as they laid the foundations of the guest lodge. Three rondavels were roof height already. Soon the Tsonga women would cut the grass and begin thatching them.

Marta felt something fall lightly onto her shoulder – a long strand of straw. No doubt dropped by one of the flock of feathered maintenance men working above her. She watched a handsome male bird, vibrantly yellow but for his black mask, making exacting adjustments to the weave of his nest.

Just like Deon. She smiled.

Then she had an idea. What if she offered to weave Koba's hair into one of those elaborate styles she'd glimpsed on the heads of the Tsonga women when their doeks slipped?

Now she thought about it, she realized Koba might well have a problem with her hair. The child had taken to wearing an old woolly cap she could only have found in a rubbish heap somewhere. It was full of holes and hardly yellow any more. Marta had longed to snatch it off her pretty head. It made Koba look so poor and – Marta cast around for the word – neglected.

Yes, that was it! Ever since the child had taken to wearing the hat and a pair of Mannie's old shorts – where had she got *them*? – she'd started looking scruffy. And like a boy, despite the breast buds, Marta thought.

She shifted uncomfortably in her chair. The thing was, though, would Koba want to have her hair braided?

Marta couldn't remember ever seeing a Khoisan woman with an elaborately woven hairstyle, but she did recall that they didn't tend to cover their heads like other African women; their hair was always close-cropped, showing off their beautifully shaped heads. Was Koba covering hers because her hair had grown too long and she had no way of cutting it?

Oh God. Marta dropped her head into her hands. She'd been so stupid. So blind. Yes the child was Khoisan – from a Jul'hoan group, Marta had now learned – but first she was a girl, a young, teenage girl, who cared about the way she looked and would want to fit in. She needed scissors and a mirror and a bath!

How could I have been so toe? Marta thought. And what to do to make it up to Koba? She stood up, began to pace. She could buy Kobatjie some clothes. A skirt and a few blouses. Ja, but was that practical for bundu-bashing? Wait. Why did Koba have to live in the bush? Why couldn't she move into the spare bedroom?

Marta hurried inside as fast as she was able, to start preparing the room.

As she worked she remembered a bitter exchange with Deon on Koba's first day at the farm:

'I thought Pasopkop would be the place for her,' she'd said as Deon and Mannie unloaded their travel bags.

'You mean make her live in a cave?'

'It's got the painting!'

'Well, that's all right then. Rock art should keep her nice and cosy.'

'What do *you* suggest then?' Marta asked through clenched teeth.

'Put her in the kraal with Selina-and-them.'

'You know, you Boere amaze me. You live in a land you think you belong to, but you don't even know the *first thing* about it. Let me put it in words you'll understand: kaffirs don't like Boesmanne; Boesmanne are frightened of kaffirs. Boesmanne and kaffirs don't like Boere –'

Deon threw a suitcase violently out the back of the truck. It landed on the drive with a thud of red dust. 'Put her in the blerry kitchen then,' he shouted.

'Like a dog, to sleep in front of the stove?'

He jumped down clumsily from the truck bed. 'Not like a dog,' he snarled. Taking Marta's arm, he steered her away from the onlookers who had gathered outside the servants' compound. 'I thought we brought her here so we could improve her situation. She needs food, clothes, education – a name, just for starters.'

'Something nice and Christian, I suppose?'

'Jissus, woman! I don't care what you call her. Anything, man, just something to make her seem more normal, so she can fit in.'

Marta yanked her arm from his grip. 'Did it ever occur to you that she might have a name – a perfectly good Khoisan one?'

'I'm sure she has, but how the blerry-hell are you going to find out what it is?'

Room ready, Marta set off to find Koba. The girl was up the jackalberry tree, balanced on a branch more than ten foot above the ground. She was wearing Mannie's cast-offs and the woolly hat. 'Be careful, child,' Marta said as she watched Koba clamber carelessly down. Koba had a handful of the yellow-purplish fruits in her hand. 'Those any good for eating?'

Koba shrugged and dropped them into her kaross, tied like a sling over one shoulder. It was lumpy with bits of bark and roots she'd gathered earlier. Also, a chipped enamel mug Marta recognized as one she'd thrown out. She looked away, embarrassed.

Koba waited. Something was in Marta's heart, she could tell. She hoped the listening wouldn't take long. She wanted to collect some jacket plums before nightfall. She fidgeted with her sling, waited a few more moments, then: 'I go.'

'Wait.' Marta kneeled down with a suddenness that startled Koba. 'Would you like to move in with us? I mean, into the house. We could get some nice clothes and I could do your hair.' She pulled the cap off Koba's head. A bush of hair sprang free, dusty and matted. Tenderly, she touched it.

Koba grabbed for the cap and pulled it back onto her head. What did Marta think she was doing?

'Koba, I think I was wrong before, trying to make you live like a Jul'hoan. Come and live in our n!ore.'

Understanding dawned on Koba. Marta wanted her to leave the cave and she wanted to do something to her hair. She touched it self-consciously. It needed shaving, but without a blade and someone to help her . . . She didn't like to ask Frog-boy for these things; she wasn't sure why.

But suddenly she knew she didn't want this woman's help either. The cave was hers; a place she'd made her own with difficulty. Her hair was her own. Something she would rather have had help with, but not from |Ton. They had taken her mother, her father, her n!ore from her, and now Marta wanted her Jul'hoan skin too. Leopard-woman wanted to eat her up, in her own lair.

No! No-and-no! They'd taken enough from her. She hated them. How could she have forgotten? Now she must show them, once and for all, how she despised them. She turned her back on Marta, pulled the shorts down and thrust her naked bottom in Marta's face. Then she pulled them up and, grabbing her sling, set off across the veld.

I 2

A year later, when Koba tried to recall landscape details from her home in the desert, she felt she was peering through the silver shimmer of a heatwave. Even massive baobab trees she'd sat under for hours listening to Zuma's stories seemed spectral now. All she remembered was searing sky, paler than here, and the sun's yellow whited out as the desert baked and burned. Her memories of the Kalahari were becoming dimmer every day, but she could still picture small black figures undulating across the sand dunes.

The trouble was, the longer she looked, the quicker they seemed to evaporate. How much longer would they be with her? she wondered.

Somewhere, far off across the veld, a wood dove mourned.

Don't cry; you can fly away, Koba thought. She watched a drongo land on a nearby sweet thorn, its two-pronged tail bobbing for balance as it avoided impaling itself on the long white thorns. That, she knew, was the thing to do.

'I must just live and live among dangerous things until it becomes easy,' she said to Zuma that night in the cave.

She stared at the mural. Soon the figures would dance with life borrowed from the fire. In the flickerings, giraffe would lope across the wall; dancers would disappear into the obscurity of the shadows, only to be licked into life again by the fire's tongues. This was a beautiful painting – even better than the one at the Forbidden Pool. She loved the patterns scratched into the rock – lines crossing as in a fishing net, or hexagoned like honeycomb. They reminded her of the pictures she'd seen behind her eyelids when Grandmother gave her gwa.

It was bitter and made her retch, but Grandmother said she must eat the root. It would help her to trance. She hadn't gone into a proper trance – for that she would need training and a drum-dance, but she had trembled and sweated and seen the patterns. It comforted her to think people had seen the same patterns in trance since ancient times. If only there had been time for Zuma to continue with her trance training. Who would teach her now?

She dropped a piece of animal fat onto the smooth stone in the middle of the fire. It sizzled before she smothered it with the clammy cold of the fish she had caught. She smelled the fish beginning to cook. For once, the aroma did not please her. She was hungry for real meat. All she ate on the farm was white meat: hare, tortoise and fish. Her stomach craved the satisfaction of gorging on the red meat of something with hooves. Like the swift buck she'd sometimes glimpsed, mostly beyond the high fence at the edge of the farm. She had seen one like it in the Kalahari, but not the same. The one from her n!ore had a black face. This one looked just as delicious. She'd like to catch this buck – impala, Mannie called it – but how? The little snares she could set wouldn't trap it.

No, she thought, the impala must be shot with a poison arrow and tracked until it dropped. She had no arrows and, anyway, it was forbidden for females and children to touch hunting tools.

As Koba picked the fish from the bones, she thought about metal. It could be fashioned into arrowheads. She tossed the fish skeleton into the flames and wiped her fingers on her bare thighs. Koba began to plan her weapon-making. If she could cut off a piece of metal from a fence, if she could find a cutting tool strong enough, she could melt it and shape it into arrowheads. She'd seen her father do it. And what was so difficult about making a bow? Already she knew where a tree with just the right switches grew. She'd cut one, carve and smooth it, then heat it in hot sand so it would curve more easily across her knees. She'd decorate her bow. It must be beautiful.

She grabbed her knife and began sharpening its blade against the hard heel of her foot. The only problem, she reflected, was the taboo. Women could make arrows – Zuma had been skilled at it – but they and children should not touch arrowheads.

Then she remembered her mother talking with awe about a woman who hunted. This woman lived near the Makgadikgadi pans, N‡aisa had said. She had a lazy husband and her craving for meat was strong so she taught herself to hunt.

'She grew fat and sleek,' N‡aisa had said. 'Her husband too!'

Koba remembered her mother laughing at that and saying nothing bad had happened to the hunting woman even though she handled poisoned arrows. She must have been as careful with them as any man, Koba thought.

'I will be too,' she shouted out loud.

And now she found herself with a clear memory of the delirious excitement that had greeted anyone who walked into camp with a buck slung around his shoulders. Along with the other children she had scampered before the hero, whooping with excitement, jumping up to sniff the carcass, yapping and scrapping with playmates like a hungry puppy. The old people had hobbled from their huts, querulous voices raised to remind the hunter of a favour owed. People stood about, salivating, while they speculated about the division of the dripping, red meat. And after bellies were full, people with faces greasy from the feast sat at the hunter's fire and begged him to tell of the chase.

It would be a fine thing to be so admired, she thought, but who will I tell my hunt stories to?

Winter left the veld bleached, but not bald, thanks to Deon's veld fire vigilance. There was little water in the river now and even the thorn trees looked bare except for the odd, tenacious corkscrew pod.

The holidays came and Mannie had whole days to spend with Koba. She was glad. It was company. She chattered like a vervet, giving him instructions in his own language as he helped her hammer out arrowheads from bits of metal she'd cut from the fence with a borrowed wire-cutter. She spoke of a Kalahari beetle whose pupae contained the poison needed for the arrow tip.

'Ja, but where will we find one?'

'None here, arrow must kill alone,' she said, noting with satisfaction his intense interest.

They spent many hours practising their stalking and shooting skills, with Mannie eager for instruction.

Zuma, garrulous in the cave that night, was the only obstacle. 'You must keep the Jul'hoan traditions,' Koba heard her urge.

'But if women can make arrows, why not hunt, Grandmother n!a'an?'

'They do not make arrow tips, as you do. It is forbidden for women or children to go near a meat-bringer tipped with poison.'

'*My* meat-bringer has no poison!' Koba crowed.

'Then how will you ask the meat animal to die for you?'

'Quickly. My sharp-sharp arrow will go straight into its heart.'

'Uhn-uhn. Still you run like an eland with its head down. You will fall, Koba. Listen to me: sure as no-rain, you will return to our n!ore,' Zuma said. 'If you have forgotten your skin, people will refuse you.'

Koba returned to her sharpening. She didn't have to listen to a spirit's whispered words.

Koba decided she and Frog-boy were ready for a buck. One morning they set off; Koba carrying a quiver full of arrows, Mannie with a long, sharpened stick. The pale soles of Koba's feet kicked up dust as she trotted in front of him. He coughed.

'Quiet,' Koba hissed. 'Walk like a hunter or never have full stomach like one.'

'Kkek-kek-kek-krrr' – the alarm call of guinea fowl. The birds fled in a flurry of blue-grey, announcing the presence of intruders.

After an hour without spotting any impala, Koba suggested they crawl through the fence and into the Kruger Park.

'It's not right to hunt there. It's a reserve. Anyway, it's against the law. If they catch us we'll go to prison for poaching.'

'Prison! Gǃaoan gave animals to feed people,' she said.

'The ones in this reserve are not for eating.'

'Hhn! Does the ǀTon of this big fence think all animals there belong to him?'

'No, Koba, they belong to everyone. But they're only for looking at – so that people can appreciate them.'

Koba placed her hands on her slim hips. 'Don't I know their beauty?' She thought about how the fluffy white undersides of impala tails reminded her of thorn tree blossom; of how graceful the backward curve of an impala ram's horns were. Just because she couldn't express it in the |Ton language didn't mean she didn't appreciate these things. She swiped viciously at the tasselled heads of the surrounding grass with an arrow. 'My people always-always love the animals we hunt,' she said mutinously.

'I know. I understand, okay?'

'What must I eat when my heart needs red meat?'

Mannie shrugged. 'Listen, we can hunt anything we find on this farm, but I can't go in there, okay? If you go, don't tell me about it.'

Koba shook her head. Truly |Ton were strange. Did they really believe that what their eyes did not see wouldn't hurt their hearts? Well, if the crazy Frog-boy wanted to hunt on the farm, she would take him on a trail he'd wish he'd never seen.

Koba set off at speed towards the densest thicket of thorn she could see. 'In there we will find a spoor,' she shouted. When they got there, she sat down with her back against an abandoned termite mound and directed Mannie towards the thicket. 'Call when you find.'

To Koba's surprise he did find something in the thicket. Or it found him. A warthog sow, disturbed by Mannie's crashing and cursing, stormed out.

'Quick, quick!' Koba scrambled up.

They couldn't keep pace with the sow as she bulldozed through bushes, but her tracks led them to a burrow in an earthbank.

'She got away,' Mannie moaned, flinging his stick down.

'Yau, you hunt like a man with a meat-tired stomach. This pig is full of fat. We can get her out. Be ready.' She handed him her quiver and took his spear. 'Warts-on-the-face, we come!'

She climbed the earthbank and began to plunge the spear into the sand. At first there was no sound but Koba's grunts as she struggled to withdraw the weapon from the earth. After a particularly vicious jab they heard a muffled squeal. 'She comes now,' she called down to Mannie. 'Be careful! Tusks like lion's teeth. Sharp on sides too.'

The warthog bulleted out her burrow, mane bristling, tail rigid as an aerial, piggy eyes murderous as they darted about looking for her tormentor. Mannie had a clear view of the lethal tusks and the warty mound under the eye she focused on him. But he stood transfixed, bow drawn, his arrow immobilized in the grip of his petrified fingers.

'Shoot, shoot,' Koba shouted, but it was all Mannie could do to jump to one side as the warthog slashed, ripping the hide of his boot, miraculously missing his skin. As the animal spun round in a fury, Koba let fly with her spear. It pierced the porcine flank and diverted the animal's attention. It squealed, but with no change to its barrelling pace, it swung in Koba's direction.

Mannie saw her look for a tree. The big marula was too far away. Almost in a dream Mannie went through the aiming ritual Koba had taught him: 'Look up – is the arrow's path clear?' He adjusted the trajectory to miss a branch. 'Stand still – the prey's ears must flap-flap in peace, not be raised because it hears you coming.' Too late! 'Look steady – hit heart or legs so the animal cannot run too far.' And then: 'Arm soft, wrist soft, ask the animal to die for you.' Mannie asked and released the arrow. 'Watch where arrow hits.'

Mannie did not see his arrow fly through the air. Nor did he see it sink into the rugose, brown chest. He was surprised when the animal stumbled to its calloused knees a few feet short of Koba.

He leaped forward and began hacking at its still-pulsating throat.

Was that his guffaw that greeted the warthog's last grunt? Could that be him scampering around the body to hug Koba, giggling when he squelched in sand soggy with blood? Was the flushed, blood-spattered boy posing with his foot on his quarry really him?

'Now you can bring meat home, you can take a wife,' Koba teased. Mannie effervesced as they skinned and gutted it. While Koba roasted a portion of ribs, he frolicked, bare-chested, in the sun. When they ate he chattered with his mouth full, spattering gristle onto his sun-warmed skin. Afterwards he lolled like a full-bellied pup watching Koba mix charred plants with warthog fat.

'No-way am I eating those vegetables.' He yawned.

'For cuts, not eating.'

'What cuts?'

'For first buck you must get cuts.'

Mannie sat up. 'What buck? I didn't shoot a buck.'

'Yes-yes, but we do the same for buck or for Eye-lumps.'

'Eye lumps?'

'Eye-lumps is warthog, Frog-boy. Didn't you see?' He nodded, remembering the grotesque mounds beneath the piggy eyes. 'Your first meat animal is female, so I must cut this side.' She approached him, pointed to his heart with the tip of her knife.

Mannie scrambled backwards. 'Hey, now wait a minute . . .'

Koba flung a leg across him and sat astride his chest, knife in one hand, tattooing mixture in the other. She pinned his arms to the ground with her knees.

He didn't struggle. He could easily heave her off his chest when he wanted to, he thought, he was bigger than her now, but she was giving one of her rare smiles and he liked the way her skin felt pressed against his.

'What you going to do?' He laughed up at her.

'Be still to respect the Meat animal.' She pinched the taut skin above his left pectoral muscle and made short, parallel cuts through the pinch. Blood welled out of the cuts, but quickly Koba rubbed the mixture into them. Only when she released the skin did Mannie feel the sting.

'Eina!' he roared. Raising his head to see where the pain was coming from he stared aghast at the smear of blood and blackened fat. 'What the fok have you done to me, you crazy girl?'

'Medicine to strong your hunter's heart.' She was still smiling, but not as confidently. 'Now I must make cuts on aim arm and on head to make eyes see well.'

'Not on my head you won't!' Mannie pushed her off his chest and stood up. 'I'm not walking around tattooed like a heathen.'

Sitting in the dust, recovering from her surprise, Koba hastily rearranged her pubic apron, but not before Mannie noticed the pale honey of thighs normally hidden from view by his old shorts. Such a different colour from the skin she exposed to the sun, he thought.

Seeing her so small, sprawled amid the debris of her ceremony, he felt terrible. He kneeled down in front of her. 'I'm sorry, man, Koba. I got a fright. I, we, er, white people, we don't do that to each other.'

Her long eyes locked onto his, searching for insincerity.

'Look, man, we're still friends, aren't we? D'you want me to make *you* some cuts for the warthog?'

Koba shook her head, sadly. 'For a woman to hunt is not Jul'hoan way. Man must hunt, woman must gather. Man must have first buck cuts; woman must have first blood cuts.'

'First blood?'

'When girl sees moon for first time.'

'Huh?'

'The moon!' She clutched her stomach, miming menstrual cramps. Mannie stared at her blankly.

Koba sighed and began gathering up her things. Frogboy was like Pishiboro, that stupid god who did not know what his wives were for until they climbed a tree above his head and called him to look upwards.

13

Mannie watched the big car bounce up the track. Jissus, a Chevy. Convertible! A real Yank Tank. Who could be visiting them in this?

The driver revved the v8 engine before skidding to a halt in front of the farmhouse with a fanfare of horn-honking. A young man jumped out from behind the steering wheel, clearing the two-tone door.

It was André – bearded and maned now like a mature lion.

Mannie unconsciously touched his own chin, where down was just beginning to harden into bristle. Realizing he was gaping, he quickly closed his mouth, but not before André noticed.

'Catching flies? You never seen a Chevy before? Bel Air, limited edition. Just fetched her off the boat at Durbs. Beauty, hey?' He patted the long, cream-coloured front seat as he lounged against the door. 'Only six in the country.'

Mannie was torn between his desire to drool over the car and his wariness around André. He still had a scar across his toes from the incident with the horse. He assessed his cousin's physique. Ja, the oke was big, but he himself was no pipsqueak now. He'd bet André was handy with those sledgehammer fists of his, but his beer boep would definitely cost him. Ja-no, if it came to it, he reckoned he could take him.

Deon emerged from the shade of the veranda behind Mannie. 'This is a surprise.'

'Ja-well,' André said, stretching his arms out wide above his head before lazily taking his uncle's proffered hand. 'I wanted to see what Uncle-and-them have done with the old place and I was in the area, so . . .' He patted the Bel Air's bonnet. 'It's a nice spin up here. I took it easy, got twenty-five to the gallon.' Deon obliged with a whistle. 'Monday morning, this baby gets loaded onto the train for the trip home, so while I wait . . .' André stretched again and yawned.

Mannie felt shocked, not by the decadence of a young man who owned a car that needed transporting by sea and rail, but by his cousin's disrespect towards Pa. And to demand a tour of the farm like he owned it! Mannie's hackles rose.

But Deon was all smiles. 'Good idea to take a look round, nephew. And you visit as long as you like, hey. Now, how long since we last saw you? Five, six years? At Weltevrede? You've grown just like your pa, hey?' He led André off on a tour.

Prosperity was coming slowly but surely to Impalala. Where Etienne's business thrived on water, Deon's had flourished when it was scarce. Drought brought holiday-makers to the Kruger Park in ghoulish droves. They came to see gaunt herds of zebra, wildebeest, giraffe and antelope scuffle for space around the shrinking water-holes. Here predators lurked – lion, leopard and even crocodiles were clearly visible as they went about their deadly business in the denuded veld and shrinking rivers. To the gasps of onlookers, irritable hippo, trying to sub-merge themselves in the diminishing mud, snapped their gargantuan jaws at any intruders, even elephant. The hippo knew better than most that soon the cooling slush would dry and set hard, while the animals all around lay dying. Rest camps in the Park could not accommodate all the tourists, so private camps like Impalala benefited.

And even now, with the vegetation lush again after good rains and the savagery of nature less evident, the lodge was full. Deon was the sort of host who ensured return custom. In the evenings he was to be found mingling with guests in the communal barbeque area limping between huge Afrikaner men in khaki shorts, who held a beer in one hand and a long braai fork in the other. Their wives made curried banana salad in bowls the size of washtubs, and their sons, ears protruding from shorn scalps like unhinged doors, played rugby or climbed trees. In the play area Deon had built, little girls in shortie pyjamas squealed on swings or queued for the seesaw. The air here was blue with braai smoke and it smelled strongly of a mosquito-deterrent called Mylol. Deon declined cans of lager and listened patiently to stories of the most exciting lion kill ever seen and answered questions about the best place to glimpse rare roan antelope.

The effect of a full lodge on the famhouse was noticeable too. The tin shack was now a gracious colonial-style bungalow. Marta slept soundly amid thick brick walls, plastered and painted bright white. The green wooden shutters matched the new tin roof, complete with expansion gaps to accommodate metal movement. It was a cool, welcoming house now, with its deep veranda and cascading bauhinia. Most evenings a sprinkler chattered on the broad lawn, arcing borehole water into the sultry air. Marta kept a few beds for veld flowers, but the men did not pass these as they approached the house along a path lined with whitewashed stones, swept and watered daily by a uniformed gardener to keep the red dust down.

Mannie kept a close eye on André all the way through supper. Was he sneering at them, at their table that only seated four, at their cloth of cotton instead of lace like Auntie Lettie's? Mannie wondered. And why had Ma done the cooking? Had André noticed the gem squash was burned underneath and the stew almost dry?

But soon he realized André was too full of himself to register his surroundings, bragging non-stop about the things he'd bought – the latest rifle, the latest motorbike, some flying lessons. And he drank brandy almost as fast as Pa used to.

André said nothing about farming until Marta specifically asked him.

'Pa trained up some foremen; they know what to do.' André smiled. 'And then there's ou Twi.' He shook his head. 'Heaven only knows what Pa wanted *him* around for. He couldn't plough straight to save his life, and the other kaff –' he bobbed apologies to his aunt – 'er, Bantu won't take orders from him, him being half-Bushman.'

Marta nodded sadly.

Spurred on by this unexpected agreement from a woman he would normally avoid engaging with, André plunged on. 'Ja-no, what the Hotnot lacks as a farmer he makes up for in loyalty. Jis, but that man loved my pa. Tears in his eyes when he talks about him, even now. And every week he goes to visit the grave. Every week, hey? He likes to do the weeding out there. I've given him one of the old bakkies so he can carry the tools.'

'That's very generous of you,' Deon said, trying to imagine just what the old Bushman was up to at his brother's well-secluded burial plot. Some kind of illegal trading, he'd bet. And now the cunning fellow had wheels to aid him in his enterprise. Well, good for him, he thought, and he looked at Marta as he raised his glass of water to André's brandy tumbler.

Boisterous from too much alcohol, André began to tease his aunt. 'I hear Auntie's got a pet Bushman too. Ma says that wild one we found is still here by you and that you treat her like a daughter.' He turned and winked at Deon. 'I thought she might be sitting next to me at the table tonight.' He roared with laughter. Deon smiled thin-lipped while Mannie prayed his mother wouldn't start a political argument with André.

Marta was stung into silence by her nephew's jibe. She could see how her treatment of Koba would look to outsiders. In another society she would have adopted the child immediately, but here, inter-racial adoption wasn't permitted. Also, Koba's Khoisan identity was at stake, she reasoned to herself. And in any case, she thought, looking down at her plate, Koba had refused the offer of accommodation in the farmhouse. She sighed. There was no point trying to explain all this to the young man sitting across the table from her. André had inherited his father's wealth and brutality, but without Etienne's intelligence and occasional compassion, Marta thought. Had *he* been here instead of his stupid son, Etienne would have challenged her for not having the courage of her convictions and including the girl as a guest at the table.

No, not just as a guest, Marta chided herself. They all thought of Koba as family now; they didn't need a piece of paper to make their relationship official. And she certainly didn't need approval from the likes of André. Marta thought proudly how Koba could hold her own. The young woman spoke Afrikaans fluently now and had even, on occasion, appeared at the house wearing a yellow dress that Marta had made for her, laboriously unpicking and resewing the frilled yellow collar. It still didn't lie right, Marta thought, though she was touched that the girl chose to wear it. She wished she could afford a shop-bought dress for her, one that fitted properly, but it would seldom be worn; dresses weren't practical bushwear. A pair of Mannie's old school shorts and shirt were much more sensible. Koba usually teamed these up with her beaded pubic apron, various decorated gourds attached to an animal skin belt and a small duiker-skin kaross for carrying things in. Instead of the tatty old hat, she now wore a variety of headscarves tied over her hair in interesting ways. Their source remained mysterious to Marta.

'She's really something, that girl,' Marta had said, shiny-eyed, to Deon. 'She's so resourceful. And she's got style.' He'd nodded. 'You know, it's people like her who are the future of this country.' She went on to evoke a picture of Africans of every creed and colour mingling to create a progressive, new culture.

'Dreams are nice,' Deon said, getting up to go.

'It's more than a dream. Koba and Mannie's generation can make it happen.'

He had paused at the screen door. 'Don't you encourage those children to do anything illegal, hey? You know more than most how dire the consequences can be these days.'

She hadn't demurred. Instead she'd begun to entice Koba back to the lessons they'd been having before they had their falling out. It wasn't difficult. Koba regretted insulting Marta and had missed her teaching. Soon Marta was covering a full curriculum of school subjects with her as best she could, but she became increasingly aware of her own limitations as a teacher. Koba needed stretching.

Marta approached several white high-school teachers in the area, asking them to tutor the girl privately. They all refused. A retired black headmaster she spoke to in the township came to meet Koba and told them both that the girl already knew more than most of the teachers he hired at his rural schools. 'You should share this gift with your own people,' he'd advised.

Koba and Marta had avoided discussing her future, but now, at the supper table, Marta began to see that keeping a bright, educated Koba at Impalala, as an unofficial family member or even just as a regular dinner guest, was going to be a lot more difficult than keeping a little Khoisan girl hidden in a cave.

Mannie was disconcerted to find himself assigned to taking André out shooting the next morning.

'I'll bag a few guinea fowl for the pot, seeing like I dropped in unannounced on Auntie,' André said. He borrowed a 0.303 from Deon.

'Won't you blow a bird to smithereens with that?' Marta asked.

André grinned. 'Only if I want to.'

They skirted the guest rondavels active with people loading cars or cooking coriander-scented boerewors for breakfast. Soon they'd left humanity behind and smelled instead the territorial markings of hyena that had passed in the night.

'So, bumfluff, show me this cave where your ma's precious savage lives,' André said, pushing through grass and thorn thicket.

This remark made Mannie's hackles rise. Did André want them to believe his visit was prompted by the desire to brag, disguised as family feeling, when all he was really interested in was Koba? Perhaps, thought Mannie, he should have made a fuss when André chose a powerful hunting rifle from Pa's cabinet instead of a bird-popper. That would have obliged Ma to fetch his father, and Pa would have interrogated André. After all, he reminded himself, Ma knew nothing of what had happened to Koba's mother out in the veld at Weltevrede. She had no idea of the danger André might pose to Koba.

'We can't go in without her permission, and, er, she's not here at the moment,' he said, trying to sound firm.

'Not here? Is she on a Hotnot *holiday* or something?' André sneered.

Mannie stopped and turned to face his solidly built cousin. 'It's none of your business where she is or where she lives.'

'Wooo, look who's getting snappish, acting like the Hotnot's his girlfriend or something . . .' André gyrated his pelvis, leaving Mannie in no doubt as to what the 'or something' referred to.

Mannie felt himself turn scarlet, from rage or embarrassment he couldn't be sure, but he was furious about letting André see he was rattled.

'Look, do you wanna shoot birds or don't you?'

'Birds? Oh ja, I'm always interested in *birds*,' André said, tapping his khaki-trousered crotch. I'm a real culture vulture, me. And I hear there's some special art in the Hotnot's cave. Really old stuff.' Mannie hid his surprise that André knew about them and nodded reluctantly. 'I hear there are dirty drawings of men . . .'

'Whhaaat?'

'. . . with thorns through their piels.' André laughed. 'Sounds eina. But you know all about that, don't you, boetie?'

Mannie knew he'd been manipulated, but still his eyes smarted at the memory of André slashing at his penis with an acacia branch when he was young. Another scar André had left him with.

Fists balled, he took a step closer to his cousin and realized that his eyes were almost level with André's now. 'Listen, I'm not that bangbroek kid any more. I don't have to put up with your sadist stuff. You leave Koba and me alone, okay? You get off our farm right now or I'm telling Pa . . .'

'You'll tell him what? What is it I've done, hey? Made a few jokes about sex. *J-j-jokes*, that's all, boetie. But you can't take them cos the kaffirgirl hasn't let you on for a ride yet, isn't it?' André laughed derisively again.

'Find your own way home, you creep!' Mannie said, and took off through the veld.

Out of sight, he broke into a fast jog. Koba was in danger, no doubt about it. André intended to find her cave and if she was in it . . . For a fleeting moment Mannie allowed himself a memory of Koba's mother lying in the back of his Uncle Etienne's wagon while André sniggered at what he could see. Mannie picked up speed to run as fast as his legs would take him.

André veered off and followed a path to the servants' compound. Once there, he banged on the reed fence to announce his presence, then strode into the kraal, scattering chickens, goats and mangy mongrels. 'Hey,' he shouted to Selina who was pounding maize in an X-shaped mortar, 'come help me.'

She ignored him. One of her daughters-in-law appeared, her hands still studded with the grains she'd been sifting for beer. A naked toddler trailed her and hid behind her skirt, peeping out in wonder at the sight of a strange white man being so noisy in their world.

André demanded the Bushman girl. All the Tsonga stared at him, slack-mouthed. 'Yellow girl, like this.' He pushed his nose flat against his face and stuck out his bottom. The little ones laughed and one child pointed across the veld, towards the river. Selina swooped down on him, scolding in Tsonga, pinning his chubby arms to his sides.

'Tell me what he's pointing at,' André ordered. Selina lowered her eyes and backed into a hut, taking the child with her.

Selina viewed the whites, who now owned what had until the previous century been Tsonga land, as a necessary evil. Without them she would have no work and her family would be living in squalor in the non-white township on the outskirts of town. By comparison with other boere madams, Marta Marias was an undemanding employer. Until the white woman had begun bringing the yellow tokoloshe girl to the table at the farmhouse, Selina had no particular cause for complaint against the Marais family.

But this rude, red-faced brute filling the doorway of her hut was another story. She owed him not even the pretence of respect.

'What you do in me khaya? Voetsek! Get out!'

André was astonished at being spoken to like that. He darted inside and fastened his fingers around the child's chubby forearm. 'You tell me now,' he said, smirking up at Selina while squeezing the tot's flesh until it rose like a brown balloon behind the tourniquet of his grip. The child began to cry. Selina snatched up a three-legged iron pot and swung it at André. Swearing, he let go of the child and ducked. The pot missed his skull but struck his shoulder. He heard people running towards the hut. He backed out, cursing, and stormed out of the kraal.

'You haven't heard the end of this,' he shouted. 'I'll tell your baas. I'll go to the police.' Fokken kaffirs, they'd never get away with cheeking him like that at home. And hitting him? André rubbed his sore shoulder. He'd beat the black off of them, man or woman. Jislaaik, what kind of people did his moegoe uncle have working for him?

No point complaining though, he realized. He had been trespassing, as his kaffir-loving auntie would be quick to tell him, he was sure. Well, fok them, he thought. He'd find the Bushgirl, even if it took him all day and all night; the Bushmen weren't the only ones who could track. He settled the rifle across his uninjured shoulder and set off towards the most obvious landmark, a hill that looked to him like it might be hiding a cave or two.

Koba wasn't in the cave or anywhere on Pasopkop, as far as Mannie could see. He called as loudly as he dared, not wanting to risk alerting André, who might already be in the vicinity. He crawled out along Koba's lookout ledge. Jissus, it was scary; how come she could run along it like a monkey? He scanned the land spread out before him. Koba wasn't checking snares in the guarri copse nor walking along one of the veld paths. But in the distance he could see a swaggering shape heading towards the hill. André! Quickly he lay down and, peering over the edge of the ledge, he checked the ravines below.

Nothing, and André was getting closer; only thing to do now was find Koba before André did. He'd have to search the whole farm; on foot that could take a day. He decided to go back to the house to see if he could borrow the farm truck.

André dropped heavily into Koba's cave then lit a match to look around. Must be hers, he thought – over there were the drawings he'd heard about. He stepped closer, lit another match and was disappointed to see the art was not pornographic. It looked no better than the scribbles of three-year-olds to him – just stick figures. Ja, some of them had obvious erections and lines through them, but Jissus, this was hardly enough to give an oke a stiffie. Actually, he'd seen one of these paintings before; above the pool at the Mother Hills. He'd found a human skeleton there too: small, with a very curved spine. An old woman, Twi had said, some kind of witch doctor: they'd picked up a muti stick or something right next to the bones. Not an old skeleton; some skin and her ragged clothing were still attached to the bones. Another Bushman trespasser probably, vrekked before she could get back home. Served her right, André thought.

He crossed to the fire and stuck the tip of his boot into the ashes. Cold – but it had been used last night. If the Bushman girl was away she hadn't been gone long. He sat down near a pile of skins, letting his eyes adjust to the dark. With the nose of his rifle he lifted the skins. Duiker, mostly, and one kaross made from impala hide.

What was this? André held up a pair of panties. So, the kaffirgirl had gone white down there, he thought. He pressed the thin cotton of the underwear over his nose and mouth, and breathed it in. It smelled fresh and sun-dried. Mentally, he pulled back the cover on his favourite fantasy, the one where Koba exposed herself to him. Would she have those long lips like her mother had? he wondered. He realized he'd driven all this way specifically to see them. How he was going to engineer it, he couldn't quite work out, but something would come to him. 'A boer always makes a plan,' he said to himself, standing up and pocketing the panties.

As Mannie rounded the corner of the farmhouse he saw the truck driving off, followed by a Land Rover with the Kruger National Park insignia on the door. In the back he could see armed rangers. Marta stood on the veranda looking worried.

'What is it, Ma?'

'Oh, thank goodness you're back. The warden's just been. Says a bull elephant broke through our fence last night. They're going to find him and dart him. I must go warn the guests still in camp to stay indoors for the time being. I need you to run to the compound, son, and tell

Selina-them to be careful if they go out for wood. You know how irritable an old jumbo can be.'

No vehicle; no Pa to talk to about André. And now he had additional duties.

Mannie cursed events as he ran to the kraal, not stopping to wonder at Selina's foul mood. As he sprinted back, Mannie fretted about where next to look for Koba. He passed André's car. The keys dangled from the ignition. A jumbo at large was not unheard of at the farm, but a Bel Air, he thought. And it happened to be the only vehicle available. Ha, wouldn't André have a blue fit if he used it to find Koba?

Mannie vaulted over the door and landed on the deeply padded seat, grinning. He placed his hands on the polished brown wheel and stretched his legs to the floorboard. Hell, this was lekker. He felt for the pedals. No clutch. Automatic. He'd never driven one before, but he was sure he could manage. Mannie turned the key. A purr of power. Quickly he turned it off again. He shouldn't be doing this.

He sat still, peering over the dashboard as he waited to be caught. Nothing. No one. Mannie turned the key again. He thrilled to the engine's throaty rumble. He looked around. Still no one.

It occurred to him that his mother probably wouldn't mind if she knew he was taking the car to rescue Koba. Anyway, he was only borrowing it; he'd have it back before André even knew it was missing.

Now he felt calmer, he was certain he knew where Koba would be – down among the sweet thorn near the river. She'd mentioned she was out of salt and wanted to trade. Mannie said he'd bring her a bottle of Cerebos 'see how it runs' salt from the store; they bought it in bulk now. Honey, too. But she'd looked fierce and said she didn't want something for nothing. She would get him the honey; if he didn't want to eat it – shrug-shrug with those small shoulders of hers.

He slipped the Chevy into gear and took off with just a slight jerk. Bakgat, he thought. This car was easier to drive than the truck. Mannie pressed his foot to the floorboards and the Bel Air took off down the track, dust billowing out behind it like a battle banner.

In a clearing near the river, Koba stopped to listen. Was that the honey guide chirping? Still far off. She sighed. She'd been searching since sunrise. All the familiar hives showed recent honey-badger damage. She could still smell the foul fart people said it used to stun the bees. But there had to be an undisturbed hive somewhere. She set off for the bushwillow thicket.

Had Koba been up on Pasopkop she would have seen the long veld grass parting, as it did when a lion padded through. Here, on the edge of the thicket, her view was obscured by the dense foliage. But now a honey guide appeared, making its distinctive rattling call, a sound she'd come to think of as that of a box of matches being shaken lengthwise. The bird flew in a circle, undulating and swooping upwards with spread tail. 'Chitik-chitik-chitik,' it called, guiding her to the stump of an old ironwood tree.

'You're a clever little feather,' Koba said, kneeling to examine the stump. Uhn-uhn, the hive was deep in the hollow, best to smoke the bees out. But it was hot and she was tired. She jabbed at the hive with her hare hook. It broke open. Quickly she clawed out a hunk of comb. Confused bees poured out of the breach. They massed in the air and turned on the marauder, dive-bombing her. Tossing down a piece of comb for the little bird, Koba ran, laughing. But she needed to wash the honey from her hands or the bees would pursue her all morning. And she needed to pee.

Having checked for crocodiles, she rinsed her hands then climbed back up the bank and found a secluded spot to pull off her shorts and underwear and squat down. She was happily scrutinizing the flow of her urine, watching it find its course through the grass, when she became aware that she was being observed. The skin on the back of her legs prickled; unease rippled over her buttocks and up her back. Yet the watcher was no life-threat; she had none of the uncomfortable pressure she always felt inside her chest just before her tappings started. Still, there was a force to be reckoned with somewhere in the bushes close by; something much bigger than she was.

I should leave, she thought, standing up and reaching for her clothing.

When Koba first appeared, André had hidden himself. He wasn't surprised to find her – he'd tracked her – but he was surprised to find she had an angry winged escort. He'd sustained a good few bee stings in furious silence as

187

she ran past. He'd followed her down to the riverbank, keeping his distance from the phalanx of bees that still swarmed around her. What's she doing taking bees for a walk? he wondered, seething. With his binoculars trained on her he'd seen her throw down the honeycomb that was attracting the insects. He watched with glee as she stood like a stilt in the river, bending forward from the waist to wash her hands. Slim, dark legs, but her crotch was covered with thick khaki shorts. He closed his eyes and imagined the garment away. Feeling the gratifying swelling of his penis, he put his binoculars down and unzipped his fly. When he looked up, Koba was closer and, if he wasn't mistaken – could an oke get that lucky? – her bottom half was bare and tilted towards him. André whipped his binoculars back up to his face, knocking the bridge of his nose so hard his eyes watered. He blinked impatiently, but by the time he'd cleared his vision and readjusted his sights, the girl had stood up and was looking around nervously as she stepped into her panties.

Fok, fok, fok, he thought, she's seen me. But the girl was looking in another direction.

Koba sensed that a gigantic mass was moving through the riverine bush without so much as snapping a twig. She could see nothing, but beneath her she felt the ground give, as though a colossal weight had been placed down nearby.

André felt it too and broke cover, scanning the surrounding thicket. He spotted a huge grey form, within shooting range. An elephant? Here? It must be rogue, he reasoned. It would have escaped from the Kruger Park; he'd be doing the rangers a favour if he shot it before it started wreaking havoc.

His penis hung out of his pants, forgotten, looking like a mottled pink rag, as he surreptitiously reached for the rifle, congratulating himself on the extraordinary luck he was having. Only one thing could be better than seeing Boes poes and that was shooting a jumbo, he thought, looking about for the best place to position himself. He noted Koba slipping away and briefly considered shooting her. She was within range; her body would roll down the bank and into the river where the crocs would have it, and no one would be any the wiser. But then he'd lose his chance with the elephant. In all the years he'd been hunting he'd never had a shot at a jumbo. The Bushgirl he could always come back for later, he told himself.

Approaching from the other side, Mannie had a better view of the elephant. It seemed to be dozing, resting the weight of its old head on one massive tusk. The tusk was so long it touched the ground in a graceful white curve. The other tusk was only a stump, lost in a fight many years ago; Mannie knew because this, he was sure, was the famous Mafuta. People had written books about him. No one knew for sure how old the bull was, but his tusk was worth thousands of rand and poachers had tried many times to trap him.

No wonder half the Kruger rangers were out searching for him, Mannie thought. But the jumbo looked listless. He stood dead still in the mottled shade, his eyes closed and his ragged tail twitching feebly at flies. His skin was dull and even baggier than was usual for an elephant.

Just like an old man with no arse, Mannie thought. Funny that he wasn't feeding. Perhaps the old bull had come here to die. He could still be dangerous, though.

And somehow I've got to get past him to see if Koba's in there, Mannie thought.

He drove a little closer. The elephant didn't stir. He wasn't surprised. The Kruger animals were used to engine noise; they knew it wasn't threatening.

But André had heard the engine – the unmistakable vibrato of his beloved Bel Air. Here? What-the-hell! He began to run towards the sound.

André saw Mannie behind the wheel of his car. At the same time as the elephant saw him.

Mafuta lifted his trunk and sniffed the air. With amazing agility he rotated himself, his immense tusk scything through the undergrowth. His huge ears began to flap.

Heedless, from fifty yards away, André screamed at Mannie: 'What the fok do you think you're doing with my car?'

Mannie saw André's undone fly. He was too late. 'Where's Koba? What have you done to her?'

'My car! Don't tell me you've stolen my fokken Bel Air and driven it through the bushveld. If you've got so much as a scratch on her I'll fokken kill you, I swear.'

Mafuta seemed to have had enough of the commotion. Trunk aloft, he trumpeted, a sound that silenced André mid-rant. He spun round in time to see the bull's mammoth ears flapping furiously. Then Mafuta charged.

The ground shook; pods, twigs, leaves showered down from trees as he thundered past. There was dust, the squawking of a ground plover desperate to protect her nest, and more of the terrible trumpeting. André sprinted for the car as though his life depended on it.

Mannie knew it did. Dry-mouthed, shaking, he pushed the gearshift into drive and pressed his foot hard on the accelerator. The car shot forward with a spin of wheels, passing André and bouncing towards the bull. Mannie pressed his palm on the horn as hard as he could. André stopped, horror-struck. 'No, no, no,' he shouted, arms flailing hopelessly. 'Mind the car.'

The distraction worked; Mafuta slowed his charge. He paused, one massive foot raised, and tossed his head from side to side. Irritably he brought the foot down, on a bushwillow. One of the tree trunks split under his weight and half the canopy began to shear off. The sound of cracking branches seemed to annoy the elephant. Wrapping his trunk around a massive branch he yanked and brought it down with a shriek of wood.

The Bel Air was close now. Mannie sat white-faced behind the wheel, perspiration running down his forehead. His heart seemed to oscillate, not beat, and he felt ice-cold. How much further dare he drive?

He waited until he judged himself to be almost within tusk-reach, but for the buckled tree, then he wrenched the steering wheel and skidded to a side-on halt behind its protection. The car stalled and Mannie scrambled along the front seat, kicked the passenger door open and rolled onto the ground. Then he was up and running, shouting for André to do the same.

But André stood transfixed, watching Mafuta consider this new impediment. With a swing of his shapeless foreleg and what seemed only slight pressure from his trunk, he elected to continue with his demolition work. A forty-foot fever tree got excavated, toppling over onto the car. There was a huge explosion of glass and metal as the windscreen shattered and the car frame buckled down to bonnet level. The boom echoed across the bush and bounced off the distant rockface of Pasopkop. Mafuta trumpeted in alarm and began to reverse as quickly as his tusk would allow, leaving André howling with anguish. 'Where's my gun, where's my fokken gun?'

Mannie's last sight of him was of a fool dancing with rage, undecided whether to pursue the elephant or inspect the wreckage.

14

Mannie, who should have been revising for his exams, was trying to teach himself to jive using the diagram on the back of the record sleeve. When Koba tapped on the window, he was glad.

'Come in. You can help me learn this dance.'

Koba jumped lightly onto the window ledge. She used the door when Marta was around, but Leopard-woman was clearly away, she thought, if her cub was making such a noise in the den.

Mannie took her hand and pulled her inside. She was under five foot to his almost six and her toes didn't reach the ground as he held her at chest-height for a moment.

She hadn't realized Frog-boy had become so tall and broad. It made her feel shy. He set her down and she stepped away from him.

'Hey, c'mon, Koba.' He offered her his hand again, but she stood stiffly, looking down at the carpet. He frowned. 'Okay then, I'll close the shutters.'

The gloom helped. She put her hand in his and made a fair mime of Mannie's movements. When he pushed her away from him, then pulled her back, Koba got the idea. She giggled, but kept time to the music. Mannie grinned, raised their linked arms and, with a push on her waist, spun her. She chuckled. A few minutes later and she was able to turn in both directions without losing the beat.

Mannie dropped Koba's hands the moment he became aware of the blond-haired figure in the doorway – Katrina Botha, a neighbour, in shorts and a blouse tied high under her breasts. 'I knocked, but you were too busy to hear. All shut up, hey?' She raised an overplucked eyebrow.

'Ma-and-them are out. We, er, I . . . hold on, I'll just turn off the player.' Mannie scurried over to the gramophone, his cheeks and ears red.

'I just came to ask about the homework – biology, actually.' Katrina smiled, her eyes glittering at the thought of the mileage she could make out of this scene. Mannie Marais, toast of the under-seventeen rugby squad, with his dark little secret.

'Dancing with a kaffirgirl, in his front room, *with the shutters closed*,' she'd tell the girls. And while they were still gasping, she'd deliver the final blow to his reputation. 'And guess what they were dancing to? *Bill Haley!*'

Nevertheless, Katrina thought, Mannie Marais had potential. He was handsome, in a very young way. They'd played together as kids and now the little scrawn was filling out nicely.

But his ma was a troublemaker. Probably a commie, her father said. Mrs Marais had been on that march-thing with all those kaffir women who were put in prison. And after Sharpeville she'd tried to get people to sign a petition protesting about it. She was lucky she wasn't arrested, Katrina's father had said.

Well, like mother, like son, the girl thought. Though why Mannie was interested in this filthy little scrap, heavens only knew. She looked like a caveman with that animal skin draped over her.

There had been talk about this kaffirgirl – Bushman or something. The Maraises kept her round the place like a pet, people said. But would you dance with your dog or your monkey?

Mama said Mrs Marais had educated the Bushgirl and wanted her to sit Matric next year, like her and Mannie. Apparently, Mrs Marais felt the Bantu exams were an insult for such a clever girl, so she'd already applied to the education board for the white ones. Cheeky, the women in Mama's sewing circle said. Katrina remembered her mother calming them down, saying the minister would never allow it.

'Koba and I,' Mannie was saying, '—have you met Koba?' As he turned his scarlet face from Katrina's cool gaze he heard the clap of shutters being thrown open and he saw Koba jump out of the window. Katrina laughed lightly, but her eyes were hard. How dare this boy think he could introduce her to a kaffir?

'Koba's a bit shy.' Mannie shrugged. He became aware of his hands hanging awkwardly off his wrists. He should do something with them. 'Can I . . . get you a drink? Coffee, or something?'

'No time. Pappie's taking us to the dam for the week-end. We're staying in a *hotel*.' She drummed her fingers on the doorframe. 'So, if I could borrow your biology homework book? Quickly.'

'Ja-ja, of course. I'll fetch it.'

She was leaning over his record collection when he got back, buttocks flared towards him, waist tapering above. She straightened up and held her hand out for the book. Her nails were painted a shimmering pink, like the inside of shells. He couldn't take his eyes off them. How did she keep them so clean, in all this dust? He watched, mesmerized, as she used one pristine talon to flick a long skein of hair back over her shoulder. Now he could see down the neck of her blouse; a bit of bra, very white against her tanned skin.

'Thanks,' she said, mincing over to the door. He felt his groin go with her.

Over her shoulder, Katrina said, 'By the way, Mannie, the jive's out – it's the twist you should be learning, unless you want your boswyfie to look out of place at the dance.'

Mannie cursed. She was going to crucify him at school on Monday, he just knew it. And it wasn't going to be easy with Koba either, he felt sure.

He found her up on Pasopkop, near her cave, leaning against the contorted trunk of the wild fig tree. She had a dog-eared book of fairytales in her lap. She didn't look up when Mannie flopped down beside her. 'Jis, it's baking.'

No reply.

'Too hot for hunting, hey?'

She turned a page.

'Want me to read it to you?'

Now she looked up, scornful. 'I can read myself.'

Mannie sighed. When they were younger he'd read her fairytales and she'd tell him a Jul'hoan story in exchange. The stories were funny, often rude, with small animals getting the better of big ones, or long-suffering wives playing tricks on their god husbands. In one, they gave the god shit to eat instead of sausage. He'd laughed at that.

Sometimes, Koba didn't bother with translation. She told the tales in her own language, as if he could understand her. Funny thing was, he sort of could. The clicks were all different; he could hear that. And many of them sounded just like the thing they were naming, like the galloping sound when she was telling about a herd in flight. Koba also made all the animal movements with her hands, fingers trotting rhythmically across the ground like the tireless jackal, or splayed like a heavy-pawed lion. Ja, it was surprisingly obvious. Pity there wouldn't be a story session today.

'You in a mood, or what?'

Yes, what? Koba thought to herself. Why did she feel so dejected? She stared out over the distant veld. Its blondness reminded her of the |Ton girl's hair. The girl Frog-boy wanted to have food with. A fierce face with sharp eyebrows and nostrils permanently flared, a serval cat about to pounce . . . but not on Frog-boy. He did not interest her enough. Yet.

I am alone, even with him here. Even with Grandmother in the cave every night. There is no one to touch me, to hold me. My heart hungers for people with my skin, my head whispers 'afraid' – afraid to go back to my n!ore.

Koba knew there was now money for her train ticket to Onderwater; Marta had said as much months ago. She'd even offered to accompany Koba on the journey home.

Koba hadn't responded because she didn't know what she should do.

'Grandmother n!a'an,' she said when the spirit came to her one night. 'Why does my heart lean towards our n!ore *and* draw back from it?'

'Your heart knows a dream is better than eyes-open.'

Koba nodded. 'I will be disappointed.' She sat staring into the flames, imagining herself among her people. She could see faces just like her own, chattering, smiling, but not at her. To her they turned blank faces. Some were even hostile.

'No different from here, then,' Zuma remarked.

Koba flapped irritably at the empty air. 'Stop that. Don't press your ear to my thoughts.'

'Yau, you Bone-and-Bloods are slow-slow-slow.'

'You Spent Breaths are . . .' Koba bit her lip. She made a determined effort to empty her mind. Zuma could wait to hear her thoughts when she had them in some order.

'You wish to know if the Ju!'hoansi will reject you?'

'Yau. Go away!'

'Uhn-nh-nh. Must be you are sitting on your manners.'

Koba pouted. It was infuriating the way Zuma took advantage, breaking rules that suited her, enforcing those that didn't. Spirits. Yau!

'The answer to the question you are too fat-lipped to ask is: the Jul'hoansi will accept you if you wish to belong.'

'But they might find me ugly, my tongue clumsy at their talk. The woman for whom I am named may not be alive. There may not be one kinsperson still living there. Who will know me? Who will take me to their fire?'

'Uhn, Koba. What I hear is what you have already decided – to stand still. You have time. But do not grow roots here, child. This ǀTon n!ore cannot feed you. One day you will have to leave.'

Koba shook herself out of her reverie when she felt Mannie staring. 'What's the matter?' he said.

'I am spoiled.'

'Spoiled? How?'

Impatiently Koba twitched the apron that hung over her shorts. 'By being here; not growing up among my people; not learning proper Jul'hoan ways. Here I live like a man – I hunt, I wear boy-clothes; I like dry food – you've seen me with salt; I prefer it to honey – could be because honey is wet, woman's food.' She sighed. 'I am not a proper Jul'hoan woman.'

'Ag, man, kak!'

She ignored him. 'I am like Rose Red who spoke toads.' Mannie looked confused. She tapped the fairytale book.

'Oh.'

'Like Jackal, in the Jul'hoan story. I am so unwoman, I will give birth to nǂah seeds. From my arse.'

Mannie winced, then said patiently: 'Look-man –'

'You see!'

'Ag, Koba-man, you know –'

'You said, you said it again.'

'You're just being otherwise, *woman*. You know you are.' She half smiled. 'Ja, so the way I see it, you don't eat honey because you don't like the taste; finished and klaar.' He tugged irritably at his shirt back. It was plastered to his skin with perspiration. Jis, it was hot for all this nonsense.

'Listen, ma– er, Koba, you should cheer up, hey? I mean, you're lucky, you know.'

'Lucky?'

'*You* can make up your own mind about things. Decide for yourself what you will and won't do. *I* can't do that. Pa says I need haircut' – he ducked his prickly pate for her to see – 'and look what I got – blerry sandpaper. Only jaaps still have hair like this.'

'You are a jaap.'

'I am not! I've been to Joburg. Well, through it, anyway. So have you. Do you remember? When we brought you from South West . . .' He cut himself short. That was dangerous territory. A place they hadn't ventured to since in any of their conversations.

Koba seemed not to have heard. She was staring at the patch of red earth between them. Then she lifted watery eyes to his.

'When a girl goes to the moon for the first time, the women dance for her. Rub her with eland fat, give cuts here' – she indicated her cheekbone – 'so she looks beautiful as zebra. Where are my marks, where is my beauty?' Two tears slipped from beneath her long lids.

'Ag, Koba, you don't need stripes on your face. You're fine' – the tears were coming faster – 'um, pretty even' – and faster. 'You're beautiful, man. You look like a little steenbok with your long, thin legs and soft eyes, and your face here . . .'

Gaats, he was getting carried away. He'd almost put his big, dirty finger on her face.

'You don't understand,' Koba said.

Mannie shrugged. He didn't. Girls were baffling to him and now Koba, his best friend, was blerry-well turning into one.

He stood up and offered her his hand to rise. 'I've got an idea – it's a long walk, but if we go along the riverbank . . .'

'You want to honk.'

It was a joke between them – whenever they were in the vicinity they stopped at what had become known on the farm as 'The Wreck of the Bel Air'. There they pretended to honk the horn of the car already removed by a team of amazed insurance assessors. A picture of the wreck now hung in the insurance company's boardroom, alongside one of Mafuta.

'So where you want to go?' Koba asked.

'To the Bothas'.' Mannie's eyes jived. 'For a goef. They're away for the weekend. They'll never know we've been in their swimming pool. And afterwards we'll pee in it. That'll teach Miss Eau de Cologne.'

*

The Bothas' garden was like an oasis in the middle of the scorched brown bushveld. A revolving sprinkler pelted giant palm and pawpaw trees, making a loud, papery clatter before spinning on to douse the profuse creepers: golden shower, bauhinia, bougainvillea. The gleaming kikuyu lawn felt springy underfoot as they ran towards the kidney-shaped pool.

Koba gasped as she got closer – the colour; almost like the other water from her worst nightmare, the water in the pool at the Mother Hills.

Mannie was already dipping his foot in. 'Water's a bit green, but never mind; warm as a bath. Come feel.' Koba shook her head and retreated to a spot some distance away, under the frangipani tree. It smelled wonderful there.

'C'mon, man. You must swim.' He walked over and stood looking down at the top of her head. 'What's the matter, hey?' Her fingers twirled a frangipani flower. 'Ag, man, there's nothing to be scared of. If you can't swim I can quickly teach you.'

'Not that,' Koba mumbled.

He flopped down in front of her. 'What then? Tell me.'

And because she had heard him earlier, and because she really needed to talk, she found herself doing just that; telling him all about the pool at the Mother Hills, about leaving Zuma, about watching her father and mother being shot.

It took a long time, and all the while she didn't cry and nor did Mannie. Quietly, while he too fiddled with fallen frangipani, he filled in his impressions of the day. Finally, without looking up, he admitted to her what he'd never told another soul – that he could have warned Etienne and saved his life.

She opened her arms to him and they held each other, sharing silent sorrow.

It seemed only natural to Mannie to kiss her face, along her cheekbone, down her slim neck. Her fingers explored his head, traced along his nose and caressed his neck. Then she ran them down his shirt and up under it, discovering the hardness of his young body.

Mannie moaned. The sound acted like an alarm for Koba and she stopped instantly. She needed something from Frog-boy and it wasn't this. She pulled away. 'I want you to help me with something,' she whispered.

'Sure,' Mannie said, still trying to nuzzle her ear.

'It's not food,' she insisted, pushing him away.

Mannie sat back and drew his knees up to hide his erection. Koba was talking, but there was no possibility of paying attention. She tapped impatiently on his arm. 'I had a message from the spirits,' she said. 'I must make a trance dance and try to become nlomkxao.'

What-the-blerry-hell? 'Listen, Koba, you gotta give me a minute here,' he said. 'I need to cool off.' And with that he jumped up, dived into the pool and swam five furious lengths. Afterwards he flipped onto his back and floated. Let her see that she didn't affect him.

He got out and lay on the concrete to dry off. Koba came and lay next to him. 'Sorry-sorry,' she whispered. He grunted and buried his face in his crossed arms. 'If we feast now, my muti won't be as strong,' she said.

He lifted his head, frowning. 'What muti?'

Koba began to explain the trance initiation ceremony. It was difficult and she didn't have a translation for many of the Jul'hoan words. But finally he understood and sulkily said he'd help. 'So what must I do?'

'For the dance I must have the drum-medicine song to help my blood boil. When it boils my nlom will be strong.'

'Nlom?'

'Healing power. It will make me sweat and tremble, maybe even jump in the fire or fall down like dead. Then you must care for me. You must stop me injuring my body, you must blow in my face, rub me' – he grinned – 'you must bring me back from the spirit world or I will die.' Now Mannie looked worried.

'Do you really want to risk this?'

'I must-must-must.' He could feel her body tense with determination.

'Okay. When do we do it?'

'Next ringed moon.'

15

In the days that followed, Koba made preparations for the dance. She collected a mopane stump for firewood – not easy to find, but worth the long walk to fetch it; it would burn long and sweet. Next she needed ankle rattles – cocoons from the mopane worm would do, and for the rattles, seeds. Koba tested their clatter in her shaking fist, inserted them into the cocoons and threaded the filled cocoons onto sinew.

Hair decoration was next.

'Take,' she whispered to Mannie next morning as they passed the wash line where curtains from the guest rondavels were hung out to dry.

'What you want a curtain for?'

'No, that.' She pointed to a brass ring still in the curtain. He slipped it out. 'What's it for?'

'My hair. I will put some beads, then' – she dangled the ring over one eye – 'see.' Mannie wolf whistled. She laughed. 'It's for Zuma n!a'an, not you.'

Mannie slowed his pace. 'Why do you want to be a nom, er . . .?'

'Nǀomkxao,' Koba prompted him.

'Yes, a nomkaho thingy?'

'If I am an owner of medicine I will be respect. People will welcome me.'

'But you can already cure people with plants. Didn't you give Selina some stuff for that baby with dysentery?'

'Bah, many people know plant muti. Marta even. But if I could heal illness from the spirit world, that would be big.'

'But it can hurt, you said.'

'Yau, pain!' She flapped her narrow wrist dismissively. 'Women,' she said, striking her chest, 'do not run from the pain of childbirth. Can trance pain be worse?'

Privately she was afraid, but not of pain or discomfort. What if her quest was successful, Koba thought, and she did reach the spirit world? Would she see her father there, with half a face; her mother, eyes pecked out by vultures; Zuma's bones splintered by hyenas? She shivered violently.

'What's the matter?'

'We call, a word like,' she said, casting about, 'um, Sunspooks. At sun's highest' – she pointed to the noonday sun – 'bad medicine men walk. These poisoners do not cast shadows.'

'Spirits dance! Spirits dance!' Mannie woke to see Koba's face looming over his. How had she got into his room? The window, of course. He groaned and pulled the sheet over his head. Being woken up suddenly always gave him a headache. He felt a gentle prod. Grumbling he sat up, rubbing his eyes. When they cleared he saw Koba dressed only in skins with a hoop in her carefully braided hair. He hadn't seen her hair for years. It looked nice like that.

'Showtime, huh?'

'Come-come-come.'

Mannie was still doing up the buttons of his shirt as he followed Koba's across the moonlit veld. It was a jewel of a night – stars studding a satin sky, a moon so bright even a dappled leopard would show up in it. The path up the hill was a silvery trail, but the pace Koba was setting was doing his head no good at all. He felt a stab of pain in his temple with every footstep. At the top of Pasopkop she allowed him to stop as she pointed out the distinct ring around the moon. 'That's c-cloud,' he gasped. 'Maybe it'll rain.'

'No, the Jul'hoansi say it's spirits dancing. Quick-quick. Drum-medicine dance.' She handed him a halved calabash with a skin stretched taut across it. He tapped it once. A good resonance.

Koba brought two tortoise shells over to him. 'What are those?' he asked.

She pointed to the first. 'To make medicine smoke. It will help me trance. But it can sick me. Then you must use the other' – she lifted the smaller shell and held it out to him – 'to cool me.'

'What is it?'

'San powder.'

He sniffed the pungent green powder. 'Phew, smells like what Ma used to put on my bruises.'

But Koba had no time for comparisons. 'Begin your drumming.'

Mannie sat down, gave the drum some tentative taps. Koba took a few short, shuffling steps. 'Are you afraid of the drum that you tap so shy-shy?' she called out.

'It's the dead of night, Koba. The Tsongas will think the tokoloshe is coming.'

'I need the noise.'

'Okay-okay.' Mannie thumped the buck hide. An owl flew from its perch screeching with shock. He laughed. This could be fun and might even make him forget the throb in his temples. 'Hey,' he called to Koba, 'do you call yourself the child of a Jul'hoan and you don't even dance?'

Koba smiled. Frog-boy was joking like a Jul'hoan! She began to stamp her feet in time to Mannie's improved tattoo. Her ankle rattles shook. She circled the fire, flicking her fly whisk with a rhythmical swish. She sang a few notes: 'Ehay-o, ehay-o.' Perhaps it was time for the medicine smoke.

She lit the greyish powder in her tortoise shell and inhaled deeply from the aromatic fumes. The smoke made her eyes water and her nose burn, but her head soon felt light. She began clapping in counterpoint to Mannie's beat. This was good. 'Now you sound like a real person! Now our rhythms are talking.'

Koba bent forward in her dance, breasts bare and hanging from her chest like golden pears. Mannie could see the curve of a buttock through the parting between kaross and pubic apron. Her amber skin glimmered with perspiration. He felt his penis press against the leg of his shorts.

From a shell held high above her head Koba poured water into her open mouth. Her back was arched, her breasts proud as she stood in profile. Water splashed down her cleavage. Mannie's eyes stretched wide. She glanced in his direction; he looked away. Koba returned to her dance stamping, singing, on and on, hour after hour, until she was so tired she could barely shuffle.

I mustn't cool. My nlom must boil. Warmth at the bottom of my spine. Soon it will rise up and power will flow through me. Ha. This is not painful – what was I afraid of? I do not need a healer to hang on to. I do not even need the voices of women singing. Now I am moving through water. My body is weightless. The drum beat comes from a world above. I see the |Ton boy. Tiny – a frog on the side of my waterworld.

Yau! Yau! Something grabs my insides. What is pulling at the back of my stomach? It is climbing up inside my back! I'm being dragged down – I cannot breathe, I cannot swim. A snake, from the Forbidden Pool!

Koba was shaking, shouting, contorting, as she tried to gouge the skin on her back with her nails. She threw herself on the ground and rolled towards the fire. Her dilated pupils failed to focus on Mannie as he blew into her face, but soon her gasps slowed. Mannie pulled

Koba into a sitting position and made her drop her head between her trembling knees.

Before he could reach for water or buchu powder, she'd jumped up and grabbed coals from the fire, oblivious to their searing heat. She began to hurl them into the darkness.

'Go away, you clawed things, you Cruel Cries in the Night. You will not have my meat. I will not sit and wait for you to harm me, not like the Mother Hills!'

The skin on the back of Mannie's neck prickled. What could she see that he couldn't? He scanned beyond the circle of firelight. Nothing. It must be bad memories then, he thought; the stuff she told me about from the Mother Hills. Jissus, two of them spooked, up on a haunted hill in the dead of night!

'Easy, take it easy, Koba, calm down. It's all right. You're safe. I got you.'

Koba's struggles stilled; her eyes shut, she seemed to sway. Mannie relaxed his grip on her, but suddenly she was shaking violently again, her spasm moving both of them.

'Koba, Koba, stop it, man.'

He began to wonder seriously if his friend was possessed. He didn't believe in ghosts and spirits and things, but maybe . . .

When Koba went limp, lolling like a rag doll in his arms he began to worry. What should he do? Take her to his mother? He'd have to take along the powder she took. It was obviously some kind of drug. Wait; what had Koba said? Something about blowing in her face if she got sick. Jissus, now she was thrashing like a fish on a hook.

Mannie blew and blew and eventually Koba stopped shaking. She grabbed the water bottle Mannie offered her and drank the whole thing.

Why did her stomach hurt so? she wondered. Other parts of her body too. Had she been beaten? And why was it so cold? Where was her kaross and why was she sitting in front of Frog-boy with her chest exposed?

She crossed her arms tightly over her breasts and dropped her head. She had not seen any spirits – not even a steenbuck, let alone an eland. Nothing;s no one had come to lead her to the other world where she might receive nǀom. Zuma had been wrong – she was not going to be a healer, nor did she have a powerful spirit guide. She was alone with nobody to help her find her Juǀ'hoan skin, she thought, feeling her lip tremble.

'To trance you must have the courage to die, then come to life again,' Zuma had once said. 'There is pain along the path, doubt and fear too, but if you can conquer these you will be worthy.'

Koba wiped her face and looked up at the moon. There was still a circle round it, though it was getting paler.

She stood up and walked shakily over to Mannie, who stood hunched in a blanket next to the subdued fire. 'We must try again,' she said.

He shook his head. 'No-way – you scared me half to death. I thought you were going to die or get taken over by the devil or something.'

'Please-please.'

'No!'

'I beg . . .'

'Koba-man, I'm bushed and my hands are sore.' He held out palms puffy and red from drumming.

'You don't understand. Now, when Great Star returns from his night's hunting, now is the most powerful time for drum-medicine dance. *Please!*'

'It's all right for you; you can sleep for the rest of the day. I've got to go to school.' His headache was now beating like a bongo up the back of his neck.

'I will give you honey. I will catch you red meat. My heart walks on its knees to you. You must drum for me.'

'But what the hell is it all for, hey? You dance, you get crazy, you fall down. I help you get better . . . now you want to do it all again. What's the point?'

'Is for nlom – to get healing power to cure people.' She stood closer to him and, stretching up onto tiptoe, just managed to put her hand on his forehead. 'Maybe even your head hurt.'

'Hey, how d'you know I had a headache?' He tried to recall whether or not he'd mentioned it to her. He decided he must have. He bent his knees so she could rest her hand more comfortably across his brow. It was a rough little hand, but he found he liked the feel of it. He felt his frown loosen. 'Ag, okay. I suppose a bit of drumming and dancing would warm us up.'

He picked up the drum and began to pat it, noticing that the tasselled tops of the grass were already sunlit.

Koba shuffled in the groove her feet had worn around the fire. Her torso barely moved, but under

her lean flesh her thigh muscles could be seen power-
ing her forward. Round and round she moved, like
an automaton.

'Mmm-mmm,' she intoned, 'music is heavy now. Will
help nǀom come.' She stared down at her dusty feet and
began to babble to herself.

Suddenly Koba's movement and murmur ceased.
Walking with the undulations of an underwater swim-
mer, she bent over Mannie.

He didn't like the look of her; her body was coated in
a thick sweat again and her eyes looked crazy behind
the bead curtain in her hair.

Koba's hands began to flutter near his forehead, like
double-winged mopane leaves in a storm. A single note
dribbled from her slack mouth, but once in the outside
air it swelled to a cry.

'Kaohididi!'

The shriek hurt his ears and made his heart thump.
Next to him Koba's legs were trembling, the quivering
spreading up her body, making her pelvis and shoulders
shake. Mannie felt she was going to collapse again. Then
she seemed to control the spasm, harnessing its energy.
Her shaking stopped and, though her face was screwed
up with effort, her breathing was regular. She began
brushing Mannie's neck with her fingers.

'What are you doing?' he asked.

'Throwing out the sickness,' she panted. 'Your head
hurt comes from tiny arrows shot by the great god,
Gǀaoan. I can pull sick arrows into my hands, and out
– out here,' she said, slapping her upper back.

Mannie was sceptical. Healing with just the hands? She was no Jesus. As far as he knew she didn't even believe in Him. He wondered what his mother would make of this.

Time passed; he wasn't sure how much. He could hear the guinea fowl begin their dawn patrol far off across the veld. After a while he stretched, raised his arms above his head, glanced at the sky. There was green where yellow sunrise had mixed with blue sky. Hmm, a person didn't often see that. Nice to be up before it got scorching, he thought. Funny, he didn't feel so tired now.

And hey, his headache had gone!

He turned to tell Koba. But his friend wasn't dancing behind him; she lay asleep beneath the tree, curled like a comma under her kaross. And near her, even after he'd rubbed his eyes to make sure he wasn't dreaming, Mannie saw a young eland cow, grazing placidly, hundreds of miles from her natural habitat.

16

Koba squatted on the riverbank and stared at the swirling brown water. The drought had broken. Floodwater from upcountry had turned the dry riverbed into a wild torrent. Koba watched a large, neat nest sail into view. Probably a green heron's, she thought, as it whirled into an eddy before being trapped in a standing wave. That would be the place to cross the river – there; a tree trunk held back the flow – she'd have to be quick, the log might shift, her splashing might alert a crocodile. She didn't know the creature well enough to predict its habits in unusual circumstances – crocodiles didn't occur in the Kalahari – and here she'd only seen them float, yellow-eyed and inert as logs in calm water.

Koba knew she wasn't destined to be crocodile breakfast. Nor would she catch a buck on that reed island in the middle of the river. Not today. The oracle discs had predicted something else.

The discs had been Zuma's. She had slipped them into the kaross on the last day at the Mother Hills. Koba had forgotten until Mannie shook the cloak out one day and they fell from the secret fold.

'What you keeping slices of old brinjal for?' he said.

'Brinjal?' Koba looked puzzled. As he picked them up, Mannie realized they were made from hide, not eggplant, and they had faint markings scratched into the leather.

'Hey, are these oracle discs? Ma once told me Bushmen – sorry, Khoisan people – throw them before a hunt to see what will happen. Do you do that?'

Koba shook her head. She did read the discs, but she didn't want him to know. He might think her stranger than he already seemed to.

Ever since the eland had appeared, she felt her friend stood a little in awe of her. She wanted to be just Koba to him; not Koba the magician; the Yellow One; the orphan or even the Khoisan girl.

Khoisan! She had once tried to explain that her people had no name for themselves and others who might look and live like them. Why would they? They never met any of those others; there were too few of them spread across an area too vast, she had learned from looking at maps with Marta. The only word they'd used for themselves was Jul'hoansi; Real People being the closest translation she could think of, although Marta had told her some groups called themselves the Harmless People. A curious name; nobody was harmless when provoked enough. Not even her father.

But she saw that |Ton needed a name for her people. There was much in |Ton books and newspapers about labelling people. Still, if there had to be one, shouldn't the people choose their name themselves? Marta agreed and asked which group name she would choose if she could.

'Bushmen.'

'But that word has always been used as an insult.' Marta had frowned the arrow line deep into her face.

'Yau, what's wrong with coming from the bush? We all do, here at Impalala.' Marta's eyes had grown very bright then and Koba had quickly said that from what she saw in the newspapers, the bush was safer than the city. Better to be a Bushwoman living in the bushveld. At least for the little time left, she thought to herself.

Lately Zuma had been been particularly present in the cave at night, mumbling on and on about chest-tappings and the need to heed them.

At first Koba had thought that the old spirit was jealous of her closeness to these |Ton. But now she knew it was more than that; the fear snaking up her spine told her. But running or hiding did not help. She'd learned that.

So she sat calmly next to the churning river, studying the reeds, noting the silent parting and closing as something dainty moved about in them. Just a little reedbuck or a duiker perhaps, she thought.

She cocked her head, listening for movement in the undergrowth on the riverbank. Not yet. She resumed her leisurely observation of the island – saw a group of red bishops alight on the reeds, making them bow gracefully towards the water. The vivid males, puffed out atop the pale stalks, reminded Koba of flaming match heads. Mannie regularly gave her boxes of matches. She loved the lion on the front and the convenience of one-strike fire; quick-quicker than rubbing sticks together. She would take some with her, she decided. The Jul'hoansi would be glad to have easy fire.

Koba heard cursing as someone slipped down the muddy bank. Nyanisi, youngest of Gideon's three wives, slid into view, scrabbling for a handhold to arrest her fall, her wide skirt rucked up almost to her waist, beaded headband slipping over one eye. The other eye flashed angrily at Koba.

Perhaps she knows I sat here so it would be difficult to reach me, Koba thought. Her impassive nod gave away none of her amusement.

Without the traditional courteous preamble, without even bothering to set her clothes to rights, Nyanisi blurted out, 'People say you can talk to the ancestors.'

Even though she knew what was coming, Koba felt uncomfortable. For years Nyanisi had been her most hostile neighbour. Koba knew this regal beauty encouraged the little children to throw stones at her when she passed the kraal. If the milk soured or anything went missing, Nyanisi immediately suggested that the ugly Yellow One was responsible. Koba found it difficult to feel well-disposed towards this woman. Yet she must accede to the request Nyanisi was about to make. It was the start of what would be.

She forced herself to remain calm, scrutinizing the string on her bow. 'Sometimes I hear things,' she said quietly.

She was taken aback when Nyanisi began beating her own breast.

'I am suffering,' the Tsonga woman cried. 'Six years I've lain with Gideon. Every time he comes from the mines, he chooses my hut. I work with him on that mattress he bought me, every night. Hard work – he is an old man. I work harder than a new daughter-in-law pounding the maize. Bang, bang, bang. But still nothing.' She pushed her skirt down and showed her flat, brown stomach. 'I am empty,' she said tragically. 'I've visited three witch doctors. I've put muti here' – she indicated her mouth – 'and here' – between her legs. 'Huw-ah, it burned like fire.' She gazed at Koba with brimming eyes. 'What else must I do? Who else can help me? I am suffering.'

As the woman's tears fell, Koba looked away. She heard a sniff before Nyanisi continued, 'The other wives mock me. Gideon pities me.' A longer sniff and urgent fingers on her arm that made Koba turn to Nyanisi again. 'Yellow One, you must ask the ancestors why I am without child.' Nyanisi's eyes were pleading. 'Perhaps your *little* voice,' Nyanisi said, lifting her lip in a sneer that showed her beautifully even white teeth, 'will not give offence and they might answer? Then you must ask what I can do to take this curse from me.'

'A curse? No,' Koba said quietly.

Nyanisi sprang up. 'It is! It is a curse. What are these for' – she yanked her breasts from her orange-patterned blouse – 'but to suckle children?'

Koba looked away. Nyanisi had identified the problem herself. Gideon was old, his seed spent, but to tell that to a man as proud as that puffed-up korhaan? She'd have to think carefully about this problem.

'Intercede for me with the Old Ones, little sister. Please. I will give you many presents. Fish and salt and even money.'

Koba considered. Money she had no use for, but Nyanisi's loud mouth could do much to establish her as a healer for as long as she remained at Impalala. This would give her some protection from the Tsonga, but how to achieve Nyanisi's goal without antagonizing the headman? Unfortunately, her discs did not tell her that. For that she would have to use her intelligence.

'With my weak powers I will attempt to ask,' Koba said. 'But it will take time . . . and plenty of salt. And a new headscarf – red would look well on me, don't you think?'

Nyanisi nodded eagerly.

'Come in three days and I'll tell you what I learned.'

When Koba reported back that the fertility problem was Gideon's, not hers, Nyanisi looked anxious. 'He will not believe. He has proof of his strength – nine children with the other wives.'

'But Gideon is old now. His seed is not fresh and strong.'

'No. They will say I am insulting our man, our father. The other wives will turn him against me. Gideon will send me home and ask for his cows back.' She wrung her hands. 'I cannot shame my father so. My bride-price was the highest in our village.' She crossed her arms. 'I'm not leaving. When Gideon dies I want the hut that is mine.

And I want children to look after me in my old age, like Selina. I want a son and a nice, quiet daughter-in-law. Not too clever and with a strong back.'

Koba hid a smile and said gravely, 'You must find another man to seed you.'

'Huw.' Nyanisi clapped her hand to her mouth. 'Gideon will kill me.'

'Gideon won't know.'

'But the other women will tell. Jealous-all.'

Koba had her plan ready. 'You can tell them you are working with me, who has the power to make you fertile where others have failed. They won't look for you on Pasopkop.' Nyanisi nodded. That was true enough. Who wanted to roam around a haunted hill, even in the daylight? 'Listen,' Koba was saying, 'you won't be there, but out hunting for a strong young father for your child.'

Nyanisi lifted her chin and gave Koba a long-lidded look. A smile, almost lascivious, flirted round her lips. But she knew the problems. 'People will say I am busy with witchcraft.'

'Tell them you are only using me to plead with the ancestors for a baby. They will understand.'

'Understand that I deserve pity,' Nyanisi said bitterly.

Koba shrugged. A little humility would suit those proud shoulders, she thought.

It was arranged that Nyanisi would leave the farm on afternoons agreed with Koba, who in turn would lie low on Pasopkop.

She saw Nyanisi several weeks later when the woman dropped off a cone of salt and a headscarf the colour of a watermelon. Nyanisi looked well, Koba thought. Like a woman getting lots of a certain kind of food.

'Not yet,' Koba warned, 'not before Gideon comes.'

Mannie tapped a cigarette from the packet of Lucky Strike as he listened to the latest news on the Rivonia Trial. How dumb could people be? The guys arrested at Liliesleaf Farm weren't terrorists – they were just a bunch of naive apartheid activists. Amateurs, like Pa said. Laughable to believe a nearby African state was going to send troops in gunboats. Yet the minute news of the raid broke, whites ran for their laager and tourism stopped.

Ma, of course, wanted to go to the trial. Pa put his foot down. There'd nearly been a riot in the court when that oke walked in waving his fist and shouting 'Amandla'. Ma could be arrested, just disappear, Pa said. True – everyone knew the security police could keep a person incommunicado for ninety days until they tortured information from them. Mannie took a quick, nervous puff on the cigarette. Did the police keep tabs on people even out in the sticks? Ma had demonstrated illegally a few years back, at the time of the Sharpeville killings. He'd wanted to go with her, but Pa wouldn't let him.

Mannie leaned back in Deon's armchair and took a long drag on the cigarette. Nice, having the place to himself and not even any guests to worry about. Everyone's attention was focused on Pretoria; even Ma and Pa had gone eventually. They'd compromised. Pa would take the old girl to Pretoria to see her friend, Anna De Wet, if she promised not to attend the trial. Lekker, the way the folks were getting along these days. Walks in the veld together, holding hands under the stars when they thought he wasn't looking. Pa had a spring in his step when he led Ma out to the car yesterday – like he was taking his bride off on honeymoon or something. Ag, shame.

'Yau, you.' Koba stuck her head in through the open window.

'Hey, come in.' Mannie laughed as she sprang lightly over the sill. 'Have a beer.'

She shook her head so vigorously her bright pink head-scarf slipped down over her eyes. Impatiently she pulled it off. Mannie felt relieved. He thought she looked like a housemaid whenever she wore a doek.

'So, sit down. Cigarette?'

She helped herself then made straight for the rocking chair. It was her favourite piece of furniture. She loved the lull of riding it gently, but today she wanted speed. Gideon was home from the mines and it was time to put her plan into action. Just as well; Nyanisi had the glow of a pregnant woman. Koba felt she'd handled the situation well and she wanted to share her pleasure with someone.

'So, what you been doing?' Mannie asked.

She savoured her moment, slowly dragging on the cigarette then carefully exhaling a perfect smoke ring. Mannie did his frog impression, goggling his eyes at her. She giggled, then smugly: 'I am helping Nyanisi be preg by Gideon.'

'Pregnant?'

Koba nodded.

'Ha.' Mannie slapped his knee. 'So the old cock's still got it in him, hey?'

'No, in Nyanisi.' Koba kept a straight face. 'But not Gideon's.'

An explosion of laughter from Mannie. When he could talk again, he said, 'So, Nyanisi's got a lover, hey? Gideon'll kill her if he finds out.'

'That's why she's giving him my muti and saying it's made his seed strong again.'

'Maybe it has.'

'Bah – it's only jackalberry leaves. To make his tongue burn for whispering against me.' Mannie snorted a laugh. 'Gideon's seed is dead.'

'But he's fathered children with his other wives. Or aren't they his either?'

She shrugged.

'I *bet* you know. Your nlom animal has probably talked with Gideon's ancestors and then trotted back to tell you.'

'Stop it.' She waggled her cigarette at him warningly.

Mannie laughed. 'Ja-jong, deny it all you like, but I saw that eland where it had no business being.'

'That was a gwa dream.'

'Ag, rubbish. I never smoked any of that druggie stuff. I just know what I saw. Like Shakespeare said. "There are more things in heaven and earth . . ."'

'Horatio,' Koba said as she stubbed out her cigarette.

Mannie fell silent. He'd long felt that Koba should write the matriculation board exam with him in December. She'd probably fare better than he would. But the education authorities had flatly refused her permission, despite

Ma's efforts. What was going to happen to her? he wondered. Would they grow apart once he'd left school and gone away to study?

'You ever think of going back to find your people, Koba?'

'Soon.'

'What?'

'Not now, Frog-boy. Not that talk now.'

He stared at her. What was she planning? Why hadn't she said anything before? How could she look so relaxed? He felt all churned up inside.

Koba was sprawled in the chair, one arm and leg gilded by sun lazy in its leave-taking. He let out a long sigh. Jis, she was pretty!

They'd had extraordinary experiences together, not all of them bad, he reflected. She was familiar with his history, his world, but so much of hers was unknown to him. He wanted to know more, to get close to her before it was too late. He stepped across the room and kneeled beside her. 'Koba?' She slipped into his embrace.

This had been a long time coming, and now it was here, she shook with excitement. Some dread too. A tapping had begun in her chest, but it was very faint and easily ignored. She lifted her face to nuzzle his neck. Beer, tobacco, |Ton boy . . . nice-nice. She offered him her mouth.

He sampled it, reverently savouring its guava-softness. Koba undid the buttons of her blouse then, arching her back like a bow, she offered him her breasts.

*

For days they wallowed in each other, discovering the tantalizing delights of exploring a beloved body. Mannie relished each new nuance of Koba – flesh and fluid. He found chamois on her thighs, peach skin on her bottom, the juice of new grass between her legs – fresh, herby, sour and sweet.

Theirs was a movable feast: on the lawn, under the night sky filled with stars that fizzed like champagne bubbles; in the bath, where wet and shiny they slipped and slithered on each other, over and under, in and out, like a pair of otters.

In the oven of afternoon they tiptoed into the shuttered master bedroom and played at being prison lovers as the sun fell in bars across their bodies.

Finally, drunk with loving, sore from fucking, careless of discretion, they staggered naked to the kitchen, desperate for food and drink.

Mannie wrenched open the fridge door, plunged his thumb through the foil top and glugged down half a bottle of cold milk. Koba declined. She was sucking on an icy Hubbly Bubbly bottle, pressing its pimpled coolness against her cheek, her chest, the burn between her legs. Mannie groaned. 'That looks so sexy . . . but I can't, I'm finished.'

Koba chuckled a deep-throated challenge and held his gaze with her almond eyes. Neither registered the tap at the door until it became a hammering.

Mannie grabbed a tea towel and held it over his groin. Koba dropped to the floor, crawling out of sight.

'Hold on, will you?' he called.

'No, master. Master must help me . . .' One of the Tsonga women sounding frightened.

'I just have to . . .'

'Please, master must hurry.'

Mannie yanked on the shorts Koba had tossed him before opening the door a fraction. He saw Nyanisi, wringing her hands in front of her beginning belly.

'I must speak with the Yellow One.' She leaned into the gap, trying to speak around the door. 'Koba, Gideon thinks the muti . . .'

'Koba isn't here.'

Nyanisi took a step back and looked the boy up and down, slowly and insolently, her lip lifting slightly to show her matchless teeth.

Mannie stood with his arm blocking her way. Silently, he cursed her. Damn this nuisance of a woman, he thought. Not even one of their staff and she was not just disturbing him, but also making him feel ashamed. After the best days of his life, he now felt bad – like he'd been caught doing something dirty. She was spoiling everything because of her whoring.

'Gideon will hit me if the Masarwa does not show this is his child,' she said.

'Well then, you better go find her.'

Mannie slammed the door on her furious face.

That last night they locked the house against the world. In the morning, Deon and Marta would return, Koba would go back to her cave and Mannie would go back to school. All would be as before, but different, they knew.

They lay close in the big bed, Mannie's body curved around Koba's, arms enfolding her, hands cupped over her breasts.

Ma had never discussed sex with him, but he felt instinctively that she wouldn't approve of this. Because it was Koba, or because they were too young, unmarried, he wasn't sure.

Married! He was too young for that. They both were. Anyway, he couldn't marry Koba. There was a stupid law against it.

But then should he have slept with her? Had he taken advantage of her? No-way, he loved her. He told himself he'd have been happy just to kiss Koba; *she'd* started the other stuff. And he was helluva glad she had.

Koba had other concerns. Her tappings had become insistent. Was it time to face the consequences of not leaving Impalala when she'd had the chance to? she wondered. She shifted irritably, trying to quell this palpable sixth sense. I don't need tappings or Zuma's old oracle discs to tell me that what we are doing is dangerous, she thought. But she couldn't escape the fact that she'd thrown the discs some time ago, and in their fall she'd seen love and loss. She'd decided then to gamble on the former.

She was glad she'd come to know her Frog-boy as a woman, even if only for a short-short time. His taste was in her mouth, his smell in her nose; these things would comfort her through the trials to come.

She lay staring at leaves silhouetted in the bedroom window. Something Monster, Marta called that one with the giant fingers that scratched at the glass as the wind picked up outside. It was a night for lions to walk. She got up and closed the wooden shutters then, feeling her way along Marta's familiar dressing table, she lit the candle she knew would be there.

Now she saw three flickering views of herself in Marta's wingback mirror. As a child the reflections had fascinated her; tonight they filled her with fear. Am I you? she asked her right-hand side, the one that showed where she'd braided beads into her hair. Or you? She looked to the left where a cheap charm heart, found in a lucky packet and given to her by Mannie, dangled from her earlobe. She didn't recognize herself in either of the mirror panes. She peered into the central one, trying to see into her own eyes. They were black hollows, fathomless as dark dreams. But over her shoulder she could discern the peacefully sleeping form of Mannie and, behind him, hanging from the bedroom door, Marta's soft white dressing gown.

Would Marta accept a law that said she could not be with the man she loved? Koba demanded of the right-hand mirror. Would Marta accept a life far from his side with people she hardly knew? she hissed to the left. Slowly she squared up to the front. She knew the answer: Leopard-woman would fight . . . and lose. She, Koba from the Nyae Nyae, was just a Jul'hoan; *she* must endure.

See, she said to the poorly lit reflection before her, I have not lost my skin. Here I sit and sit, waiting for my fate.

17

With the new day came the sound of a van pulling up. Koba heard only the frenzied bark of the dogs, and then they whimpered, as if they'd been struck or kicked. She shivered and backed herself tighter up against Mannie's warm chest. She felt groggy; she hadn't had enough sleep; she wasn't ready to face the morning. But it tiptoed towards her anyway, in unyielding black boots, and too late she thought to wake her Frog-boy up and hide.

Kerr-ackk-k-k, an axe blade broke through the wooden shutter. Kerr-ashh, the window glass shattered. Koba and Mannie shot up, cowering against the headboard as a large policeman heaved himself through the window, cursing as the splintered shutter snagged his uniform. From the doorway, a younger policeman approached, smirking. He ignored Koba, who had the sheet clutched to her chest, and addressed himself to Mannie.

'We had a tip-off the maid was doing some after-hours for you, young master. Let's see.' With a theatrical flourish he ripped the bedcovers off the trembling teenagers.

'Liewe magies.' The lumbering captain was now in the room, mopping the fat roll at the back of his neck with a dingy handkerchief. 'Not just a kaffirgirl,' he said, leaning across Mannie to peer more closely at a petrified Koba, 'but a minor. Shame on you.'

A black policeman hovering in the doorway spoke up. 'Bushman, baas. Small.' Message delivered, he stepped smartly back into the shadows.

'Well, just when you think you've seen it all, hey?' He shook his head and a bead of sour sweat flew from his jowl and landed on Koba's bare chest. She felt it burn, but didn't dare move to wipe it away. 'A little Boes Bessie, hey? Never seen one this far east. How d'you come to be here, girl?'

'She lives, er . . . s-she's our guest,' Mannie blurted out and would have said more but for the warning pressure of Koba's hand on his.

'Your girlfriend's right; don't say anything, son. You don't want to make your situation any worse than it already is.' Then, as if he'd had enough of playing the kindly uncle, the fat man snarled: 'Get up, both of you! You're under arrest.'

The younger man grabbed Koba's arm and wrenched her off the bed. For a moment her slight brown body dangled in the air, limp as a rag doll. Then she was chucked into the corner.

Mannie shouted and lunged at the smirker.

Smirk and his sidekick were ready for the boy. Quickly his arms were trapped and pinned behind his back, so tightly his shoulder blades cracked together. Still he struggled.

'Here, make yourself decent.' They handed him his underpants. In his haste, Mannie tried to put two feet through one leg hole. They sniggered. 'Always happens,' the captain sighed. Talking between themselves, they stripped the bed, bundling the bottom sheet into a bag for evidence.

'You know, Captain, I read the other day that some Tukkies professor advised kaffirs against using sheets. Something about it being bad for the shine on their skins.'

'Don't believe everything you read, Jordaan. Now, we'll need your FL, son.'

Mannie stared aghast at the captain.

'You didn't use one, did you? Honestly, you kaffirlovers! Aren't there enough poor coloureds in this country? How would you like to be born neither one thing nor the other, hey? Don't suppose you thought of that when you broke the Mixed Marriages Prevention Law.' He took his cap off and wiped the back of his porky hand across his moist forehead. 'Never mind, the district surgeon can probably get all we need from inside the maid. Right, men, just a quick look round in case we've missed anything . . .'

Smirk began ripping open drawers and flinging their contents onto the floor, not even pretending to look through them. The black constable got down on all fours and peered under the bed. Mannie noticed that the window was unguarded. Koba could easily slip through it and take off. He could start a scuffle to delay the chase. She'd find a place to hide, knowing the farm as she did. He caught her eye, used his to point at the window. Almost imperceptibly she shook her head. Mannie stared. What was the matter with her?

Then the search charade was over and they were shoved out of the room and into the back of the police van outside.

'Normally, we don't expect a white man to ride in the back with the kaffirs,' Smirk said, 'but under the circumstances . . .'

The grille banged shut, the van shot off, its acceleration throwing Mannie and Koba together against the sharp metal of the wheel housing. He wanted to grab her then, shout in that imperturbable face that she'd missed her chance of freedom. She'd rejected the only chance she had of escape. Now they were trapped, locked in the cage, with a police escort following the van. The driver seemed to be seeking out the worst potholes in the farm track, while his colleagues jeered and pointed from the car behind as the lovers were tossed about. Mannie tried to hold Koba's hand, but that made it more difficult for them to maintain their balance. Nor could they talk above the noise of the engine. 'It will be all right,' Mannie mouthed to her.

It broke her heart to see her gentle boy trying to be so strong. It wasn't going to be all right and they both knew that now. She decided that the only way to make it easier for her Frog-boy was to withdraw from him. She turned to face the direction they were travelling in.

Mannie's mind was racing, trying to work out how he could get a message to his parents. He clung onto the back door, fingers through the grille like a desperate monkey. They'd soon be passing the Tsonga compound. That was their last chance.

Only one figure stood outside the reed fence. She seemed to be waiting for the van. It was Nyanisi, upright under the enormous bundle of kindling she carried on her head. But her face looked strangely misshapen, one eye swollen closed.

Mannie pressed hard up against the scoring grille, and bellowed.

'Police station. Tell the baas, please!'

Nyanisi smiled, revealing her broken front teeth.

18

'Deon, I'm very grateful to you for taking me.'
Marta put her hand over his as it rested on the steering wheel.

He stared at it happily. The five-hour trip was the perfect end to a damn good week, he thought. It had been years since he and Marta had taken a holiday; years since his wife had been this relaxed.

Mind you, he thought, they'd both been busy: him establishing the rest camp, her getting all those drawing commissions from Donker's. Then there was her protest work.

Thank God she'd given up her petitions to the minister for education. They were flouting the law by harbouring Koba; why draw attention to it? What good will a school-leaving certificate do Koba anyway? he'd asked his wife. She won't get a job, not even in the Bantu trading store. No one will employ a Bushman, er, Khoisan.

Marta had conceded defeat on the school exam, but he knew it wouldn't be long before she took up her cudgel about some other apartheid issue. Despite all the trouble it caused, he admired her spirit. Marta, hot with indignation, was sexy as hell to him. Now they had time, he'd like to show her; he'd like to stop the car right now and kiss her; make love to her in the back seat of the Vauxhall, here, on the side of the road.

He raised an enquiring eyebrow.

Marta laughed. 'I know that look, Mr Marais. But I'm too old to be caught in a compromising situation on a national road.'

Deon pulled a face, which made her giggle like a girl. The trip to Pretoria had been such fun, she thought: shopping; dinner-dancing at elegant Ciro's; going to the bioscope three times – a bioscope where patrons dressed up even though they'd be sitting in the dark.

Now, however, she felt guilty. This was a tense time for the country. Nelson Mandela was going to jail and grave injustice was being condoned by the highest body in the land. She should have been in mourning, not in evening dress.

'Will you look at that?' Deon said as they crested the last rise of the Highveld escarpment. 'A storm coming; at this time of the year!'

'No, it can't be. Not in winter. Maybe locusts?'

'No. There's big weather up ahead, I'm telling you.' The sky darkened further as they began their descent to the Lowveld. Impalala was still more than an hour away and a warning wind was beginning to agitate the stiff leaves of mango and orange trees as they drove past orchards. Now the sky was an engorged purple. It pulsed with sheet lightning. Then a bolt zigzagged down to the valley and crackled angrily up again, iridescently white. Marta counted to five before she heard thunder.

'Five miles away, the storm.'

Deon had to raise his voice because of a roll of thunder. 'No-way. It's just above our heads.' He smiled. 'My ma used to say it was the angels moving their furniture.'

'That settee must be big enough to seat the whole host,' Marta shouted back as a mighty rumble drowned out even the engine noise. Wind was buffeting the car, tree crowns looked like umbrellas blown inside out and the rain began to pelt down, the drops zinging into the bonnet like birdshot. The wipers fought to clear the veil of water across the windscreen, but when it turned to sticky hailstones, Deon pulled off the road and switched the ignition off. They sat, unperturbed. The car was a relatively safe place to be in an electrical storm and the rain would soon stop. With a squeak of leather, Marta shifted along the seat towards Deon. He put his arm around her shoulders. 'Aren't you the lucky one with the weather? I wouldn't be at all surprised if the car windows didn't steam up soon,' she said, snuggling in.

The rain stopped as suddenly as it had started, though they didn't notice. The sun began to steam the puddles off the tarmac.

Back on the road half an hour later, Marta said to Deon, 'I'm glad I'm going home. I'm not brave enough for subversive politics, like Anna and them.'

He stroked her hair. 'You're as brave as a lioness, Martjie.'

'No. I just write letters or demonstrate. Anna goes to court and tries to visit detainees in jail. She says they use electric cattle prods to extract information from the prisoners. One has died in custody, supposedly from hanging himself.'

'*Himself?* My eye! He would have had assistance from Verwoerd's ever-helpful security boys.'

'Maybe he did hang himself – to put an end to the torture.' Marta shuddered. 'Can you imagine?'

'Hell-no. Rather give me six rondavels with blocked toilets to deal with.'

'Ja. Or twelve meals to cook.'

'Cook!' Deon laughed. 'Are you sure you wouldn't rather be tortured?'

An hour later, the Vauxhall rattled over the cattle grid at Impalala.

'Tomorrow I must get started with rethatching. Number five's the worst,' Deon said. He clicked his tongue in irritation. 'Will you look at that light, left on in the middle of the day? And what's the matter with the dogs?'

As soon as Marta walked into their bedroom she knew something was very wrong. Paper, powder, clothing were scattered everywhere, drawers upturned. What, in heaven's name, had happened to the shutters?

Heart hammering, she ran to Mannie's room. Tidy, and the bed unslept in.

Oh my God, he must have been in our bed when he was attacked.

She tore back to her room, cast about for signs of blood. Nothing. But the bedclothes were missing. Had the attackers used them to bundle the body up in? She must find them. Koba. Koba could help. Weren't her people the best trackers?

Marta ran from the room. 'Koba! Koba!' she screamed.

Selina appeared. With an I-told-you-so expression, she announced that the police had taken the Yellow One away in a van early that morning.

'But Mannie?'

'Kleinbaas too,' Selina replied, looking less triumphant. Manfred wasn't a bad boy. He said please and thank you and always made his own bed, she thought.

Unable to process the information, Marta stared at the Tsonga woman as though she'd never seen her before. When she registered the uneven clump of Deon's hurrying footsteps Marta flew into his arms.

'What's the matter? W-who's hurt?' Then, seeing the disarray in the bedroom: 'What the hell happened?'

Patiently, as though talking to toddlers, Selina explained what she'd gleaned from Nyanisi.

Deon focused immediately. 'When did they take them? Where to?' he demanded.

But Selina had said all she was going to. Folding her arms across her massive bosom, she only offered: 'Nyanisi, she know. You ask her.'

*

Deon pushed past the sergeant hurrying out from behind the charge desk and burst into the captain's office. 'My boy, Manfred Marais, where is he?'

The captain rested his hand on the putter he'd been swinging.

'And you'd be, sir?'

'His father!'

'Well, sir, I'm sorry to have to inform you that your son has been arrested and will be charged under the Immorality Act. We caught him, "in flagrante" with your little maid.'

'She is not a maid,' Marta hissed.

'I don't care how you caught him, take us to the children. Right now.'

'I'm afraid that's not possible.' The captain looked directly at Marta for the first time. He'd heard rumours she was a communist, but to him she looked just like any other farm wife. The sort of woman you'd trust with your chickens or your children. 'Special Branch has taken the opportunity to question them. They're on their way to Johannesburg now where they'll be held under the General Law Amendment of 1963.'

Deon's face bleached. 'The Ninety Day Act?'

The captain nodded.

At first they were too tense to talk as they drove with reckless speed back to Johannesburg: through valleys where the Crocodile River ran mud-brown after the downpour; up the mountain pass, two-wheeling round hairpin bends, Deon with his hand on the horn to warn unseen traffic. A long race across the escarpment passing dusty fields around lone farmsteads, the odd copse of gum trees, windpumps that turned creakily in a listless breeze. Marta stared unseeing at the blood-red cattle behind barbed-wire fences; the kites perched periodically on the unending telegraph lines, raising and lowering their tails as they watched the ground intently. She didn't even blink at the black widow bird flying off across the veld, a snake dangling from its beak.

Please God keep them safe. Not the cattle prod, not cigarette burns on their genitalia, not their heads in suffocating bags. Please, please. It's my fault . . . if I'd never brought her to Impalala . . . I shouldn't have left them. They're just children.

Deon, meanwhile, gnawed at a knuckle, thinking it unlikely the security police would allow them to see the kids. Under the Ninety Day Act they weren't compelled to – not even to admit they were holding anyone in detention. He'd have to think of something, make a plan. And he'd have to get back to the farm soon. He couldn't expect Selina to keep an eye on things for long, even with no guests in camp. Man, he could do with a drink. Helluva lot of driving this, for one day. Nine – ten hours? He was dog-tired. Marta, too, he shouldn't wonder.

'Deon, do you think those two, Koba and Mannie, have been, er . . . lovers, for a while?'

'Hell, Marta, I don't know; can't say I'm too happy about the idea, though.'

Marta sat very still. She didn't want to hear this. Not from this man she'd felt so close to just a few hours earlier on this very same stretch of road.

She spoke, hoping to pre-empt him. 'I ask because, if Mannie is sexually inexperienced, well, he might think he was *in love*.' She saw Deon's mouth move to form words. She rushed on. 'But Koba's got a strong sense of her destiny, I suspect. I wouldn't be surprised if she could foresee certain things . . . you know; I mean it's not uncommon among the Jul'hoansi. Not that she's ever told me anything like that, mind you. You know how private she is. Such a dignified little person.'

'Ja-no, but . . .'

'Ja-well, all I'm trying to say is, she'll *know* they have no future together and not just because of the law of this land. She's clever, but it's more than book learning she's got. It's like a wisdom she's inherited or something.' She turned her body to face him as an idea occurred. 'You know what it reminds me of? That thing they say about elephants; about how a new matriach just knows where the waterholes are even if she's never been there before. She just knows what to do for the survival of the herd. Instinctively.'

'You're doing it again.'

'What?'

'You know. She-Tarzan, we plain-Jane.'

'I am not!' Marta turned away and stared at the empty road ahead. 'All I'm saying is, I think Koba knows her place is with her people. But Mannie?' She lifted her shoulders in a helpless shrug.

'One thing's for sure, it'll be hard for him to cope with the gossip there'll be about him,' Deon said. 'Socially, he'll be isolated. No self-respecting father's going to let our son date his daughter, is he?' Marta's lips became very thin. 'But the thing that really bothers me about this is, dammit-all,' he said, smacking the steering wheel, 'our boy, with *her!*'

Marta's heart sank.

'Jissus-man,' Deon pressed on, 'she's like our daughter and like a sister to him. I mean, it's practically incest.'

For a few moments Marta was stunned. Then she leaned across and kissed him.

19

'A grocery store! They are going to torture my children above a shop selling sugar.' Marta leaned her forehead against the dark display window, staring in disbelief at the Hulett's packets stacked neatly there.

'They are not going to torture them, Martjie. They're only kids. And we don't know if they will be held here, up there . . .' He indicated lit windows on the second and third floor of the building that rose blandly above them. The discreet entrance was locked, no uniformed policemen or even security guards in sight, no police vehicles, no blood stains on the pavement. Just a notice stating hours: 8.30 a.m to 5 p.m.

Perhaps the children weren't even here? But where, where was she going to find them? Where could she begin to look? She turned to face the road. Light traffic; comfortable family sedans driven by comfortable men, driving their wives to dinner or the bioscope while their children were tucked up safely in bed. How could they be so heedless? Marta thought. Didn't they know the danger they and their children were in? The evil being done in this boring building they drove by every day. But the truth was that the occupants of the cars and their families were all safe. They were white. She wanted to run into the road, screaming and screaming and screaming.

They checked into a boarding house nearby and were served supper. They didn't notice the twice-boiled meanness of the soup, or the stickiness of the oilcloth beneath their cracked bowls. That night they lay in bed, holding hands, staring at the neon light shining through the threadbare curtains. VACANCIES it flashed.

'She can't stay here,' the man with two brass buttons on his shoulder had said, when finally Koba's papers were presented to him. He hadn't even looked up at her. There was no need. After four hours at Jeppe Street police station all that anyone in authority needed to know about her was contained in the sheaf of papers in front of him. By then she'd become an accumulation of thin white sheets that had been filled in, crossed out, typed up, stapled together, pushed across dusty desks and, finally, stamped CRIMINAL. She was therefore to be detained not here, but at a prison in Pretoria, until formal charges had been brought against her by the state. A case would be made by her arresting officers and eventually she would be brought before someone called a Prosecutor. Koba gathered that she would be accused of contravention of a law which prevented mixed marriages.

Who said me and Frog-boy were planning to marry? she thought, but it seemed having food with a ǀTon led to marriage with one and so to the downfall of the whole Afrikaner race. She'd kept her incredulity to herself. She'd already decided that the way to survive this ordeal was to act as though she could neither hear nor speak. That way she could avoid giving these ape-like men the satisfaction of seeing that their racial jibes riled her. They were calling her stupid when she could see that the officer whose bald head was bent over her charge sheet was accusing her of immortality rather than immorality.

There had been other incidents she'd have liked to share with Mannie, but they'd been separated the minute they arrived at the police station. He was taken through the wide entrance for whites and she was pushed through the narrow non-whites one. When the duty officer grabbed her fingers and rolled every tip in black ink, then made her press onto a sheet of paper, she'd longed to prod Mannie in the ribs and laugh about the fact that thousands of years ago one of her ancestors had left such a San print on the wall of her cave at Impalala. That the ǀTon of this big, bright city were still doing it seemed funny to her. Had they finger-printed her Frog-boy too? she wondered. Were his white prints also black?

She'd lost her ability to see the funny side of the situation when they bundled her back into the cage of a police van and set off on a long, straight road north to Pretoria. Her tappings, quiet at the station, had started up again, and again she cursed her prescience. What good was an early warning system to someone whose feet were shackled together with an iron chain and whose wrist was handcuffed to the mesh of a cage? she thought. She looked despairingly at the lights of Johannesburg, fast diminishing as the van raced down the dark road. She was aware of tall trees on either side. Their leaves rattled like a sheaf of papers in nervous hands, as the van sped by.

At the blackest part of the road, the van veered off the national road and bumped down a short dirt track. It halted next to a concrete picnic table with a bench on either side. Its freshly painted whiteness dazzled Koba when the door of the cab opened; light spilled out along with a policeman carrying a six-pack of Lion lager. He clunked it down on the table, ripped open the cardboard carrier and extracted two cans. His colleague, after laying his truncheon on the table, sat down opposite him.

The men were in good humour, laughing and saluting each other's health with clashes of first the one, then another and another can of beer. Koba couldn't tell what they were talking about; they were speaking a South African black language she was not familiar with, but she knew their partly inebriated state was dangerous for her.

Finally, one of the men needed to pee. When he moved towards the back of the van, taking his time to unzip himself, looking in her direction all the while, she guessed what was coming.

Koba retreated deep into herself. She used her tappings to block out the sound of him swinging open the cage door, unlocking the padlock of her leg chains, jumping into the back of the van, his heavy black boots thumping onto the metal bed and making the wire cage shudder.

She sublimated all her senses so she wouldn't feel the rough serge of his uniform chafing her, or smell his beer breath or hear his grunts. She willed herself to soar above her body, above the roof of the rocking police van, to inhabit the eucalyptus-scented treetops. It was dark up there; tonight the moon wasn't shining down on the Highveld. No one would see; no one would know. She did not bite when the man's colleague climbed into the cage with his own requirements. She endured, determined not to provoke these animals into murdering her. They were ruining the pure thing she and her Frog-boy had had together, but they would not kill her.

Koba registered she was choking, but she would not swallow, no matter how hard the baboon in the police suit clamped her jaw. And, after they'd climbed back into the front of the van and started up the engine, she spat and spat and spat through the rusty, bitter-tasting mesh. Then she curled up as small as she could and closed her eyes; she had burned a memory of their names and numbers into her brain for ever.

She couldn't help but feel glad when the enormous door of Pretoria Central Prison banged closed behind her thirty minutes later. She was amid brown serge uniforms stretched across white bodies: fat, thin, young and old, but all the warders here were female. Koba's brusied legs buckled and she sank onto the concrete floor on the far side of the admissions desk.

At eight the next morning Deon and Marta Marais were outside the grocery store on Main Street. To its left an entranceway led to a small lobby with a three-person iron-grille lift and a staircase. They chose the stairs and had to join a sedate ascension of ordinary-looking businessmen in suits and ties, distinguishable as security police only by their brutal short-back-and-sides haircuts.

The headquarters was already open for business; the long wooden bench in the barely furnished waiting room already held three occupants: two black women, who held hands, and a young man. He looked relieved to see Deon and immediately struck up conversation, telling him that he was setting up in the jewellery business.

'I need a gold licence, you see, sir. Trading, not prospecting.' He giggled. 'Are you here for papers, sir?'

'Er, ja, that's right –'

Fortunately Deon was interrupted by an announcement from the clerk. 'Anyone requiring a licence or making application for citizenship, first door on your right; the officer will see you now.' The young man stood up, lifted his hat to Marta and left. The clerk raised his voice: 'Anyone here about a suspect detained under the General Law Amendment of 1963?' He ignored the raised hands of the two black women and stared at Marta and Deon over his glasses.

'Ja – er.' Deon stood up, hat in his hand.

But Marta was already at the desk. Gripping the edge with both hands, she said, 'We'd like to speak to someone about the detention of our son –'

'– and another minor,' Deon said.

From an open office door they heard a command barked: 'It's the Marais boy and the Boesman girl; came in last night. Girl's been sent to Pretoria Central. Give them the next-of-kin letter about the boy.'

Next of kin? Was Mannie dead? Marta sat down so hard the impact jarred her spine all the way to her neck. She heard herself sob.

'Tula, tula,' she heard one of the women whisper in comfort. But there was none to be had. A man emerged from the open door. 'Now, now, lady. He's not dead. If you'd taken the time to read the letter the clerk has provided you with, sir, madam, you'd see your son's being held at Jeppe Street station, no more than two miles from here. A nice modern facility, cells on one side, charge office on the other. Even a little court room.'

Marta's breathing felt constricted. 'Can we see him?' she managed to say.

'I'm afraid that won't be possible at the present time. But you can leave fresh clothes for them with the sergeant at the desk, and food. No news materials, of course.'

Deon gripped the policeman's tanned forearm. 'Captain, please, what about the girl?'

'You'll have to make enquiries there, in Pretoria, sir.'

'Listen, man, we're both men of the world. My boy having er, sexual congress with . . . ag-man, it's hardly a matter of state security, is it?'

Steyn withdrew his arm as if from an open sewer. 'I'm afraid that the General Law Amendment Act prevents me from discussing the case with you at the present time, so if you'll excuse me . . .'

Deon and Marta realized pleading would be fruitless. And they needed to establish that Koba was alive. They would drive to Pretoria Central Prison, straight away. It would take just over an hour, they calculated. As they hurried down the staircase, they heard heavy footsteps behind. The larger of the two black women had followed them from the waiting room.

'Sew; the madam must sew a letter in the shirt,' she said, panting.

'Excuse us?' Deon said.

'For the boy; you' son. They never will let you see, but pol-is, they give the clothes. We put the letter, small-small, in the collar of the shirt and sew closed.'

Marta recovered herself and addressed the woman in Zulu. It was a lucky choice. She was from Natal, but had been in Johannesburg for a month trying to secure the release of her son, Jabu Zondo, arrested under the terms of the Sabotage Act. She had recently received a letter from him saying he was well and being fairly treated. She pulled it from her bra and, unfolding it carefully, showed it to Marta. The handwriting looked shaky.

'That is not his hand,' Mrs Zondo said. 'Jabu would never go out of the lines like that. He was my firstborn. He was very good in school. Since he was that high.' She pinched three fingers and held them at knee-height. 'Now I want to know, what have they done with him? When is he coming home?'

Captain Steyn appeared at the top of the stairs. 'Mrs Zondo,' he barked, 'I haven't got all day you know.'

The prison wardress at Pretoria Central confirmed that a Bushman female was being held in custody there. She seemed astonished that they wanted to visit her. 'Well, anyway, you'll have to get permission; you're not family. It can take months, you know.'

Back in Johannesburg Deon said he was going to telephone an old hotel chum who'd gone into the police force. 'You coming?'

Marta shook her head. 'No. I'm going to buy a shirt for each of them, and a needle and some cotton. I'll see you back at the boarding house.'

But Marta found she couldn't just walk away. She wanted to stay near the police station and walk around the building, just in case.

In case of what? she thought, on her fourth circuit. Would she be able to catch his body if he was pushed out of a window? If she were back in Pretoria, could she shout 'Marta's coming' if she heard Koba scream? Here she heard only the sound of cars, buses and motorbikes buzzing by in an unending, unknowing stream.

Eventually she went off to OK Bazaars to make her purchases.

Back in their room, Deon found her unpicking the collar of a school shirt. 'Myburg will do what he can, but he's not optimistic. He says our best bet's someone in government. I know it's a long shot, but we could ask Lettie. See if she keeps up contact with any of Etienne's old party choms?'

'Ja-ja, go call her.'

Though they hadn't seen Lettie since their visit to Weltevrede, they'd stayed in touch; cards for birthdays and Christmas. Marta was a conscientious letter-writer, while Lettie preferred to telephone. Marta was sure that everyone on the Onderwater district party line was glad of Lettie's preference. Her sister-in-law was still famously indiscreet.

'Wragtig, what a scandal!' Lettie said now on hearing the news. 'But I can't say I'm surprised, Deon. It's what you must mos expect if you insist on treating them the way Marta does. Give a kaffir an inch and they take a whole yard.'

Deon thought he could hear a chorus of agreement down the line.

'But, ja-no, children are such a worry, hey? There's my André with hair down below his ears.' Deon found himself gripping the receiver very tightly. 'Dankie tog, his father isn't here to see it.' She sighed. 'Anyway, no good crying over spilled milk, hey? Look, I'll have a think about what I can do. If I can help to keep the Marais name out of this, ja-no, I will.'

Deon stepped through the door of the first bar he passed on his way back to Marta. He sat down, willing himself to order only a Coca-Cola. If he started on brandy it wouldn't be for show. He must get back, but he needed a few minutes on his own. Marta would understand. She needed him strong now.

His eyes sought his reflection; found it behind a battlement of bottles stacked in front of the mirror. He smiled sardonically to see his old stalwart, Klipdrif brandy, in such close proximity to his mirrored mouth. Klipdrif – Stone Ford. And what was that English expression?

Between a rock and a hard place. Ja, that was how he felt now.

He ordered a Coca-Cola.

By the next morning, Lettie had sprung into action. She called Deon to report her progress: 'I spoke with Denis Bezuidenhout –'

'Denis!'

'Ja; a Rooinek Bezuidenhout, but toemaar, his heart's in the right place. He's an MP – Nationalist, of course. He did a lot of shooting with Etienne. Etienne always called him 'Anyone-for-tennis-my-name-is-Denis'; ag, you know how funny Etienne could be? Shame-man, Denis was very kind when Etienne died. Came to the funeral. All the way from Cape Town, hey? You remember him? Tall, handsome man and he's got a good chin. His wife died not so long ago; thyroid. I sent a lovely tribute; carnations, red and white. Denis remembered and said –'

'Lettie! What did he say about getting the children out?'

'There's no need to shout, Deon. I've done my best and it can't be done. Parliament's got no say over the security police. But Denis says old Senator Bosch is your best bet. The man's very big on Bushmen.'

'D'you know him?'

'Ja-well-no, not actually. But I did sit next to him once. Magies, he was boring! Talked about separate development all night long. But I don't think he'll remember me. Didn't even want to dance and, anyway, he and Etienne didn't see eye to eye. He thought Etienne shouldn't have any tame Bushmen on the farm. Send them all back to the desert, he said. It's their homeland.'

Deon felt a glimmer of hope. 'He's the one, Lettie. He's the man we've got to tell about Koba. Can you do it?'

'Ag-no, I don't think so.'

Deon thought for a minute. 'What about if Denis Bezuidenhout helps you? I mean, maybe you wouldn't mind speaking to him again and arranging a meeting?'

'Ooh, naughty boy.' Lettie giggled.

'Sorry, ousus, I know he's a rooinek, but I just thought it might be a good excuse for you to get away from the farm for a bit. I remember how much you enjoyed your trips to South Africa when Etienne was alive.'

'Ja, it was sooo lovely. He'd take me to Ansteys for a cream tea and buy me a new dress at Miladys. We'd walk in the garden at the Union Buildings and all the jacaranda blossom would be falling on our heads, like purple confetti.' She began to sound tearful. 'He was a good man, that brother of yours. Why did he have to be taken so young?' She began to snivel. 'Christmases are very hard for me and André.'

Deon heard party-line sympathy. 'Poor Letjie. You've been very brave all these years. If he were here, Etienne would it say it was high time you had a treat. Come to Pretoria, ousus. We can drive over from Joburg at a moment's notice.'

She sniffed loudly. 'I've got so much to do here. It's the Women's Federation meeting next week and I've promised to bake for the church bazaar. Then André . . .'

'And of course I'll pay.'

'Oohh, it would be so nice to stay in a hotel and be waited on. I could do a bit of shopping at Miladys.'

'I'm sure the budget could stretch to that.'

Dinner at a hotel in Pretoria was arranged. Denis would be invited, Lettie would wear a new outfit and Deon would get a chance to present his case.

Marta, meanwhile, had delivered two parcels, one to Jeppe Street and one to Pretoria Central. Both contained a shirt, dried apricots and some biltong in each. Sewn into the collars of the flamboyant shirts were long, narrow notes written in light pencil, which she'd agonized over, trying to fit as much love and encouragement onto the strip as she could. She was sure the children would get the shirts, and she was sure Mannie at least would realize that it must be significant, being the kind of garment they both knew he'd never wear. But would he or Koba think to un-pick the collars? Her only hope was that they would notice an unusual stiffness around the neck, something the sergeant who inspected the contents of each parcel had failed to feel. And Koba might notice the stitches, Marta thought, and think of the first time Marta had sewed for her, repairing her mother's skin cloak, all those years ago in the storeroom at Weltevrede. She fervently hoped the gift would sustain Koba, even if the girl did not discover the note. Marta crossed her fingers and prepared to wait.

She devised a routine for herself; small ceremonies she could perform daily to control her rising sense of panic. She rose, having hardly slept, splashed cold water onto her face, stared into the fly-shit-spotted mirror and told herself it would be all right. On even-numbered days she set out to patrol the perimeter of Jeppe Street station. Four times round the block. On odd days she and Deon drove to Pretoria Central Prison and knocked on its massive wooden door. The face at the grille always turned them away.

One day Marta stepped into a public phone booth. She tried her friend, Anna De Wet. Anna was oddly abrupt, but they arranged to meet outdoors, in a place Anna described cryptically as 'where we had that picnic'. It could only be Joubert Park, Marta thought, remembering one of their sunny outings from just a week or so ago. She made her way there.

The news wasn't good. Anna warned that their telephone was being tapped and, for all she knew, she and her civil rights lawyer husband were being tailed. 'I was very careful coming here. I'm sure no one followed. But for Mannie and Koba's sakes we shouldn't be connected. Last thing you need now is an association with suspected commies.'

They made an arrangement to keep in touch via public call boxes. Anna said there was talk of the so-called Ninety Day Act being extended to one hundred and eighty days without trial. She also said that Jabu Zondo was likely to be released soon if his mother had received a letter from him.

'Lately they make them write one of those letters so that if the detainee accuses the authorities of torture when he gets out, they can produce a copy of the letter to disprove it.' Marta looked white. 'Don't worry. I'm sure they won't be torturing Mannie. He's just a child.'

'Jabu's only seventeen,' Marta said.

Afterwards, Marta went back to the phone box near the Security Police headquarters. Let them keep an eye on me all they like, she thought. From here she could watch them too.

She opened the telephone directory and began to work her way down the list of government departments: Prisons; Police; Justice; Education; even Bantu Affairs. She argued with telephonists, secretaries, aides, deputies and, once, a minister, all the while frantically feeding the hungry coin box. They told her to put it in writing, to call back next day, next week, next month. When Deon found her, she was standing with her forehead pressed against the glass.

'Never mind. Lettie might help.' Marta pulled a face. 'No, really. She's got a good heart –'

'I know. And she can't resist a good drama.'

'Ja, especially if she can star in it in a new outfit.'

Marta nodded. A smile was more than she could manage.

A few days later, she was back in the phone booth. She didn't lift the handset. There was no one else she could call. She just wanted to stand there, in that cramped, defaced, urine-stinking box.

'It might be like this, their cell,' she explained to a puzzled Deon. 'No bigger than this; the smell might be the same if they only have a bucket to use.'

'But you're getting cold, Marta. You're shivering.'

'They might be cold.'

Deon had to leave her. He went to see if he could secure them an interview with Steyn at Security Police headquarters. Marta stayed in the booth, emerging only when the irate tapping of someone wanting to use the phone roused her.

She headed for a bakery where she bought a big box of doughnuts. She carried it, unopened, to the Non-European entrance at Jeppe Street police station. She wasn't allowed inside, but the black women who waited there every day trickled out, eventually. She enquired after a Mrs Zondo. Someone told her she'd returned to Natal because her mother was sick. Jabu had not been released. At Marta's insistence, and because she was that most unusual thing, a white woman fluent in a black language, the woman helped herself to a Sugarbun and advised her friends to do the same. 'This might be the only food some of them have all day,' she said.

As the days passed Marta became a familiar sight with her box of buns outside Jeppe Street station and at Pretoria Central. The other mothers talked to her – always about their missing children; how they'd never let them out of their sights when they got them home, how they would cook them their favourite dishes and make them concentrate on their school work. Never about how they'd bury their bruised, broken bodies.

Deon sat through an insufferable meal with Denis Bezuidenhout and Lettie, listening to a shot-by-shot account of the man's recent 16–14, 12–10, 11–9 victory. Now he understood Etienne's nickname for this bore.

'The old bugger would just not give up,' Denis said. 'Eventually I had to resort to disguised topspin and sneaky drop shots. Not exactly cricket, hey, but all's fair in love and war, what?' He winked at Lettie.

Neither of them seemed interested in raising the issue of Koba with the senator. Deon left frustrated. He hoped that Tennis Denis would be too.

Another week passed with Deon increasingly concerned about expenses. With no money coming in and a stream of bills to settle from Lettie's hotel, he needed to get back to work. He must reopen the lodge, do some advertising, get customers back in. And Donker's might have sent some work for Marta. Shouldn't they leave Johannesburg for a while? he asked. 'Mrs Zondo has and she knows her way around the system. You said so yourself.'

'You go if you must. I'll stay.'

'But, Martjie, you can do nothing here. At home there'd be things to take your mind off –'

'I do *not want* my mind taken off the children. Can't you understand that I can't go back to normal? There is no normal when governments can do this to their citizens.'

'Ja, but money's getting tight and –'

'I'll sleep in the doorway at Jeppe Street if I have to. I don't care. I am not going to betray the children by –'

'Betray the children? Is that what you think I'm doing just because I've pointed out that we have to have money? I resent that, Marta. I really do.'

Deon left the next morning and didn't return to Johannesburg for three weeks.

Back on Impalala he worked like a Trojan, setting the lodge to rights, making deals with tourist boards to get customers in, trying to keep Mannie's whereabouts secret from those who asked. When he returned he brought fresh clothes for Marta, avocados from their tree, and a commission from Donker's. Marta didn't even open it.

Deon said nothing about how empty the farm was without her and the children, nor how tempting the bar in town had looked. He couldn't fail Marta. Not again.

That night they lay against each other, forced to by the dip in the boarding-house mattress, but they didn't hold hands.

As soon as Deon left for the long drive back, Marta resumed her new work.

She was collecting details of the detainees from their families and preparing a petition to send to the minister of justice. That was all she wanted to talk about, even when Anna called her. 'This is something I can do, Anna. I'm not a revolutionary, after all. Just an administrator.'

'Ag, Martjie, you don't have to make a grand gesture. Listen, you remember Nelson Mandela?'

'Of course.'

'Ja-well, I once heard him say that the best contribution to "the cause" that people could make was inside their own homes, in their own families. You and Deon treat the people who work for you fairly; you've brought your son up to have no prejudice about blacks. Quite the opposite.'

Marta began to laugh.

'Ag sorry.' Anna giggled. 'I didn't mean . . .'

But now Marta was laughing so hard she had to hold onto the side of the phone booth to support herself. It was part hysteria, she knew, but when she'd wiped away her tears and said goodbye, she felt better.

Silver-haired Senator Bosch met them in the waiting room of Security Police headquarters.

Looking every inch the patrician above the grocery store, Marta thought. 'Tall and sure, like he's got God and the government on his side,' she whispered to Deon. Next to him, Steyn wore the sulky expression of a man who has been outranked and outmanoeuvred.

As they were led down the passage, Marta could still hardly believe that Lettie's coquetry had opened doors that had been firmly shut on her pleas and on Deon's persistence.

Lettie had been working the government cocktail and dinner party circuit, all dimples, country charm and new frocks. Even so, Marta wasn't sure exactly why. Yes, Lettie had been enjoying the glamorous social life she'd missed since Etienne's death, but she knew Lettie, knew how she hummed as she baked and pickled and sewed at home. At heart she was a farm girl. Had it simply been a matter of pride, of trying to keep the Marais name out of the glare of publicity, Marta reasoned that Lettie would have been better off remaining out of sight at Weltevrede. The attraction must be Denis. But would Lettie be seriously interested in what Deon called a 'not-quite' – not-quite English, not-quite Afrikaans?

Such a very different man from Etienne, Marta thought. Was his seat in parliament the attraction? She gave herself a mental slap on the wrist; unkind to think that of her sister-in-law. Hats off to Lettie for engineering a meeting between Deon and the senator, though: Once Senator Bosch understood that Koba was an opportunity to show the Homeland Policy at work, he'd written the necessary letters.

Marta, feeling wan and crumpled, was beyond caring who was making mileage out of the situation – as long as the children were freed.

They were ushered through a reinforced glass door to a hospital-green office. Seats were proffered, but it was a crush. Steyn stepped behind the desk and, without looking up, said, 'I've prepared all the documentation for you. If Mr Marais would just sign for him here . . .'

Deon knocked the pen off the desk in his haste to comply. While Steyn scrabbled around on the floor for it, the senator proffered his own gold-nibbed fountain pen.

Then it was done and, with mixed feelings, Marta watched Deon's humble gratitude when Steyn said they'd be dropping all charges and weren't interested in questioning any other members of the family 'at the present time'.

The senator nodded gravely. Then came a respectful knock on the door and a uniformed policeman stuck his head into the room. Steyn beckoned and seconds later the policeman pushed a boy into the office.

Mannie stood there blinking. He looked pale and very young in khaki school shorts and a gaudy shirt with torn collar. His feet were bare. Marta leaped out of her chair. 'Liebchen, liebchen!' She swooped, searching his exposed skin for injury. He seemed blemish-free, but his eyes carried a sorrow she couldn't bear to see. She made to pull him to her, but the rigid way her son stood, as though the tightening of his tendons was all that was keeping him upright, stopped her.

Not in front of these people, his haunted eyes begged.

Marta watched Deon clasp their son's thin shoulders and smile at him too long.

'You've grown, son,' she said. Then she had to fall silent as the senator delivered a lecture on the importance of Afrikaner youth 'keeping pure'.

Marta quivered with suppressed rage.

They were escorted back to the waiting room.

'Koba? Where's she?' Mannie asked.

'The Bushman female is back from Pretoria and is being loaded now. She'll be taken to the station and put on a train back to her homeland, courtesy of the government of the Republic of South Africa,' Steyn intoned, 'after the senator's press conference.'

'But where's the loading place?' Mannie's eyes were wild; his feet stamped with impatience.

Marta grabbed his cold hand. 'Come, son. We'll go look.'

Outside the Non-White section, they saw a figure swathed in a blanket, being bundled into a police van.

Mannie broke and ran. By the time he reached the vehicle, the doors had been shut. He banged on the grille. 'Koba, is that you?'

'Yau, you.' He heard the words spoken softly by the shackled shape.

Then he was shoved aside by a black policeman who barred his view.

Mannie felt himself being pulled backwards. Behind him he heard noise – the babble of black women, a soup of Xhosa, Zulu, Sotho words, and his mother's voice, greeting them.

Rough hands stroked him, patting and congratulating. Over the bereted heads of smiling women, he saw Koba's white wire cage shudder as the van started up.

'Thank you, thank you, Sissie. Yes, this is Mannie – yes, my firstborn. Many thanks. Yes. And may *your* wait soon be over. May Sipho soon be home safe. And for Mrs Zondo, for her Jabu, I am praying, please tell her, Mama.'

Marta tried to detach herself from the group. She felt as though she'd cheated. She'd acted like one of them, been accepted as a fellow sufferer, but clearly she wasn't. Even here she was privileged, advantaged, thanks to her race. Should she have refused the senator's help? She knew none of these women would have expected her to. It didn't make her feel any better.

She stared over the beaming faces at her son. There was desperation in his bloodshot eyes. 'Please, please, we must go,' she said to the women.

'Ladies.' It was Deon, pushing politely through the crowd. 'If you'll excuse us, our' – his eyes caught

Marta's – 'our daughter is in that van. We must follow.'

The crowd parted. Women clapped. A voice called in Zulu: 'You, you sir, and the Sugarbun family, hamba kahle.'

Marta kept her head down as Deon led her away.

Lettie was waiting for them round the front, under the WHITES ONLY sign. She wore a baby blue crimplene suit, with matching hat and gloves. To Marta she looked dressed for the official opening of parliament. She had her arm linked through Denis Bezuidenhout's. He wore a dark blazer and cravat.

Lettie tripped forward and kissed the air near Marta's ear. Then she patted her sister-in-law's cheek with a gloved hand. 'Don't you worry, Martjie, there's nothing here that a good oatmeal face pack won't fix.'

Marta's neck blotched, her eyes glittered dangerously. Deon stepped between them. 'Come, ladies. We must get to the station.'

'There's going to be an official send-off. With photographers.' Lettie's eyes danced under the wide brim of her hat. 'I know the way; I'll drive,' she said. She set off up a one-way street, against the flow of traffic. Facing cars hooted at the Mercedes. 'Oops,' she giggled and, grating the gear into reverse, she tried to back up the street, tacking right, then left.

'Bit like a sailboat,' Denis said tensely.

'Ag, I'm sorry; it's this hat.'

'Take it off!' Marta hissed.

'Ag, even if I take it off, the hairdresser's used so much spray, I feel as though my head won't turn on my neck.'

'Watchit,' Denis said, his foot pressed hard against the floorboard on the passenger side.

'Oopsie, was that the kerb?'

Deon groaned as they heard the scrape of hubcap and suddenly, inappropriately, Marta had an overwhelming urge to laugh. She groped in her handbag for a handkerchief and held it to her mouth. Stupid, she thought; it must be a relief. After six of the worst weeks of her life her son was back with her, safe and sound. He was thinner, filthy and so much older in his eyes, but he was alive. And so was Koba.

Mannie craned forward on the long back seat. He felt as though he'd walked out of prison and onto the set of a slapstick film. His auntie, dressed like the prime minister's wife, was using a Mercedes Benz to wreck parked cars; his mother, who looked ten years older than she had a few weeks ago, was killing herself with laughter; his father, whose Sunday-best suit seemed to have grown too big for him, was agreeing with the complete stranger in the front seat that the 'Boks had the best rugby side anywhere in the world, and all the time Koba was leaving.

Had the country gone mad while he'd been in prison? How could it be that a world of muffled screams, slamming cell doors, sobs in the dark and literally shitting one's pants under interrogation could seem more normal than this?

It was insane. He wanted no part of it. If Koba was going back to the Kalahari Desert then so was he. There they could live away from this lunacy. There they could love each other without fear and shame.

At the station, Lettie parked with maximum fuss. Mannie drummed his filthy fingers on the backrest of her seat. Deon stilled his son's agitated hand. 'Thanks very much, ousus,' he said to Lettie before she'd turned off the engine. 'We'll see you inside if that's okay?'

'Ja-ja. You go. I've got to powder my nose. I won't be long.'

'Well, er, we don't want to miss the senator's statement – separate development. Very important, being seen to practise what we preach. Good opportunity with this, er, Khoisan girl. Quite a find, what? So, I'll just run along in the meantime,' Denis said, already half out of the car.

'No wait, I'm ready.' Lettie snapped her powder compact shut. 'Now, where's that Mannie? We don't want him getting his picture taken by the press. We don't want the Marais name in the papers, hey?'

Mannie was long gone, thrusting through the crowd in the station concourse.

But it felt weird. Like stepping into a pinball machine: blaring noise; flashing signs; constant movement; people and their baggage obstructing his route at every turn. Which was his route? He stopped, bewildered. He felt giddy and sick. He longed for his dark cell.

Then he felt a strong hand on his forearm, steadying him. 'Come on, son. It'll be this way.' Deon led him through a doorway marked NON-WHITES. They were at the bottom end of a long platform. Above a WHITES

ONLY barricade, uniformed porters pushed trolleys of matching luggage for white passengers: men in suits and hats, women in floral dresses and gloves. Down below the barricade it was every man and woman for themselves as people scrambled to load bundles, boxes, babies and cardboard suitcases into the dingy carriages. Mannie spotted blue serge uniforms. But they were above the barricade.

'She must be there.' His parents and aunt watched him race away, ricocheting off people in his path. When they caught up, Mannie was arguing with a young policeman.

'You can't go any closer, sonny. That's a senator there talking to the press.'

'Fok the senator. That's my girl . . .'

'Hey, you watch your –'

With a waft of L'air du temps, Lettie was among them. 'If you'll excuse me, officer.' She inserted herself between Mannie and his adversary. The policeman stepped back to avoid her hat brim. She tilted her head back and dimpled up at him. 'I'm supposed to be there next to the senator for the photos, but it's such a crush I can't get through. I'm counting on a big strong man like you to help me.' She tapped his shoulder with her pale blue, gloved hand. He immediately shoved that shoulder into the tightly packed crowd of onlookers and heaved like a prop forward.

Mannie took his chance and ducked through the crush.

He saw her at once, very small next to the senator, her face impassive, her hair wild. Koba didn't flinch as the senator placed his hand on her head and flashbulbs popped.

Mannie wanted to run to her, wrap her in his arms and take her away from this. But the five feet separating them felt like five miles. He hesitated. He felt afraid. Not because of the police presence, but because of the way Koba was gazing past him, her eyes focused on some point on the distant horizon where the railway lines converged.

He smiled and raised his hand to waist level, waving surreptitiously. Koba ignored him.

Lettie arrived with Denis now in tow. She slipped one hand through the arm of the senator, the other through Denis's. The senator looked disconcerted; Denis, not-quite. Lettie flashed a dazzling smile at the cameras.

When the photo opportunity was over, the senator and his entourage, including Lettie and Denis, left. Koba was handcuffed to a black policeman and pushed towards the Non-White section. 'Koba,' Mannie hissed, following her. She didn't look over her shoulder. The policeman lifted her up the carriage steps. Mannie saw her black buckled leather shoes disappear into the train. It juddered into life as the engine started up.

Mannie stood stunned. He knew she'd heard him. He'd seen the muscles at the top of her back tense. Why wouldn't she acknowledge him? Did she blame him for their imprisonment? What had they said and done to her in there? Didn't she love him like he loved her? He felt his heart tear.

'You have to let her go, liebchen.' His mother was beside him; he could feel her aching to hold him. He swayed. He felt tired, so tired, but he squared his shoulders.

'Ma, have you got sixpence for me?'

Marta looked surprised, but taking out her purse she handed him the small coin.

'Thanks.' And he was off, running up the platform, under the barricade and out of sight.

Koba, installed in a window seat on the train, watched him run away. It surprised her. She'd felt the pain of his heart in her own. It had cost her all her remaining strength to keep her eyes from his when she saw him at the front of the flashing crowd. Now her Frog-boy was running away. Well, perhaps it was better like this.

Marta tapped on the glass. The policeman lowered the window and indicated that she could lean out.

'Oh my girl, my girl, are you all right? Ag, I'm so sorry for what happened. For everything, you know; from the beginning.' Marta wrung her hands. 'I probably didn't do right by you, Kobatjie. I think I made it worse, the way I kept you on Impalala. Deon was right, all along. He always saw you clearly, without labels, like I never did.' Marta was crying, tears coursing over her spots like floodwater over pebbles.

Koba touched her hand as it rested on the window edge. 'A good person who follows their heart can't stray too far from the path, Grandmother says.'

'Ah, I would have liked to have known your grandmother. I'm sorry I never asked. So many things I didn't do – would have liked to have done –' Marta raised her hand and placed it on Koba's hair.

'I should have let you braid,' Koba said softly. They heard the conductor's whistle. Marta stepped back and stood next to Deon. He took her hand, then lifted his hat to Koba. She smiled at him. 'I still have your gift.' She held up the old pocket knife he'd left outside her cave so many years ago.

The conductor walked past with a green flag. From behind him came Mannie, vaulting over the barricade and sprinting toward Koba. She leaned further out of the window. He thrust a packet at her. 'Here,' he panted. 'Not mangetti nuts. But they are salted.'

Koba looked at the peanuts and felt her resolve beginning to melt. She lowered her face to his. Timidly, he cupped it in his hands. He saw her lids close, tremble, like satiny brown butterfly wings. Two small tears became trapped in her upturned lashes. He reached for her lips with his, but Koba pulled back.

'No.'

Mannie sprang away, his features a mosaic of misery. Now he knew for sure; Koba didn't want him. Even given the choice, she would have gone back to her people. She had told him, long ago. He just hadn't listened properly.

He balled his fists up in the pocket of his shorts. Why, why had she let him love her? Why had she let him believe she loved him? Why had she clung to him so desperately those nights in the big bed and told him he had her heart? He'd been tortured because he'd screamed he loved her and would marry her.

But Koba didn't need him or want him. She belonged to her tribe and he never could. His mouth set as he took a last look at her face. That gentle, concave profile. It was beautiful, but already it looked less familiar to him.

Koba drew her head back into the carriage. She felt like a bulb too long uprooted – dry, sour, beginning to shrivel up, draw inwards. She couldn't have kissed Frog-boy. She had no juice left to give.

I've been exposed too long, she thought. There has been too much of me for clawed things to tear at.

By now word had spread around the packed carriage that there was a prisoner on board. Curious passengers craned their necks to see the black girl so precious to whites she had to be guarded by a policeman. Koba felt their stares. She didn't care what they thought – a train and its occupants no longer terrified her. But she was frightened of what lay beyond this journey, of people who would look at her with more than idle curiosity. Would her kinsmen accept her or reject her?

The driver gave a short blast on the horn and the train jolted into motion. She steadied herself. There was nothing she could do now. She had chosen this path when she chose to remain for the nights with Frog-boy. She could have heeded her tappings, taken money from Marta and gone away by herself – before the policemen came. But she knew, even after all the torment of prison, that she could never have left Impalala of her own free will. The place and the people had grown into her, slowly reaching into her heart like a fig tree forcing its way between rock. Uhn-uhn-uhn, the roots were deep.

She sighed. No help to have the sight and foresee that it would end with sorrow. Neither Grandmother nor the discs had told her how much Frog-boy's hurt would cost her.

She leaned back out of the window. 'Mannie!'

He started. She'd never used his name before.

'You gave me salt. I gave you honey. It was not nothing. Don't forget.'

As the train pulled out she kissed her palm and blew across it towards him.

Glossary

amandla	power (a Xhosa and Zulu word used as a rallying cry against apartheid)
bakgat	marvellous, great
bangbroek	scaredy-pants
blerry	bloody (used as a swear word)
bliksem	(literally 'lightning') a term of personal abuse, such as swine, bastard
boep	a paunch
boerperd	a muscular, sturdy South African breed of horse
Boes	the Bush, as in Boesman (Bushman): used to describe those who are part of the Khoisan group of the indigenous people of southern Africa. A term with a problematic history, now considered by many to be offensive, with San preferred in official contexts
boet	a brother
boetie	a diminutive of brother
brak	a mongrel
bundu-bash	to travel over rough, difficult ground
chom	a chum

dankie tog	thank goodness
dopp	to booze, usually spirits
eina	'ouch'
finished and klaar	'and that's that'
gaats	an exclamation of surprise or dismay
goef	a dip, a short swim
gwa	a hallucinogenic mix of plants
hamba kahle	goodbye: 'go well' (Zulu)
hokaai	halt: 'whoa!' to an animal
Hotnot	(abbreviation of Hottentot) an offensive term for a Khoisan person
hxaro	the San custom of creating partnerships between people, cemented by the reciprocal act of giving gifts
jaap	a country bumpkin (denotes a boorish stereotype)
jislaaik	an expression of astonishment: 'good grief'
Jul'hoan	the name of Koba's group (plural: Jul'hoansi)
kaffirboetie	(literally: 'kaffir brother') a very offensive term
kak	crap
kaross	a cloak made of animal hide
kleinbaas	a little master
kleinboet	a little brother
knopkierie	a round-headed stick used as a club
koeksister	a syrup-coated doughnut in the shape of a plait
liebchen	darling, sweetheart (German)
liewe magies	good heavens, goodness gracious

Masarwa	a pejorative term for the San/Khoisan people
mielie	an ear of corn
miesies	a mistress or missus
moegoe	an idiot
mos	in fact, actually
n!a'an	a form of respectful address
n‡ah	a fruit found in the Kalahari Desert
n|om	a spiritual energy harnessed for healing
n|omkxao	an owner of medicine (plural: n|omkxaosi)
n!ore	(literally: tree-water), territory
oke	a person
opa	grandpa
opsaal	'saddle up'
ouboet	an older brother
outa	a form of respectful address to an elderly black man
padkos	(literally: road food) snacks and provisions for a journey
piepie	child's term for penis
poes	the female genitalia (obscene slang)
rondavel	a circular hut with a conical thatched roof
thunderstick	a rifle
toe	(literally: closed up) impenetrably stupid
toemaar	never mind
|Ton	a white person
voetsek	'get lost' (highly contemptuous, used for dogs)
vrek	to die
weltevrede	well satisfied
wragtig	an exclamation of incredulity: 'oh hell'

Note on the Jul'hoan People and Language

From the evidence of paleontological finds and scenes depicted in ancient rock art, experts believe that groups of hunter-gatherers have inhabited parts of southern Africa for 40,000 years or more. The San people of Namibia, Botswana and Angola are thought to be descendants of the stone-age artists. They have been labelled Bushmen, Hottentots, Masarwa, Khoisan and San by westerners and other Africans. However, these people have no collective name for themselves. The particular group in this book have always referred to themselves as Jul'hoansi, translating as 'real' or 'ordinary people'.

From their perspective, the world outside their camps was a hostile place. Water and food were scarce, they faced natural predators, such as lion and hyena, and they were persecuted by invading pastoralists, both black and white, for centuries. The San (as some anthropologists now refer to Bushmen) were not blameless, however, sometimes provoking attack from the settler pastoralists by poaching their livestock and stealing the goods of returning migrant workers. It became common practice to shoot 'Bushmen', abduct their children and use them as indentured labourers on settler farms in what was then German South West Africa. Modern times have seen no let-up in the problems faced by these formerly nomadic people, and nowadays the Jul'hoansi are unable to live solely by hunting and gathering.

To this day, the Jul'hoansi use a trance dance ceremony for community healing purposes. Jul'hoan shamans claim to derive their healing power from spirit guides, usually antelope, whom they meet in a mystical world when they trance. Some shamans say they have an ear for the voices of their ancestors, who might make their presence felt in the form of mini dust tornadoes, or 'dust devils'. Some members of the Jul'hoansi are able to heal certain physical ailments using their knowledge of medicinal plants, a skill known as muti.

San languages and dialects are unique in containing the largest inventory of consonants found in any known language. They also have a particularly complex phonology of implosive consonants or 'clicks', which westerners have historically struggled to master. However, the sophisticated verbal arts of click-language-speaking peoples are recognized today as among the most intricate and beautiful in the world.

Only in recent years have linguists developed orthographies – ways to write San languages. These languages have clicks, made when the tongue is drawn sharply away from various points on the roof of the mouth. The main examples found in this novel are:

	Dental click, as in ǀTon, white person. (Sounds like the reproach: 'tsk'). Place the tip of the tongue immediately behind the top front teeth and pull gently away.
ǂ	**Palatal click**, as in Nǂaisa. Similar to above, but made by pressing the front of the tongue to the roof of the mouth (on the ridge just behind top front teeth). The tongue is then withdrawn quickly from the ridge.
!	**Guttural click**, as in Chu!ko. A popping noise made at the back of the mouth, by drawing the end of the tongue away from the curve where the alveolar ridge meets the hard palate.
ǀ	**Lateral click**, as in Khaǀ'an. (Similar to the sound one uses to urge a horse forward.) Suck one side of the tongue sharply away from the alveolar ridge.

The language is rich in wordplay, metaphors and euphemism. Conversation is entertainment for the San; they are skilled storytellers and mimics.

Acknowledgements

The scholarly works of countless researchers have informed my reading about hunter-gatherers, past and present. Sometimes, in the service of character or plot, facts have inevitably given way to fiction in this story.

To read more about the present-day Jul'hoansi visit www.kalaharipeoples.net.

My thanks to George Bizos for sharing his memories of South African detention facilities of the 1960s and for his expert legal opinion.

For research help, thanks to Professor M. Toolan, Bev Schram and Gary Travlos. Also, officers of what was then the Nyae Nyae Foundation and the Jul'hoan people living in that area of Namibia, who tolerated my company and were gracious enough to myth-swap with me around their campfires at night in the Kalahari.

Appreciation for the production of this book is due to the team at Tindal Street Press, especially to Alan Mahar.

Finally, my love and grateful thanks go to my patient family: Yiannis, Louka, Xanthe and Myra.

About the Author

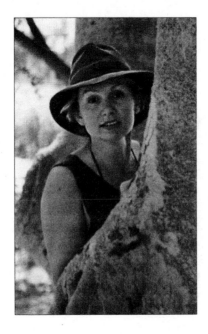

Candi Miller, born in Zambia and brought up in South Africa, has been a journalist and advertising copywriter, and now lives in Staffordshire where she teaches Creative Writing.